CANTICLE CREEK

CANTICLE

CREEK

ADRIAN HYLAND

ultimo
press

First edition published in 2021.
This edition published in 2022 by Ultimo Press,
an imprint of Hardie Grant Publishing

Ultimo Press
Gadigal Country
7, 45 Jones Street
Ultimo, NSW 2007
ultimopress.com.au

Ultimo Press (London)
5th & 6th Floors
52–54 Southwark Street
London SE1 1UN

Canticle Creek
ISBN 978 1 76115 155 2 (hardback)

10 9 8 7 6 5 4 3 2 1

Cover design Design by Committee
Cover photograph KHBlack/Bigstock
Typesetting Kirby Jones | Typeset in 13/17 pt Adobe Garamond Pro
Copyeditor Deonie Fiford
Proofreader Ronnie Scott

Printed and bound in Great Britain by Clays Ltd, Elcograf S.p.A.

Ultimo Press acknowledges the Traditional Owners of the country on which we work, the Gadigal people of the Eora nation and the Wurundjeri people of the Kulin nation, and recognises their continuing connection to the land, waters and culture. We pay our respects to their Elders past and present.

To Siena

The birds are a filament of
white and gold against
the shadow roads
the burnt blue north
Kenji Takada (1926–1980)

PROLOGUE

She heard the siren scream out over the valley and her father came hopping from the workshop, pager in one hand, boot in the other. He got a foot into the boot and ran for the Prado.

'What is it?' she yelled.

'Car accident.'

He jumped into the vehicle and roared out onto the main road, turning in the direction of the Canticle Creek fire station.

She checked the emergency services app on her phone. The incident was described as a high-angle rescue and fire, up on Crowcall Road.

High-angle rescue and fire? That sounded bad. Had a car gone over the edge and burst into flames?

She went down to the yard and whistled up her horse, Atomica. She slipped a bridle onto him and set off, bareback.

Ten minutes later she reined in fifty metres away from the incident. There was no sign of fire or smoke but there were a couple of fire tankers on scene, as well as a cop car and an ambulance. A few locals, one of whom glanced around, spotted her and smiled.

'Hey, Poss.'

It was Daisy Baker. She was wearing her usual Nepalese silk hat, with an indigo scarf and a cotton top.

With her was a young man, one arm around her in a casual, intimate manner that spoke volumes: her new beau. He was barefoot, wearing a blue shirt and jeans, with a mop of scraggly hair flowing out from under a stockman's hat.

'Possum,' she said. 'Meet Adam.'

'Possum?' The guy had an enthusiastic laugh. 'Better keep out of my country – somebody might eat you.'

'Adam's from a place called Kulara,' explained Daisy. 'In the outback. I met him when I was up there a few months ago.'

Daisy had spent much of the past year trooping around the wilder parts of the world: she'd climbed mountains in Nepal, canoed down wild rivers in Sulawesi, driven across the Tanami Desert. That must have been where she'd come across this bloke.

'Did you see what happened?' Possum asked, nodding at the accident. The fireys were manhandling a stretcher up the shallow slope.

'Feller was in the car with his missus,' said Adam. 'Tried to light a smoke, but he was so pissed all he managed to do was set his beard on fire. Then he jumped out of the car and fell over the edge.'

'Was he badly hurt?'

'His leg's a bit smashed around, but when we tried to help him he told us to fuck off – even swung a punch. Thought we'd leave him to the professionals.'

Another emergency vehicle came past, and Atomica shied in fright.

The horse was quick, but Adam was quicker: he sprang forward, caught the bridle, steadied the animal with a powerful arm and a gentle word.

Embarrassed at losing control of her mount, Possum murmured her thanks and said she'd better be getting home.

* * *

The next morning she saddled up and set out for a ride. She went south along the Cockatiel Track, then cut across country, pushing into the scrub alongside Ryan's Mill. When they reached open pasture she urged Atomica into a canter that morphed into a gallop.

She eased him up, took pleasure in moving in and out of the shadows that flickered across her path. She called good morning to a few old friends: the coal-faced watch dog, the albino kangaroo. Atomica glared at the alpacas on Brady's farm, jumped at a whirring wood pigeon, whinnied at a golden horse in a green paddock.

A truck came rumbling down the road. She recognised it: Christie Looms, the water carter. That was okay – he was a careful driver, but then some idiot in a big black F2-something, all halogen spotties and fat alloy wheels, decided to overtake him on the bend. The ute hit a post, kicked up an arc of dirt and fish-tailed down the road to town.

'Dickhead,' she growled.

She spent a minute settling Atomica down, then let him have his head to distract him.

When she reached Messmate Lane, the track that led to Daisy Baker's, she eased him up. She checked the time. Why not? Daisy always seemed to have some treat, fresh from the oven, on the table.

Atomica trotted up the driveway, but the signs were far from promising. There was no smoke slipping out of the chimney, no ute in the carport.

'Hell-o-o!' she called.

Nothing.

She dismounted and knocked on the door. No answer. She peered through the stained-glass window. The front room was empty.

Damn.

As she was launching herself into the saddle, she spotted something unusual in the ditch that ran alongside the house. Curious, she stood up in the stirrups.

It looked like a scrap of material, an indigo of the same shade as Daisy's scarf.

She jumped down, walked towards the bank. She felt a premonition, dark and clammy in the guts.

At the water's edge, she stopped. Fell back, stunned.

She put her hands to her head, trying to silence the rushing roar within, so fierce it felt like it was going to crack her skull.

Some of the dirt fell into the ditch. Possum came close to falling in herself.

Daisy was lying in the mud, face up, mouth frozen in a silent scream. Her eyes were open, lifeless. There were weeds in her hair and bruises and blood all over her head.

Possum did what she could to get her out. She dragged the body as far as the bank, lay her in the dirt. When she slid away Possum caught a strap and hauled her back. She tried pumping and breathing life into her, the way they'd taught her at the fire brigade.

Nothing. Daisy was as cold as ice, as far away as the moon.

Possum found her phone. She started to punch the numbers and was surprised to hear a siren in the distance, getting closer.

Already? she thought.

CHAPTER 1

Central Australia,
three months earlier

We pulled into a waterhole for a break and a fox shot up from the rocks like a bolt of red flame. Danny Jakamarra whipped out his old twenty-two, though it was a tricky shot. He was only half-serious, but Adam let loose with a whoop of amusement.

'Go for it!' he yelled.

Danny fired as the animal dashed up the opposite slope. He missed, of course, and the animal glided away, swift and low.

But then another shot exploded from the mulga scrub to our right and the fox somersaulted and dropped. Lay still.

A Range Rover, its duco as bright as a new two-dollar coin, came rumbling out of the mulga and circled the waterhole. A stranger in a red cap and khaki battle-jacket climbed down from the cab, collected the animal and drove back towards us.

'Excuse the interruption,' he said, getting out. 'Thought somebody might like the trophy.'

He dragged the carcass from the tray and dropped it at our feet. The shot had taken off the top of the fox's head.

'Roly Mitchell.' Handshakes all round.

'Jesse Redpath,' I said.

He was an American – overweight, over-armed but amicable enough. Somewhere in his fifties, with a blistered face and a blunt nose.

'You the law out here?' he asked. He seemed surprised. There weren't many women in uniform running round this neck of the desert.

'Depends on what you mean by law,' I replied. 'I'm officer in charge of the station back at Kulara. Danny here's our Aboriginal Community Police Officer.'

Roly looked in the direction we'd come from. 'Kulara? That the shithole I drove through a couple of hours ago?'

'Hopefully.'

Adam was examining the dead fox. 'That was some shot,' he said.

'Technology, mate.' Roly reached into the cabin and pulled out a weapon with a scope that wouldn't have looked out of place at Mount Stromlo Observatory.

'Seven mil Weatherby Magnum.' He ran a hand along the stock. 'This baby's bagged kudu bulls in Mozambique, muskox in the Arctic –'

'You got a permit for it?' I interrupted.

He pulled out a Blackhawk carry-case and plastic folder: four weapons on board, a range of calibres and firepower. They were all legit, paperwork up to date: international visitor's permit, firearms licence. He told us he'd been hunting buffalo in the Top End.

'Where you heading now?' I asked.

'Place called Saddlebag Springs.'

Danny turned to the west and frowned. 'Didn't anybody mention you got three hundred k's of the toughest country on earth between Saddlebag and here?'

'Officer, I'm *equipped*.'

And we had to admit, he was. He gave us the guided tour: satphone, GPS, PTO winch, long-range tanks, plenty of water and fuel. The Rover was better set up than my police Landcruiser. Even the watch on his wrist was like a medieval astronomer's dream, full of exposed sprockets and springs, star wheels, crown wheels, half-a-dozen dials doing god-knows-what: giving him the weather in Mozambique, the snowfall in the Arctic?

I caught the look in Adam's eye. He was staring at the watch, entranced.

'Don't get too excited,' I warned him.

I liked Adam – liked him a lot. He was tall and lithe, long-haired, always ready with a quip or a witty observation. But he was also restless, wild, often in trouble. The week before, he and a mob of mates had gone into Willoughby River, loaded up on goonbag hooch and any other illicit substances they could find. They'd borrowed – stolen – a car, raced it up the town's only hill, missed a turn and driven over the town's only cliff. That was bad enough, but there was a house at the bottom of the cliff. A house belonging to the mayor, who failed to see the funny side of a runaway Holden landing in his bed.

'At least he wasn't in it,' Adam pointed out when the Willoughby coppers charged him.

Adam Lawson had grown up in Kulara – father a FIFO miner who'd F'd O, mother a hippie horticulturalist whose produce had gone increasingly feral over the years, and whose parenting techniques followed a similar trajectory. A few years earlier, she'd run off with the percussionist in a passing Peruvian folkloric band. Adam had stayed in Kulara and run wild. He'd had a few jobs, but he and his little gang mostly concentrated on enjoying themselves.

The visiting magistrate, Lenny Bartlett, had looked at me askance when I supported Legal Aid's request for a suspended sentence. I told him I had a job lined up for Adam.

The magistrate adjusted his glasses and raised his head. He was a tall, spare man with cavernous nostrils that must have given him hell on windy mornings.

'What job is that?' he asked.

'Yard hand at the Nickel Creek roadhouse.'

He frowned and called me up to what passed for a bench in these parts. Lenny had been on the travelling circuit for thirty years; he knew the falls, both pit and prat. He expressed concern that living at a roadhouse would get Adam into more trouble than he was in now.

'He won't be living at the roadhouse, Your Honour,' I explained. 'He's found board with a respected local family.'

He fixed me with a look. 'Jess,' he said. 'I've been passing through Nickel Creek for more years than you've been alive, and I've yet to notice that there are *any* families in the vicinity, respectable or not. Who is this family?'

'My father, Your Honour.'

He raised his brows. 'Ben? He's the family?'

Dad was living in the old Nickel Creek telegraph station. I explained that he'd had a few health scares of late and that we'd all be happier if he had a fit young man about the place to give him a hand.

I had an ulterior motive, of course. I'd caught Adam scribbling his tag round town and his efforts showed spark. My father was a professional artist. I was hoping that he might provide a settling influence, maybe even some inspiration; direct Adam's talents towards more positive forms of expression.

Lenny listened carefully, stared at his desk for a moment then sent me back to my table. He turned to Adam, who'd put on a clean shirt and boots – normally he got around in bare feet – for the court. 'You're fully committed to this arrangement, Mr Lawson?'

'Certainly am, Your Honour.'

'You'll work at the roadhouse? Stay with Constable Redpath's father?'

'Yes, Your Honour.'

The magistrate gave Adam a suspended sentence, provisional upon his living at Nickel Creek for a year and keeping his nose and the roadhouse clean.

I was pleased. Jail-time would have only exacerbated his appetite for life on the edge. All very exciting when you're twenty, like Adam, but you tend to end up dead in a ditch by thirty.

And that was how we found ourselves driving up to Nickel Creek and conversing with this cocksure American.

Roly put his weapons away and checked his watch, keen to be on his way.

I pulled out a map, made some suggestions about tracks and threats. Danny Jakamarra warned him about flash floods; there was rain about, and when it hit, the country could quickly become treacherous.

Roly showed little interest in our advice. He had everything he wanted in his digital devices and equipment, his sleek weaponry. Ten minutes later we went our separate ways – he to the west, our little party to the north.

It had been a brief encounter, but the damage was done. I couldn't say what it was: the guns, the watch, the overall impact of Roly Mitchell and his extravagant rig. Adam's gaze lingered on the disappearing Rover and I knew what he was thinking. That there was another world out there, gold-plated, alluring, light years beyond these windswept plains, and he wanted a look at it.

'You stay out of trouble,' I warned him. 'And town!' I tapped the release papers. 'This is a court order, not a Christmas card from your parole officer.'

'No worries, Jess.' He grinned, flashing a beguiling Adam smile.

CHAPTER 2

Nickel Creek was an hour's drive to the north-west, up where the yellow Mitchell grass cattle country began drying out into spinifex desert. When we reached the roadhouse we turned left and drove the kilometre out to the telegraph station. There was a waterhole lined with ghost gums and bloodwoods, a row of fence posts subsiding into the sand. The station itself was over a hundred years old: it had broad verandahs, stone walls and a miserable geranium contemplating its own mortality beside the stairs. Dad always was a shithouse gardener.

'Stay in the car,' I told Adam.

I knocked on the door. No answer. I stepped inside, suppressing my usual fear – that I'd come across Dad's body on the floor. He was seventy-three, and last year had what sounded to me like a transient ischaemic attack, though he'd refused to see a doctor.

No body.

I checked out the rest of the house. Nothing. Adam materialised beside me, gazing around the chaotic studio with interest.

'People pay for this?' he asked, looking at the studies and sketches on the benches and walls.

'Sometimes.'

I was being modest on Dad's behalf. A qualified hydrologist, he'd come to the Centre with the Geological Survey forty years before and been so fascinated by what he saw, he quit the job and devoted himself to what had always been his real passion in life: art. He'd struggled for years, supported himself with a succession of odd jobs, but now he was represented by major galleries in Melbourne and Sydney.

'Stay here,' I said to Adam.

I went out the back door and walked the couple of hundred metres to the crater.

The Nickel Creek crater was three hundred metres wide and fifteen deep, ringed by cliffs of nickel and sandstone split by deep crevasses. Formed by a meteorite strike a hundred thousand years ago, the crater was the real reason my father had chosen to live here.

I reached the edge and shaded my eyes against the mineral glare. I saw Dad's regular *plein-air* set-up – a beach umbrella, an easel and palette, a wicker chair and the metal trunk in which he kept his gear – down on the crater floor.

But where was the man himself?

I scanned the hollow then spotted him on a ladder halfway up the rock wall directly below me. That would have had him – what? Seven? Eight? – metres from the ground.

I cupped my hands and yelled, 'Didn't anybody tell you there's a law against old blokes climbing anything over knee-height?'

He looked up. 'Fuckin hell, it's the jacks.'

Dad had never hidden his disapproval of my career, figured with a degree to my name I should have been able to come up with something better. He'd also spent years living among rough and rowdy outback characters who had an inbred antipathy towards the law.

'I've brought your boarder,' I said as I worked my way down the rough steps that had been chiselled into the crater.

'My what?' he replied.

'Adam.'

'Who?'

'The young feller who's gonna stay with you. We talked about it on the phone. Don't fall off,' I added when I noticed him scratching his jaw.

I walked across to the foot of the ladder and steadied it.

'Maybe you did say something,' he said as he descended. 'Didn't realise it would be this soon.'

'I said today.'

'I wasn't paying much attention,' he said when he reached the ground. 'Just wanted to get rid of you.'

That didn't surprise me. When Dad was at work – and he was rarely at anything else – he was oblivious to everything except the canvas in front of him.

My father was a wiry feller with a shock of white hair, a dicky knee (and a needy dick, he tended to add at the most inappropriate moments) and the leathery skin of a man who'd absorbed too much sunshine and beef jerky in his life.

'Oy!' he yelled. 'Don't touch that!'

I looked around. It was Adam. He'd followed me down into the crater. He'd picked up Dad's palette and was examining it with interest.

'I told you to stay back at the car.'

He glanced up, smiled, then resumed his examination of the palette, clearly fascinated by its array of intermingled pigments. He ran a finger through the paint and seemed to find pleasure in the cocktail of colour and texture that resulted. For a moment I thought he was going to lick it.

'For fuck's sake, son, put that down,' said Dad. 'Every shade's got its place.'

I looked at the cliff he'd just descended. 'What were you doing up there anyway?'

He pulled a handful of metallic fragments from his pocket.

'It's the laterites in the rockface,' he said. 'The way they absorb and scatter the light. Gotta get up close to see how they do that.'

'Terrific. Ben Redpath, meet Adam Lawson.'

The two studied each other warily, Dad doubtless contemplating the invasion of his solitude, Adam wondering whether Ben-time would really be better than jail-time.

'You two should have a lot in common,' I said.

'Aye?' asked Dad. 'What would that be?'

'You're both artists.'

'Oh?' A flicker of interest flew across his face.

'After a fashion.'

Dad turned to Adam. 'You paint, lad?'

'Sometimes.'

'What?'

Adam shrugged. 'Fences, mainly. Walls if I can get em.'

Dad appeared momentarily disconcerted. He scratched his head and shuffled in his roomy boots. 'Graffiti?'

'Some people call it that.'

'Jesus. That's not art.'

I shot him a look. 'Well, I suppose it *could* be,' he added. 'Theoretically.' He dusted off his hat. 'Anyway, I gather I've signed up to be your landlord. Or warder. Come and I'll show you to your cell.'

We walked back to the house. Danny Jakamarra had stayed with the car. He was leaning against the bull-bar, hat low, boots crossed. He and Dad greeted each other warmly. They'd known each other for years, had even worked together for a while at Mantulyu Station.

We went into the house and discussed the arrangement. Adam would walk up to the roadhouse every morning. He'd sweep floors, wash dishes or cars, do whatever Val, the owner, wanted. He'd sleep in the bungalow behind Dad's place and do odd jobs to pay for his keep.

'You can start at the top and work your way down,' said Dad. 'The roof's leaking.'

'No worries,' Adam chirped. 'Maybe we'll do some painting while we're at it, eh?'

'Like hell we will,' said Dad. 'And don't touch that!' he added when Adam picked up the FitzRoy storm glass he kept on his bench and gave it a shake.

My radio squawked. There was a brawl at the Cape Kennedy roadhouse. The manager said he was under siege and wanted the riot squad.

Danny stood up. He and I were the riot squad. I was grateful to have him with me. He hardly ever had to swing a punch but he tended to calm things down, just by being there.

Dad followed us to the car.

'Just give him a chance, will you?' I said quietly. 'He's a good kid.'

'We'll see.'

I called back at Adam, who'd followed us out onto the verandah.

'You make yourself useful!'

He made a mock salute.

'Aye, aye, Sarge.'

'You think he's gonna stay?' I asked Danny as we drove away.

He glanced back at Adam.

'Maybe.'

* * *

A week later I was awoken by a call from my father.

'Adam's gone,' he said.

I groaned. I shouldn't have been surprised. I thought about that hungry look in his eyes as he gazed after Roly Mitchell's disappearing Rover.

'When?'

'No sign of him when I woke up this morning. Val at the roadhouse reckons he was chatting up some woman in the bar a few days ago. She thinks he might have taken off after her.'

His voice sounded flatter than I would have expected.

'Least you'll get your solitude back now,' I said.

A drawn-out pause, then he muttered, 'I liked that boy.'

'You can go and visit him in jail,' I said, perhaps a little harshly. Adam did have a knack of getting both under your skin and into your heart simultaneously. He'd sneak under the back fence at the drive-in, steal the watermelon you were secretly growing at the tip, turn up at your barbeque and eat half the food. But then he'd flash a smile or crack a joke and your anger would vanish.

I drove round town, checked Adam's usual haunts – the Westside Camp, the Community Cultural Centre – but drew a blank. I asked around the truck stop and heard he'd been spotted climbing into the cabin of a southbound road train.

A week later we heard he was in Adelaide, getting up to god knows what. Then, rumour had it, Victoria. A warrant went out for his arrest, but nobody expected much to come of it. Somebody's second cousin said he'd been spotted in Glenroy, in Melbourne's northern suburbs. The bookkeeper at Lillian Springs Station, where he'd worked in the past, said he'd rung her up, drunk and asking for wages he thought he was owed, then thanked her and hung up before he could tell her where to send it.

CHAPTER 3

Three months passed. Three long, thirsty summer months. Danny Jakamarra and I spent them chasing drink and drug runners along the back roads of Kulara and dragging their sorry customers out of what would have been the gutters, if Kulara had gutters.

This was the most senior posting of my short career, and I was determined to make a go of it. Outsiders might have seen Kulara as a dump, and maybe it was – a cluster of run-down buildings in the middle of a rough-red scoria plain. But it was my dump.

Kulara was a hardscrabble outback town with a population of four or five hundred, most of them Indigenous, and most living in one of two town camps on either side of the highway. It had a store, a school, a bakery, a community centre and a police station. Not much else.

I'd been here for a year now. I played it hard, but I hope I played it fair. The changes were beginning to show. The smugglers were moving on to greener pastures; school attendance was on the rise, crime, the decline. We'd just had our fourth film night in a row not interrupted by a punch-up. Apparently that was a record.

One blazing afternoon we got word of a brawl out on the El Dorado gold diggings, on the other side of our region. Nothing unusual about that – the miners often got a little frisky as the mercury rose and the blood alcohol levels followed suit. But somebody had reported shots being fired.

The incident was a day old, and our chances of coming across a smoking gun were miniscule, but it wouldn't do any harm to get out there and fly the flag, remind the gougers that there was such a thing as the rule of law.

It was also, of course, a good excuse to get away from Kulara.

I stepped out onto the verandah of the police station, shaded my eyes and looked out over the sun-blasted town. We'd had months of no rain, fat black clouds that dumped their load everywhere but here. The thermometers were hitting forty every day. Just walking to the car left you wet and sweaty.

Bandy Quayle, the baker, came out of his shop, stood there smoking a cheroot and scratching his balls, a wonderful advertisement for his bread. Like most of the whitefellers in this godforsaken little town, he looked like he was wondering what on earth he'd done to deserve a place like this. The generator was broken down, yet again: no water, no air-con. Toilets would be blocking up all over town.

From the scrub on the hill came a chorus of raucous noises that needed investigating. There was always a noise that needed investigating, often with unpleasant consequences for both investigator and investigatee.

A bonus of the trip to El Dorado, of course, was that I'd be getting out bush with Danny Jakamarra.

'Getting out bush' with people like Danny was what drew me to this job in the first place. Not that I'd had many options. I'd grown up in the yellow grassland outer suburbs of Melbourne's west with my mother, Helen, the second of Ben Redpath's three wives. A second-rate law degree from a third-rate university hadn't set me up for much more than the dubious job – barmaid-cum-kickboxing instructor – that had sustained me through my studies. I applied to twenty-two firms, received three interviews and an intern position that lasted about as long as the junior partner's drunken attempt to get into my pants at the High End Happy Hour. My legal career outlasted his right incisor, but only by an hour or two. No criminal convictions on my resume, but it was made clear to me that if I wanted it to stay that way, I'd best consider a different career.

That night I drove down to Altona Beach and parked on the foreshore, sat there brooding and gazing out over the choppy waters. I fiddled idly with the dial on the radio, looking for something to distract me from the heaviness in my heart. I heard snatches of jazz, Indian ragas, old pop songs: Lucy Jordan, Ruby Tuesday. Then a lone voice scattered and sent them all packing with a ballad that floated over the bay like a sea eagle. It was Gurrumul, singing one of his magnificent paeans to his country. The song brought to mind the time

I'd spent at Warluju when Dad was working there as an arts advisor. My mum had sent me up to him from time to time, when I got too hard to handle, and I realised how much the desert and its people had seeped into my being. There and then, I decided to return to the Territory.

But what employment options were there for a failed lawyer whose most notable attributes were a roundhouse kick and a motor mouth?

Only one came to mind and three months later I found myself on the Recruit Constable training course with the Northern Territory Police Force. To everybody's surprise, I'd thrived. I actually enjoyed the responsibility. The grief I got from the odd sexist Neanderthal – colleague or customer – served only to remind me of the axiom I'd developed growing up in Laverton: when you run into a brick wall, put your best shoulder forward and run again.

I spent a year in Darwin, two in Alice, another in Willoughby River. I'd been given the Kulara job – and the promotion to leading senior constable that went with it – a year ago.

* * *

Danny and I set out for El Dorado the next morning.

We travelled south, turned onto the Gunshot Road and drove for hours. We didn't talk much – Danny was a quiet man at the noisiest of times. It was a slow journey, made slower by the fact that the farther we went, the keener he seemed to get out, look around and frown.

We reached El Dorado early afternoon and spent a couple of hours driving around talking to the miners in their dusty demountables and dingy rabbit holes. We didn't learn much, of course. Yes, there'd been a scuffle. No, nobody was injured, and nobody knew anything about any shots being fired. Nobody knew anything about anything. All good here, now piss off.

Danny stayed by my side, asked the odd question, made the occasional comment, but I could tell his mind was elsewhere. He seemed distracted, on edge. When we were ready to head back home, he asked if we could go out to Kalaringi, a waterhole half an hour's drive to the east.

'Is there something wrong?' I asked.

'I'll tell you when we get there.'

Danny Jakamarra was the best bushman I'd ever known. He was in his fifties now, heavily built, arthritis setting in, but he'd grown up on Mantulyu Station and spent his early days in the saddle – he'd seen the country close up and could read it like nobody else. His tracking skills were in constant demand: stolen beef, on or off the hoof, disoriented grey nomads, the odd bungled burglary or wanted man.

The drive to Kalaringi was a slow one, Danny pulling over every so often to scour the bush. When we reached the waterhole he took off again, walking alongside the track, up into the sandhills, kneeling down from time to time.

I made a fire and boiled the billy. When Danny came back he picked up a stick and scratched out a drawing in the sand, then studied it intensely.

'So what's troubling you?' I handed him his pannikin and an Anzac biscuit.

He took a sip and a bite then looked around. We were at the western end of one of the tracks that crept out of the desert there. A gust of wind stirred a willy-willy, a bug-eyed lizard looked on with interest.

'What do you see here, Jess?'

We did this sometimes; it was his way of passing a little bit of his knowledge on to the ignorant white woman.

I took a few steps across the clearing, then crouched down, reading the surface as best I could. It was a good time to be looking at country: the slanting afternoon light made things stand out.

'Goanna tracks there,' I said. 'Old – eight, maybe nine months.'

'How do you figure that?'

'That was the last time we had decent rain. There's scuff marks on the windrow, and a white feather: couple of magpies fighting? This here's a *mulurr* bush – good for cough medicine. There's been a fire come through, scarred the branches, year or two ago.'

I looked at him expectantly.

'Very good,' he said. 'Though one of the maggies was a mudlark. Now what *don't* you see?'

Jesus. How do you answer a question like that? Where do I begin?

Danny helped me out. 'That American feller,' he said.

I had to scratch my head to remember. 'The one with the guns?'

'I'm worried he never made it out of the dry country.'

I hadn't given Roly Mitchell a moment's consideration since we'd left him at the waterhole all those months ago. But Danny had. As we'd traversed the complex set of scratches and scuffs that form the desert crust, the footprints and paw prints, the claw prints, wheel tracks and scuttle marks, something had clicked. Not a presence but an absence.

'I been lookin the whole way,' he explained. 'If he'd come out of the dry country, we'd have seen something. Those fat tyres o' his, they stand out.'

He noticed I was puzzled and muttered, 'It isn't always what you see, Jess.'

The unspoken corollary: sometimes it's what you don't.

'We better track him down,' I said.

He gave a bleak smile that said 'No rush'.

I'd seen that expression before, most recently when we were searching for a poor disturbed woman who'd disappeared from Solar Well. Danny had started in a whirlwind of activity, running, climbing, scrambling over rocks and sand. But mid-afternoon he slowed down, realising he'd been called in too late.

'How do you learn to read country like that?' I asked him.

'Takes time.'

'Sure, but what else does it take?'

He ran a hand through his stubble, gave the question a moment's consideration.

'You gotta listen,' he said at last.

'To what?'

He gazed at the desert sky, clearly wondering how to put it in words I would understand. In the end, he chose a story, as was his wont.

'When I was a kid at Mantulyu,' he said, 'the manager got me to look after this old donkey engine.' I'd seen a donkey engine out there – a kind of early, steam-powered winch. 'When it was working properly, it just glided along, all the parts interlocking smoothly. But if you heard a knock – even a little one – you knew that, sooner or later, it was gonna come back and bite you on the arse.'

He finished his biscuit and tossed the skerricks of his tea into the red sand.

'That's it?' I asked.

'Sorry to disappoint you, Jess, but that's about it, far as I know. If you hear that knock – doesn't matter what you're doin, whether you're hunting a man or a turkey, whether you're maintaining a motor or digging for water – something ain't right. Something's out of place.'

We sat there quietly, then packed up and drove back to Kulara.

CHAPTER 4

The next morning we retraced our journey out into the del Fuego desert. We reached the waterhole at noon and picked up the Rover's distinctive tread marks as they headed west.

I couldn't exactly say we followed him. Roly had barged through the bush with all the finesse of a rampaging Panzer. Danny took the wheel, carved a delicate path through prickle-bush and ti-tree, didn't get a single puncture.

'Feller don't know the tracks,' he commented, shaking his head.

We found the Rover soon afterwards. It was out on a vast expanse of gibber I knew to be criss-crossed by sharp gullies and washouts.

We pulled up twenty metres away, got out and walked.

The cab was empty, but a quick assessment told me what had gone wrong: everything. He'd spun out in a flash flood, hit a concealed crevice and damaged an axle. A couple of broken stumps and a loose cable suggested he'd tried to winch himself out of trouble and failed. The satphone was still in its case.

Where was the man himself?

We spotted a line of footsteps to the west. We followed them and found what the scavengers had left of the body at the bottom of a steep gully. He'd obviously tumbled in, broken something vital. Had it happened at night? Had he gone to gather more wood to brace the winch? The Magnum lay beside him. He must have brought it along as a protection against … what? Snakes? His shattered jawbone suggested that the weapon hadn't been as reliable as he'd hoped, that his precious technology couldn't do everything for him.

I climbed down for a closer look and was taken aback. Not by the death – I saw a lot of that in this job. It was the watch. The bloody thing was still going, its wheels clicking and spinning, its face grinning in a weird, digital rictus.

Danny Jakamarra's words came to mind: 'Feller don't know the tracks.'

I've been roaming over these spinifex plains for a few years now, and the further I go the more I feel the significance of those words. Reality assembles itself in patterns, like iron filings on a magnet. We all travel, and when we do, if we know what's good for us, we follow the tracks of those who've gone before. A feller in a pub told me even the vast highways of southern Australia follow ancient songlines. Tracks.

There were procedures to be followed, formalities to be observed. We went back to the radio and raised Willoughby River. Got our boss, Sergeant Tom Vallence. I began to give him the news but he got in first, his tone grim.

'We just got some bad news,' he said.

Bad news? Common as red dirt round here.

'Young Adam Lawson.'

Danny clicked his tongue and caught my eye. I should have been expecting this. The bloody city was a deathtrap for someone like Adam.

'How'd it happen?' I asked.

'Car crash.'

I sighed.

'It gets worse,' said Tom.

How could it?

'Seems he murdered somebody down there. Woman. Stole her car, ran off the road trying to get away.'

I leaned back into the seat and closed my eyes. What had I done?

The static rustled and pulsed like a sandstorm battering a tin roof.

'Redpath!' he snapped. 'You there?'

'Yeah.'

'This is radio. Silence doesn't work.'

I reported my own news, which really made Tom's day.

'Three months?' he repeated dismally.

'Bout that.'

'Past stinkin?'

'Pretty well.'

We arranged to meet back at the highway. He said he'd be out there with the ambos in a couple of hours.

As I signed off my attention was caught by a couple of crows parked in a nearby ghost gum. They were gazing down at me, their eyes opalescent.

One flapped its wings and carked; the note drifted out over the spinifex plains with a long, dying cadence.

CHAPTER 5

It was dark when we pulled up in front of the Kulara police station.

Danny grabbed his swag, said he'd see me tomorrow and headed off to the house next door, where he lived with his wife and a fluctuating posse of kids.

I went into my own place, grabbed a water bottle from the fridge, guzzled it down and gasped for air. Second bottle, same thing. I stripped off, showered, pulled on a singlet and shorts. Made my way to the little gym I'd set up in the shed.

First port of call, the punching bag. I skipped the foreplay: kick, slam, double punch, grunt. Kick, slam, double punch, grunt. Over and over, faster, harder, building up a head of sweat and steam. Feeling the recoil bouncing through my bones. I took a second or two's rest then went at it again, lost myself in a blizzard of fists and feet.

Somewhere in all the fury I must have yelled, because when I paused for breath I heard the door scrape. Danny was standing there, a pannikin in each hand.

'You okay, Jess?'

'Just letting off a bit of steam,' I gasped.

'Looked more atomic than hydraulic,' he said. 'Heard the racket, figured you were having a party or a punch-up.'

I bent over, elbows on knees, breath short. Felt it coming on: the tightening of the lungs, the rasp and wheeze. Bloody asthma. I'd managed to conceal it when I was recruited, but it was getting worse. The dusty desert winds were playing havoc with my lungs.

I found the inhaler I kept on the shelf and gave myself a blast. Took another for good measure. My chest felt better but my head was spinning.

We took our teas and sat on the back verandah. 'It's not your fault, you know,' said Danny.

'Isn't it?' I wheezed.

I licked a little of the sweat from my lips, hawked and spat into the dirt. 'I'm the one who took him out to Nickel Creek. If he'd been in jail, none of this would have happened.'

'That was the magistrate's decision, Jess. You think he's lying awake worrying about it? It was what people round here wanted. You never said we'd provide twenty-four-seven security. We were just the taxi.'

I stared out through the doorway, up into the lively outback sky. You could almost see the stars orbiting. The iron rooftops glimmered with reflected light.

'Doesn't make sense,' I said.

'Not much of what you whitefellers do makes sense to me,' he said. 'But you're right. I've known Adam all his life. Wouldn't have thought he had a nasty bone in his body. Plenty of funny ones, nothing violent.'

Tom Vallence had given us more details when we met him at the highway. The victim was a 21-year-old woman named Daisy Baker. She lived in a little bush community called Canticle Creek, in the Windmark Ranges, north-east of Melbourne. She and Adam appeared to have been in a relationship. All the evidence supported the story: Adam had bashed her to death, stolen her car and made a panicky getaway. He'd driven hard and fast. Too fast. He'd ended up at the bottom of a cliff a kilometre from the crime scene. The autopsy report said he had a cocktail of drugs in his system.

'And those coppers down there, they're sure of all this?' asked Danny. He had little faith in forensic science, his trust never straying far from the evidence presented by his own senses.

I shrugged and said I wasn't sure of anything. Tom Vallence had a mate who worked for Homicide in Melbourne who'd promised to keep us informed.

I looked out over the community, momentarily distracted by the radiant geometry of the streetlights and their orbiting insects. A road-train rattled past, its cargo of doomed Brahmans mooing mournfully through the bars. I took a sip of tea and shook my head.

'This was the job I wanted, Danny. I was gonna make a difference. Make up for the troglodytes who came before me.'

'And you have.'

'Sure – for the worse. If Scully was still here, he'd have given Adam a smack in the mouth, beaten a bit of sense into him. Might've had a few less teeth, but he'd be alive. Him and the woman.'

33

Danny frowned. 'Jesus, Jess, you start comparing yourself unfavourably to Brent Scully, you must have taken leave of your senses.'

He may have had a point. Scully, my predecessor twice removed, had been convicted of rape and drummed out of the force. Last anybody heard of him he'd been drinking and boring himself to death in a bar in Chiang Mai.

We heard a horse whinny, a set of hooves pound the earth.

'Settle down, you mob!' Danny yelled into the darkness. He kept a couple of horses in the yard behind his house. On his days off, he sometimes rode with his kids to the family outstation west of here.

He stood up and began to walk away, then paused.

'You try to get some sleep,' he said.

He knew me too well. I spent a restless night on sweaty sheets, then rose early. I stepped out onto the back verandah, still yawning. Hardy, the rainbow-feathered rooster, squawked and strutted in the yard.

There was one more job I had to do and I wasn't looking forward to it. I thought about the surprising note of melancholy in Dad's voice when he rang to tell me Adam had absconded. Best to do this face to face.

I kitted up and drove out to Nickel Creek. When I pulled up in front of the telegraph station Dad's car was there, but he wasn't. I walked to the crater, but there was no sign of him there either.

I returned to the house and waited.

Scattered across the kitchen table was a pile of papers: bills, notices, letters from agents and galleries.

A thump at the kitchen door and Dad appeared, his arms laden with firewood.

'Turning me into a social fucking butterfly,' he said as he dropped his load next to the stove.

'Hello to you too.'

We exchanged a few more unpleasantries, then he peered at me suspiciously. 'Okay, girl. What's wrong?'

No hiding anything from my father. He might have been a little lacking in social skills, but not observational ones.

'It's Adam.'

His eyes brightened. 'He's turned up?'

'Turned up dead.'

'Fuck,' he muttered. His mouth drew tight. 'I had a bad feeling the moment he disappeared. How'd it happen?'

'Car crash.'

'In Melbourne?'

'Nearby. Place called Canticle Creek.'

I took a deep breath and told him that the police were saying Adam had killed a woman.

'What! In the crash?'

I began to give him the details of the incident, but I hadn't got far before he interrupted me.

'Bullshit. Who told you all this? Your band of bloody brothers?'

'Homicide are still investigating, but I gather the evidence is clear-cut.'

'Clear-cut to some idiotic southern fucking flatfoot, maybe.' He shook his head angrily. 'Not to anybody who knew the boy. Somebody's got their wires crossed.'

He sat there, brooding, then got up and headed for the door.

'Want to show you something,' he said.

He led me to the five-thousand-gallon concrete water tank out back. When we got to its western side, he put his hands on my shoulders and turned me around.

'What do you make of that?'

There was a mural on the tank wall that hadn't been there last time I looked.

It was an elongated portrait of Nickel Creek; not just of the meteorite crater, but of the entire community: the roadhouse, telegraph station, highway. And its inhabitants: there was Val in the kitchen, her husband Frank changing a tyre, a mob of ringers laughing in the bar. I even spotted my father, standing on the rim of the crater, soaking up the glare of its reflected minerals.

Some of the details were rough, the paint splashed around wildly, but the overall effect was extraordinary. The characters – and I'd have to include buildings, fences and power lines in the term – were moving in a kind of frozen dance that seemed to illuminate something inside them.

'You didn't tell me,' said Dad, 'the boy was *good*.'

I shook my head. 'I didn't realise he was *that* good.'

'He was always hanging round, watching me work. That got annoying, so I started showing him things: the colour wheel, shape and line. Took me a few days to realise I was wasting my time – he had more talent in his little finger than I've got in my whole body. Tried to teach him perspective, but he had his own perspective – based on speed and light. All the energy of the desert sky – the stars and the sun, the creeks and crystals – came out of his brush. He learnt so *fast*. Must have picked that up from painting on the run in the backstreets.'

I listened carefully, even though what I was hearing was making me feel worse. He told me how Adam had stayed late at the roadhouse one night and Dad had growled at him. Dad had spent the next day working down in the crater. When he came back he found the mural on the tank and a note on the table.

He fished it out of his pocket and passed it over.

Sorry, man, gotta go. Thanks for showing me what you do. It's brill. Borrowed some of your gear, pay you back when I can. Adam.

He waved an angry hand at the mural. 'Look at it. The life! The colour! You're saying somebody capable of doing work like that is capable of beating a woman to death? I say bullshit.'

I turned back to the painting, lost for words.

After a while, we went inside. I made some tea, pulled out the lamingtons I'd picked up at the roadhouse. Dad had a nibble of one, but I doubt he even tasted it. Coconut fluttered onto his chin.

'You shouldn't have left him with a silly old goat like me,' he muttered. 'Boy like that, he needed room to move. He was right to hit the road. No telling what he could have done if some bastard hadn't killed him.'

'Far as I know, Dad, he killed himself.'

He poured himself a shot of rum and stepped out onto the verandah.

I stayed at the table, feeling frustrated, useless.

A flash of colour among the papers caught my eye. I picked it up. It was an invitation to an exhibition from the National Gallery in Melbourne. The event was called 'The Illuminated Lake: Journeys into Australian Landscape'.

Dad got a lot of these, generally filed them in the bin.

I took a closer look at the invitation. It featured one of his crater paintings, *Nickel Creek 15* – a stratified wall of scarlet rock, shot through with silver sparks and facetted arrows. Below it was another painting, one I didn't recognise. It wasn't one of Dad's, but its vivid blues and greens were a surprisingly effective counterpoint to his red-dirt fire and light.

Curious, I checked the identity of the other artist. Kenji Takada. Takada? The name rang a bell: a Japanese painter who'd settled in Australia years ago.

But it was the title of the painting that stopped me in my tracks.

Canticle Creek. The place where Adam died.

Coincidence or omen?

I knew straightaway what I was going to do.

I took the invitation outside and showed it to Dad. Like me, he was struck by the connection between Takada's painting and Adam's death. He listened carefully while I explained my plan. He would accept the invitation, and I would attend the launch on his behalf, meet anyone I could from Canticle Creek and use whatever connections I made to visit the area and investigate Adam's death.

When I'd finished talking he stared out into the scrub for a minute then checked his watch. 'When are we leaving?'

'We?' I groaned quietly.

CHAPTER 6

My sergeant, Tom Vallence, approved the leave. He'd known Adam, arrested him on the odd occasion, always been amused by his cheery insouciance.

Dad and I drove up to Willoughby River the day before the flight. I dropped him off at a mate's house and went in to the station, where I found the boss in his office.

After a minute or two's chit-chat he asked what exactly I was hoping to achieve in Melbourne.

'Not quite sure,' I replied. 'Look around. See if it makes any more sense down there than it does from up here. See how much of this fucking mess I'm responsible for.'

He snorted. 'It's the job, Jess. You make decisions. Show me somebody who says he's always made the right ones, I'll show you an idiot or a liar.'

He shuffled through his in-tray and pulled out a file.

'Bit of reading for the trip,' he said.

I opened it up, closed it fast. Opened it again, more carefully: a woman, blonde, mouth agape, eyes staring at infinity. Too much colour. There were more photos and they didn't get any better. The look on her face was one of crushed innocence. So much violence visited upon one so young; her beauty was still visible through the bruises and blood.

The pictures of Adam were worse. I barely recognised what was left of him.

I flicked through the rest of the file: medical examiner's report, witness statements, photographs, forensics.

I looked up at Tom. 'Your mate from Melbourne?'

'Compliments of.'

I found a spare desk and started reading. By the time I'd finished, I had to admit that the case against Adam looked damning.

Ms Baker lived in a cottage on Messmate Lane, Canticle Creek, an hour's drive north-east of Melbourne. She was an artist. The community, the author of the report noted, was 'full of artists', as if they were some kind of vermin, rabbits or cane toads.

Daisy and Adam were apparently in a relationship. They'd met when she was travelling through the Territory and he'd followed her down south. They'd been spotted by a local teenager at a traffic accident the evening before. Next morning, the teenager – one Alice Kelly – had come across Daisy's battered body in a ditch beside the cottage.

The lead investigator, a Detective Senior Sergeant Wallace, suggested there'd been some sort of drug-fuelled altercation, a lovers' tiff gone ape. Adam bashed her to death, fled in her HiLux. The road was described as 'treacherous and windy'. He'd missed a turn, flown over the edge and through the windscreen. He wasn't wearing a seatbelt – his head was almost severed.

They found her blood on his hands, his prints on the rock with which she'd been bashed, a baggie in his pocket. The autopsy had detected traces of ice in his hair, marijuana in his blood.

Damning.

I read the file again. An hour later I went out onto the back porch for a break. Collingwood, the station cat, curled around my feet and purred. An inebriated ringer with a big hat and a bad voice was strumming a guitar in the yard and serenading some unlucky bastard in the cells.

Why was I doing this? To assuage my guilt? Or was it that I just couldn't reconcile the cheeky young man I remembered with the vicious killer portrayed in the report? But what did I really know about Adam? He'd been gone for months, lost and sinking into the cesspit of the city. He'd been running wild, using ice. God only knew what that had done to him. I was letting my heart rule my head.

I turned to go, then hesitated. I scratched my temple, dredging something up from the bog hole of my brain. I pushed Collingwood away, went back and scrambled through the report, found the detail that had snagged in my memory.

A minute later I was knocking on Tom's door.

'The report said he was high on ice.'

He barely looked up from his computer. 'Isn't everybody down there?'

I explained the anomaly I'd spotted in the case notes. Forensics had found traces of crystal meth in Adam's hair but not his blood. It lasts ninety days in hair, but only three in blood. That suggested that he hadn't been high when she was killed.

Tom took off his reading glasses, breathed on them, gave them a rub and put them back on.

'You figure they don't know that down south? Bunch of ignoramuses?'

'People jump to conclusions. We knew Adam. They didn't. I couldn't imagine him killing anybody unless he was affected by drugs.'

Tom leaned forward, elbows on the table, ran his hands up into the receding hairline. He looked like a man dreaming of retirement, the Queensland beach block and its azure waters beckoning. Most of these old desert coppers seemed to have a beach block waiting for them somewhere; it was the waterbag that saw them through the dry times.

'Bit of an artist, wasn't he?' he said. 'Young Adam.'

I nodded, unsure of where this was going.

'You're an artist too, Jess. In your own weird way.' He turned back to his computer, punched the keys, cop-style. 'You still doing that Chinese kicking thing?'

'Thai.'

'Whatever.' He shook his head. 'God help Melbourne.'

* * *

During the flight down south I read through the information an online search had given me about Kenji Takada. The surname, I learnt, meant 'hawk'.

Widely regarded as one of the formative spirits of the post-war generation, Takada had come from Japan in the fifties to work at a pottery studio in Windmark, sixty k's north-east of Melbourne. He built a shack at the nearby Canticle Creek, painted it blue, took to taking long walks through the bush. And, intrigued by what he saw around him, he began to paint: first on clay, then on packing boxes, cardboard, finally canvas.

Over the next twenty-five years – until he succumbed to the tuberculosis he'd carried with him from Japan – Takada produced a flood of landscape art his biographer described as 'a subversive intrusion of Asian sensibility into the Great Australian Rawness'. He married a local woman, Marina, but the current guardian of his legacy was their daughter, Lucy. She was in her forties and still lived in what had become known as the Bluehouse.

Dad spent most of the flight relaxing under his rabbit-skin hat or sipping Bundy and Coke. After a couple of drinks he asked what my mother was up to.

'Budapest, according to the last postcard,' I replied.

My parents had met when Mum was working as a nanny at Mantulyu Station and Dad was out there sinking wells. He swept her off her feet for long enough for me to be conceived, but by the time I made my appearance she'd figured out that she'd got the station dud. Instead of the romantic cowboy she'd imagined, she'd teamed up with a man whose only interest in life was slapping paint onto the canvases that were gathering dust in the annex of the caravan in which we lived. 'Rocks!' she'd growl if ever I asked about him. 'That's all he ever did. Paint bloody rocks.' She fled for Laverton North, from whence she'd come, did a six-week course in aged care and spent the next twenty-eight years working in a hostel.

I'd always imagined that the rocks Dad was painting were like the ornamental two or three we had in our little patch of garden, but when I did finally get to see his canvases I found them strangely compelling. That said, we'd learnt never to expect anything from him, and nobody was more surprised than we were when he began to send us small amounts of money. Those small amounts gradually turned into big amounts. Mum thought he must have been robbing banks, but eventually it emerged that somebody had decided his rocks were works of genius. She adjusted to the money without much difficulty, as you do, buying a house and making an annual overseas holiday, both firsts for her.

'She's on something called the Crystal River Cruise,' I explained.

Dad harrumphed, took a swig of rum and returned to his hat. From time to time he'd emerge for long enough to take note of the burnished plains below.

'Dry down there,' he commented.

'It's desert. Meant to be dry.'

'Not that dry. Whole country's turning into a desert. Fucking hot too.'

I suggested it would be cooler in Melbourne, but he didn't look hopeful and took another swig.

'And go easy on the booze,' I added. 'We're here to do a job.'

He growled again but I was pleased to notice he didn't touch another drop for the rest of the flight.

We touched down and made our way through the exit. Among the waiting crowd I spotted a needle-thin hipster with a sign that said 'Redpath'. He introduced himself as Edgar Winters, said he was an assistant curator at the gallery.

'Bit warm today,' he said apologetically as he piled our bags and swags onto a trolley.

'We're from the Territory,' I assured him. 'Think we can handle it.'

We stepped outside and were nearly blown off our feet by a blast of burning red wind that must have followed us down from Willoughby River. Coffee cups, dust and dirty food wrappers whirled through the air, battered our bodies, scratched our eyes. The only unaffected thing was Dad's hat, which had been known to stay in place through cyclones.

Edgar waved, exposing a sweaty armpit. 'And it's a warm welcome to Melbourne.'

I sniffed. The air stank. The horizon was a grey blur. People were wearing masks. There were particles of carbon on the wind.

'Smells like the end of the world,' said Dad.

Edgar explained that there were out-of-control bushfires up in the Wimmera and the smoke shouldn't be here for long.

He delivered us to a fancy hotel and signed us in. A couple of hours and a hot shower or two later we strolled down to the exhibition at the National Gallery.

CHAPTER 7

'There's you,' I commented to Dad as we approached the gallery. A reproduction of his *Nickel Creek 15* was on a banner to the left of the entrance.

It was a simple image but, as you gazed at it, the picture seemed to hum, like a distant generator, or galaxy. The Nickel Creek crater was formed by an ancient meteorite strike; Dad's painting was like a particle or spark thrown up by that falling object's explosive impact.

On the opposite side was Takada's *Canticle Creek*. If my father's work was about energy, Takada's was a study in grace. It was an underwater scene – among its lilting imagery I made out a basket of light, a fringe of aquatic plants, the shadow of a platypus. The banner seemed to be rippling in the breeze, then I realised there was no breeze, that the wind had died down and the sense of movement came from the painting itself.

Whatever lift the banners gave me evaporated as we entered the gallery and looked out over the noisy throng. We'd both spent years in the desert and large congregations tended to overwhelm us.

'Here we fuckin go,' Dad grunted.

There were sulphur-crested women with orange skin and hazardous heels, feral businessmen with titanium teeth and statement ties. Around them surged chicken-skin widows with screw-tight eyes and come-along toy boys. Investors looking for a bargain, artists for a feed.

There was a promising spread on the tables, but a cordon of po-faced waiters to make it clear that the food was off-limits until after the speeches.

'Ben Redpath!'

The flamboyant fellow cruising in to greet us turned out to be Clive Carpenter, the senior curator. He was flaxen-haired, with a wheat-bag belly, a bright blue suit and a nose like a burst sausage.

He said how thrilled he was that we could make it, asked about our journey and accommodation then introduced us to some of the nearby guests. We met a bloke named Ice with eyes like wheels of fire and a performance artist who 'worked with balsa and glue', a conversation killer if ever I heard one.

Soon afterwards Clive's plummy voice boomed through the speakers. 'My friends – if I could have your attention please.'

He was up on a dais. I was worried he was about to make the speech himself, but a few minutes later I was wishing he had. The real launcher, a cutting edge professor from a chipboard university in the city's west, was leaping from one academic apercu to the next so swiftly that he reminded me of Hardy, the spangled rooster who strutted about my yard picking bugs out of the dust.

The speech may have been the best since Gettysburg, but I had very little idea of what the bugger was talking about. Other members of the audience clearly felt the same way – they began glancing at their watches, exploring their nostrils, chewing their lips.

They may have had to eat their own heads had not the Professor inserted into his discourse a rhetorical question: 'Is there anything as vital to the rejuvenation of a culture as the persistence of the artist as *wild* man, as alien jester-spy, as feral emissary from the barbarian frontier to the king's court?' – and a young female muttered a response that somehow cleaved the room.

'Yeah – dinner.'

People laughed. Dad looked around appreciatively – a heckler after his own heart.

The culprit was a teenage girl standing with a couple off to my left; she was staring at the ceiling with an expression of such doe-eyed innocence it had to be contrived. The woman beside her was frowning, the middle-aged man was struggling to suppress a smile.

The professor lost his place. Clive Carpenter, sensing the mood of the room, stepped up and thanked him for the speech, then let slip the dogs of dinner.

The teenager was as quick with her feet as she was with her mouth. She was one of the first to emerge from the crowd at the table, piled plate in hand. She re-joined the couple who were standing next to a painting I realised was Takada's *Canticle Creek*.

Edgar, the assistant curator who'd met us at the airport, approached them and gestured at the painting. The woman replied curtly, casting her gaze across the canvas with such a casual, almost proprietorial, intimacy that I knew at once who she was.

When Edgar moved on I went across and spoke to her.

'You wouldn't be related to this painting, would you?' I asked.

She gave a fleeting smile. 'My father always told me I was in it.'

I'd been right – she was the artist's daughter.

I followed her gaze and gestured at the closest approximation I could see to a living creature. 'Thought that was a platypus.'

'It is.'

I put out a hand and introduced myself.

'Lucy Takada,' she replied.

She was cool-eyed, dark-haired, elegantly accoutred in a tight black dress and a pearl necklace that shimmered against her tawny skin.

When Dad introduced himself her smile was contained but genuine. She said how pleased she was to see his work alongside her father's and then introduced us to her companions.

The bloke was her husband, Sam. He was wearing a ragged suit and a lopsided smile, with more hair sprouting from his ears than his scalp. He appeared to be enjoying the gathering about as much as Dad and I were.

The teenager was their daughter. Did I hear the name correctly? Possum? Eyes like that, I could see why. She had wild, blackbird hair, slim white pants and a jacket sprinkled and lit with mirrors. Fifteen, maybe sixteen.

When she heard we were from the Territory, she studied us with a thinly veiled suspicion.

'Which part?' she asked.

'Small town you've probably never heard of.'

'Try me.'

'Kulara.'

Her frown darkened. She was about to say more, but before she could do so we were joined by another couple, Dominic and Sheree. They were from Windmark, the regional town closest to Canticle Creek.

Dad was polite, but subdued – until he shook hands with Dominic.

'I've met you before,' he said, studying the bloke's wrist. I followed his gaze and spotted a little bird of prey tattooed there. 'You're Dom Talia.'

Dominic raised a brow.

'Warluju,' Dad explained. 'I was working there as an arts adviser. You ran a clinic – taught the young boys how to do a banana kick.'

I rolled my eyes. Bloody football. There was no escape. Even my old man couldn't help but get swept up in the game.

'My god,' said Dominic, 'that was twenty years ago. Club sent us up there during the off-season.'

Not a surprise to me – an excellent memory and an eye for an image were common denominators in Dad's various pursuits.

'Dom was one of our local stars,' Sam explained to me. 'Played with the mighty Hawks.'

'They weren't that mighty when I was with them,' Dominic said, 'and I was never a star.'

'Pulled on the guernsey, mate. Makes you a star in the eyes of a lot of people.'

'What position did you play?' I asked him.

He gave a modest smile and said he was just an odd-job man they used to plug holes in the defence.

'Ah, mate,' said Sam, 'don't put yourself down. Maybe you weren't the most naturally gifted player on the ground but, my god, you were the most determined. Not to mention resourceful. Remember the time you pulled down Denny Hartung's pants while he was going for a mark?'

'Still hasn't forgiven me, Denny.'

'Woulda worked if they hadn't caught it on camera.'

Dominic's deep belly-laugh rolled over the gathering like a breaker. 'Silly bugger should have worn a jockstrap. Pixel-dick they call him now. That picture's as close as I got to football immortality – been dining out on it for years.'

Another man joined the group. He was introduced as Christie Looms, also from Canticle Creek. He was a tall, podgy individual with fiery cheeks, spectacles and a scruffy beard. Maybe in his early thirties, he was wearing new jeans and an op-shop shirt that did little to flatter his figure. There was an air of isolation about him, something everybody else seemed to take for granted.

Christie was apparently a sculptor. In response to a question from Lucy Takada, he explained that he'd just finished working on a commission for Dominic's company.

'It's an installation for the new estate we're building,' added Sheree Talia.

'Installation?' queried Sam. 'Saw a turd in Gladwrap once, catalogue said it was an installation. What is yours exactly, Chris?'

'It's a sculpture of a blue wren,' replied Christie. 'Metal and glass on a stone base.'

'It's a masterpiece,' said Dom. 'The boys are putting it up this week. You'll be able to judge for yourself.'

Christie scanned the room, a thirsty look on his face. 'What's a feller gotta do to get a drink round here?'

I'd been wondering that myself. Dominic nodded at a passing waiter and managed to secure refreshments for us all. Christie's first drink vanished as soon as it arrived and was quickly followed by a couple more. The noise level went up a decibel or ten as the booze kicked in. A string quartet in the corner belted out a mercurial melody. Waves of laughter rolled through the room.

I caught Dad's eye; he was thinking the same thing I was: time we weren't here. We made our farewells. Lucy gave us a card and invited us to visit the Bluehouse if we were ever in the Canticle neighbourhood.

As we headed for the exit, I felt somebody's gaze drilling me in the back. I glanced around. It was the young girl, Possum. She held my eye for a moment, then returned her attention to more important matters on her plate.

We headed up St Kilda Road. Stood for a minute on Princes Bridge, gazing into the glittering cityscape: flashing clocks and trains, the green–gold dome of the station. The river shivered, a neon snake rolling out into the bay, the strait, the lonely Southern Ocean.

I glanced at the card: *Lucy Takada. Ceramic Artist. Bluehouse Road, Canticle Creek.*

I checked it on my phone. Bluehouse Road was a few minutes' drive from Messmate Lane, where Daisy Baker died.

'Tomorrow morning, Dad, fancy a little run up into the hills?'

CHAPTER 8

The morning sky was an improvement. Most of the smoke that was stinking out the city had been blown away. The horizons were still hazy, though, and the weather steamy.

We checked out of our hotel and hired an SUV. We drove through the crane-riddled CBD, out into the brain-dead outer suburbs and the parched, yellow paddocks, up towards the distant Windmark Ranges. It was mixed agricultural and forest country: we passed paddocks dotted with Herefords and alpaca, undulating vineyards, orchards and pick-your-own berry farms. Massive timber trucks ran down from the heavily forested slopes that lined the road. Half an hour into the ranges we entered a winding valley, then the town of Windmark.

The main road was lined with plane trees and Victorian-era buildings, with covered verandahs and brick chimneys. The community looked like somebody had drawn a line through it: timber mills and industrial workshops on one side of the road, galleries and wine cellars on the other. The right and the left, the gritty and the green, the old and the *ye olde*. The division must have made for some interesting town council meetings.

We bought coffee and pies from a bustling bakery then sat on a bench overlooking a river that, according to the Rooftop map I'd picked up at a servo, was called the Flinders. We studied the map, trying to get our bearings. The vehicle had GPS, but one thing I'd learnt from years of running around the outback was that no device could replace the myriad observations, interactions and specks of experience we call instinct. You have to feel a country and its inhabitants, feel it in your gut, learn from your mistakes, listen to the wind, walk the slopes. You don't find that in a machine. I did, however, have a pair of binoculars I'd brought from home.

'What's the plan, officer?' asked Dad.

I put the map aside. 'Dunno if it's anything as grandiose as a plan. Just have a bit of a sniff around. See if anything stinks.'

'Where do we start?'

'Up there.' I indicated the jackknife ridges and tall timber to the south-east. 'According to the map, Canticle Creek is four or five k's that-away.'

He raised his eyes to the hills and snorted.

'That oughta be easy enough,' he said wryly.

After dicking around with the map, a Melways and the case notes, we set off in the general direction of the southern slopes of the Windmark Valley. On the outskirts of town we came to a Robinwood Road. I pulled over and checked the map.

'This is where we go left,' I said. 'I think.'

There was a little white ute in the shade of a billboard, a little white man at the wheel munching his lunch and reading *The Herald Sun*. The billboard said *Robinwood Lakes Estate*, the sign on the door of the car: *Geordie North Construction Management*. In the paddocks beyond the sign, a squadron of earth-moving vehicles were busily moving earth and blowing smoke.

We walked across to him. 'Excuse me, sir.'

He looked up, mouth full, jaw working overtime. 'Aye, lass?' Geordie himself, from the sound of that. White bread, pink ham, pickles and spittle.

I told him we were looking for Messmate Lane. That was my first mistake. 'Ye go up the road as far as ye can see,' he began, and it was all downhill from there. Something about crossing a wee bridge, taking a left turn at a fork in the road, looking for a tyre – or some attire – in a tree. A lot of other things I missed amid the general splutter and grunt, the brackish brogue.

The main thing I learnt was never interrupt a Scotsman while he's masticating.

'You make any sense of that?' I asked Dad as we got back into the car.

He nodded and indicated the ranges in front of us. 'You see that tower on top of the hill?'

A mobile phone job.

'Yes.'

'Just below it, a big old tree.'

'Maybe.' I found it, but only with the binoculars. Dad had excellent vision for a man of his age.

'Head for that,' he said.

'How'd you figure that?'

'Bloke looked up there, first time you asked him.'

I patted him on the shoulder. 'Earning your keep already.'

We set off. The road was winding and steep, mostly dirt. After a ten-minute climb we came to a sign that said *Canticle Creek*.

We got out and had a look around. That didn't take long; it was clearly more of a locality than a town. The most interesting feature was a haphazard orchard of apple and plum trees dotted about the intersection. We ate a few pieces of fruit, decided they were delicious and filled our hats with them. A flock of rainbow lorikeets burst out of a scribbly gum and whirled overhead. Other than that, there was just a crossroads, a corrugated-iron fire station, a concrete water tank and a few weatherboard houses shyly poking their noses out of a tangle of lush green bush. We did spot a tyre halfway up a tree, an arrow painted on it pointing right.

We followed the arrow. After a dead-end lane, a hairpin bend and a close encounter with a fat timber truck on a skinny bridge, we found ourselves pulling in under a magnificent old eucalypt. We got out and stared down a long dark drive I recognised from the crime scene photos.

Buried under the branches was a sign: *Messmate Lane*.

Dad gazed down the lane, his eyes wary, scanning the undergrowth. I knew how he felt. This was a place of violent death. Acacia branches arched over the lane like giant bats' wings, their leaves a black shroud.

A gust of wind ruffled the upper branches, stirred some birds. Choughs. I watched them move, branch and bird, rise and fall.

Another timber truck swept past, rocking us with a rolling tailwind and showering us with dust. The driver – John Deere cap, fat red face, nose that appeared to be pressed against the glass but wasn't – glanced at us for long enough to let us know who ruled the roost up here. The logo on the door said *A. Gaunt & Sons*, with a cartoon figure of a beaming gum tree, hands on hips, beneath it. Poor little bastard wouldn't be beaming if it knew what A. Gaunt and Sons had in mind for it.

We drove down the lane and came to a mudbrick cottage. It had leadlight windows, sculptures in the garden, birdbaths on the lawn. The only sombre note came from the blue and white crime-scene tape still sealing off the building.

We stood in front of the cottage for a minute or two, absorbing a little of its radiant gloom. There was no sign of occupation, but I knocked on the door, just to be sure. Nobody answered.

I opened the folder, examined the photos and used them to locate the hollow in which the body had been discovered. I stood at the edge of the shallow ditch, surrendering myself to the whirlwind of impressions that blow about a place like this. I'd attended a few such scenes over the years. One thing I'd learnt: treat them with respect and they'll treat you the same way.

I tried to conjure up the woman who'd lived and died here, her broken dreams, her lost friendships and affections. What did the setting tell me? That she was independent, practical, creative; that she cared for the bush. I thought about Adam, his enthusiasm, his naivety, his own unfulfilled talent. I promised them both I'd do my best to find out what happened to them.

How to begin? I'd seen Danny Jakamarra do this dozens of times, but doing it on my own was something else. I made a preliminary sweep of the clearing, trying to get a sense of what went where.

The investigators had kept the cars away, for which I was grateful. The reports said Daisy drove an old HiLux, so that was presumably the source of the majority of the tyre tracks that scuffed and rutted the soft yellow clay in front of the building. There were also hoof prints trailing through the dirt, coming to rest at a hitching rail on the verandah.

I crouched down and made a more detailed examination of the surface: the cracks and crevices, little ridges and footprints. Close to where Daisy had parked her car, I came across a pair of tracks that spoke volumes, even to someone as deaf as me: they were made by bare feet, long, narrow, cracked in the heel.

Adam's, surely. Between them was a pair of small sandal prints that had to be Daisy's. They were up close to Adam's, as if the couple had been leaning against the car, embracing. I took another look at the position of the prints in relation to each other – maybe more than embracing.

I scouted farther afield, came across more of Adam's prints. None of them, I noted, were anywhere near the ditch in which the body had been found.

On the far side of the parking place I came across a print that stood out: a depression made by the ball of a bare foot, a sunken big toe. Then, over a metre away, something similar. Then a third.

He'd been running.

I looked in the direction he'd come from and found myself staring into a lemon tree in front of the cottage. I went over and examined it.

At around waist-height, on its far side, was a broken branch. No, not broken. Sliced – neatly. Behind it was another, the lean of its frayed edges suggesting that whatever severed it had been heading in the same direction. I pushed into the tree and studied the damage up close. There were other, more subtle, signs: the pattern of holes in the leathery leaves, the notches and tears in the twigs.

Something had slammed through this tree. A bullet. Fired by somebody in the yard. Where had it ended up? I searched the wall of the cottage. No sign of it there. It must have shot across the verandah and over the car.

I tried the front door. Locked, of course. I circled the building. There was a back entrance, but it was locked as well. I noticed a track leading off into the bush, a rock alongside it that looked promising. I turned it over. There was a key beneath it that fitted the door. I glanced around cautiously. Nobody in sight but Dad, who appeared to be as up for a spot of breaking and entering as I was. A risky course of action, perhaps, but I was going to have to take a few chances if I was going to get anywhere, given that I was starting a mile behind the eight ball.

The interior of the cottage was a storm of concentrated colour, a beautiful chaotic space, full of marine blues and greens, splashes of indigo and gold. Sunbeams angled in, illuminating an array of bottles and brushes, palettes, tubes of paint, trestles and benches.

Scattered across the shelves were artefacts of what had clearly been a nomadic life: Buddhist chimes, Uyghur beads, a Tibetan saddle blanket. Even the clothing held to the theme: Chinese dresses, purple scarves, a black hat studded with turquoise and silver.

And then there were the works of art themselves.

Daisy had been described as an artist, but nobody had bothered to mention what it was she painted. The pictures on the table and easels were all of plants. There were flowers and fronds, creepers and ferns, bulrushes and ground covers, all drawn with intricate detail, subtle flourishes and bursts of colour.

Correction. All but one. On the table beside the bed was a small portrait of a blonde woman in a bright hat sitting on the front step of the cabin. Her face was crafted with such tender care, we both knew who'd painted it.

Dad picked the painting up and studied it. Maybe he was seeing what I was: a lonely boy, far from home, struggling to connect.

'It's a gift,' he said. 'For the woman.'

Maybe, I had to remind myself, but it wasn't exactly proof that Adam didn't kill her. Drugs do weird things, jerk your head around like a cork in a cataract. He may not have been using for a few days before the incident, but he evidently had been at some stage since he left Kulara. Could the drugs have changed his personality in such a short time? I had to admit, I wasn't sure. I didn't have much experience with crystal meth. Largely because of our aggressive policing, it had gained little traction in Kulara.

Our search revealed little else of immediate interest. A few minutes later we stepped outside and I put the key back where we'd found it. I sat on a ramshackle couch on the verandah and studied the scene, trying to weave the scattered fragments into a coherent narrative. Dad went poking around the outskirts of the clearing.

I'd been sitting there for a minute or two when I heard hoof beats, then a jangle of metal and voices, coming down the drive.

Two horses appeared, two girls in the saddles – one familiar, the girl from the gallery.

'Morning, Possum!' I called.

She looked around, startled.

Dad appeared. 'What's this – the Light Brigade?'

The girl blinked. 'Mr Redpath?'

'G'day, Possum,' he replied.

Possum returned the greeting and introduced us to her friend, whose name was Karly.

'Nice-looking animal you got there,' said Dad.

I wouldn't have called it nice. 'Big, black, stomping nightmare' would have been my personal description, a cross between a Clydesdale and Mike Tyson. Possum's looked just as intimidating: an Australian stockhorse with an aristocratic demeanour. I had climbed onto the odd station nag since moving out bush but wouldn't have fancied my chances with either of these monsters.

'Thanks,' said Karly in a raspy, enthusiastic voice. 'She's called Red.'

The name would have been better suited to Karly herself. She was tall, broad-shouldered, with a thick auburn ponytail and a saddle of freckles across her nose.

The girls dismounted and Possum asked what we were doing here.

'We wanted to have a look around,' I said.

'But why?' she pressed.

I shrugged. 'We knew Adam Lawson.'

Her face lit up with a fiery gaze, and her rising index finger suggested that the conversation was about to morph into an interrogation, but before she could say any more we were distracted by the roar of a car coming down the lane.

A police four-wheel drive barrelled into the clearing and shuddered to a halt in front of us.

CHAPTER 9

The first cop was plain – but not too plain – clothed, powerfully built, somewhere between burly and fat. There were purple pouches under his eyes, a furry rodent under his nose. He glanced around, clearly out of his comfort zone in this environment, with its mudbrick walls and sculptures, its beams of light and wood. He looked like somebody whose idea of a comfort zone would involve beating up badly-tattooed people in urine-stained alleyways.

A baby constable with taxi-door ears jumped out of the driver's side and trotted along at his heels.

The moustachioed one strode up and loomed over me.

'Who are you and what are you doing here?'

'Am I invisible?' said Dad. 'We're here because it's a free fucking country.'

This was why I'd been worried about bringing him along. 'Settle down, Dad,' I said.

The policeman snorted and turned on him.

'You said what?'

His speech was grunty, clipped, a quality that gave it punch, like a sawn-off shotgun. I imagine it worked in the alleyways. Not so much here.

'I'm in the job, sir,' I said.

I pulled out the wallet and showed my ID.

His eyebrows shot up. 'You're a leading senior constable?' Possum's eyes narrowed.

'Jesse Redpath, Sarge. NT Police. This is my father, Ben.'

He scraped his jaw and shook my hand.

'Neville Wallace. Detective Senior Sergeant, Homicide.'

I remembered the name. He was one of the investigators whose reports I'd read back in Willoughby River.

'Had a passer-by call you in,' he continued. Passer-by? The truck driver on Messmate Lane? 'Sensible to let the locals know you're on their turf, Redpath.'

'On holiday, sir,' I improvised. 'Don't normally drop in and flash the badge at every police station I pass.'

He wasn't satisfied.

'Holiday?'

'Yes, sir.'

'Where are you stationed?' he pressed.

'Place called Kulara.'

Wallace put his hands on his hips and looked around the clearing. 'Right. And you just happen to be spending your vacation at the scene of a crime connected to a deceased crook from your town? Popular spot with your holidaying Territory copper, is it? Harbour views? Beach parties?'

'We came to see what you mongrels are covering up,' said my father.

Wallace rose to his full height; there was a decent amount of it, and a matching amount of bulk.

'We did know the boy, sir,' I said, trying to insert myself between them. This could end badly. 'We were just trying to get a better picture of exactly what happened.'

He returned his attention to me, displaying some heavy dental work. 'Pretty clear what happened. Hadn't he done something similar in the Territory? Stole a car, drove it over a cliff. Breached a correction order. Kid was out of control.'

He paused, then clicked his fingers and stared at me.

'What was your name again?'

'Redpath.'

'Knew I'd seen it somewhere,' he said. 'You're the bloody idiot who recommended a community order for him.'

I shifted on my feet, a little lost for words. This guy came across as some sort of turbo-charged gorilla, but he clearly didn't miss much.

'And you're here to convince yourself,' he continued, 'it wasn't your fault.'

Dad stepped in to what he doubtless thought was my defence, though all he was doing was making things worse. 'We're here to find the fucking truth,' he said. 'Something that seems to be seriously missing from your investigation.'

Wallace poked a fat finger into his chest. 'You, mate, are sailing perilously close to a charge of hindering police.'

'For god's sake, Dad,' I said, 'settle down.'

Wallace turned to Possum and Karly. 'And you two girls, what are you doing out here?'

'We were just riding by,' said Possum. 'Saw a flash of light, come to see what was going on.'

'Does your old man know you're here?' he asked Karly.

'He knows I'm out riding.'

Wallace frowned, poked around his moustache, came away empty-handed. Then he turned to me. 'Not proposing to go inside, are you, Redpath?'

'No, sir.' Technically correct. Not proposing.

He checked his watch and scraped his jaw, thinking. He mustn't have come up with much, because he said he'd be on his way. He warned me not to make a nuisance of myself and did a bit of metaphorical chest-thumping with Dad.

Before he left, I asked if he could tell me where Adam had gone over the edge. He pointed at a track running away to the south and explained that the accident had happened a kilometre down there. The wreckage had been cleared away, but the signs of the crash should still be there.

I asked where the track went.

'Place called Grinwood,' he replied.

Another anomaly. If Adam had just committed a murder, surely he'd go back the way he came, try to lose himself in the city?

Wallace returned to the car, constable in his wake. I watched until they disappeared. Dad resumed his exploration of the scrubland.

Possum stood near me, hands on hips. 'You didn't tell me you were a cop.'

'I didn't say I wasn't.'

'So what are you really doing here?'

I retreated – figuratively, at least. She may have looked sixteen, but she was interrogating me more forcefully than the Homicide detective had done.

'I like to make sure things … connect, before I put em away.'

'And do they?' she replied. 'Do you think Adam killed Daisy?'

'I'm yet to be convinced.'

She lowered her eyes and snorted.

'Thank god,' she said. 'At last somebody else's having doubts.'

The second girl muttered, 'Oh come on, Poss.'

'Karls, your dad's the town's top cop,' she replied. 'Course you're gonna take their side.'

Top cop? That explained Wallace's reference to her father.

Karly was indignant. 'I'm not taking anybody's side. I'm just talking common sense. They found him at the bottom of the cliff in a stolen car,' she persisted. 'Daisy's … with *her* blood on his knuckles.'

'She's got a point,' I said to Possum. 'What's your problem?'

She took a couple of steps to the west, then turned round. 'I met Adam and Daisy around the time they died.'

She said she'd gone to look at a car accident down near Canticle when she came across the couple. They'd seemed happy, relaxed, laughing – in love. She told me how Adam had made a joke about her name – said if she visited his hometown somebody would eat her. She was struck by the ease with which he'd settled her horse when it shied at a passing vehicle.

'And they're saying he killed her a few hours later?' she concluded. 'I don't think so.'

That was when it finally twigged.

'What's your real name?' I asked her.

'Possum.'

'The one on your birth certificate.'

'It's Alice,' said Karly, who copped a withering glance for her troubles.

Alice Kelly. She was the one who found the body. Poor kid. Hell of a shock. From what I could recall, she'd done well for someone of her age: called triple zero, attempted CPR.

Dad came back and joined us.

'What do you reckon?' I asked. 'Learn anything?'

He opened his hand to reveal a cluster of crushed leaves.

'Hard country, this.'

'Hard?'

'Dangerous. Ready to explode.' He let the fragments float away. 'Green on the surface, but that's just canopy. Underneath, it's desperate. Trees are dying, the litter's inches thick.'

'This is our fifth year of drought,' said Possum.

I glanced at the dense vegetation, then at the girls. I had a sudden vision of raging flame and fierce winds, of wildfire biting at the horses' flanks.

Possum didn't share my fears. 'You get used to it,' she said, with all the nonchalance of youth. 'I heard you asking about the crash. Want us to show you where it was?'

'Sure.'

The girls rode on ahead. Like the detective had said, the location wasn't hard to find. A kilometre down the road we came across skid marks on a sharp bend, then shattered glass and a broken railing, a steep fall.

Possum and Karly watched from the shade of a tree as Dad and I pieced together the fundamentals of the site. We traced

69

the vehicle's path, located the impact tree, the spot – five metres ahead – where the emergency workers had found the body. Then Dad sat on a rock and wiped his brow.

'You can do the fine-tooth work,' he said.

I carefully stepped out a pattern across the incline: back and forth, up and down. I did my best to work out who'd been where. The cops seemed to have stood watching while the fireys and ambos did the grunt work. I identified the taut metal coil of the tow-rope, the ruts left behind when they'd hauled the stretcher up the slope, the tracks the wreck gouged as it was dragged through the dirt.

Then, in a patch of sand close to where the body had lain, I came across another print. Just the one, but it stood out from the ubiquitous emergency services boots. In the middle of its ellipse was a shape like a spider. It had broken curves that might have been legs and a distinctive crack in its abdomen.

Who did that belong to? The towie? No reason for him to come all the way down here. Most tow-truck operators I'd come across just wanted to snatch the wreck and move on to the next job.

I asked the girls if they knew who came across the crash.

'I heard it was the water man,' said Karly.

'Water man?'

'Christie Looms.'

The name rang a bell. 'Wasn't that the bloke we met at the gallery last night? The sculptor. Heavy guy with glasses?'

'That's him,' she said. 'Drives a water truck for his day job.'

That made sense, from what I knew about the economics of the artist's life. My dad had never made any money until the past few years. I made a mental note to track the water man down and check him out. Especially his boots.

'Would you like to come back to our house?' Possum offered. 'Sure Mum could rustle up a cup of tea.'

She was a lot friendlier now she'd decided we were on the same team.

I glanced at Dad. He nodded his agreement.

CHAPTER 10

We cruised on ahead, pulling over from time to time to wait for Possum and Karly. Whenever we stopped Dad went poking around the scrub, chipping at rocks, tearing off bark, kicking divots. At one point, he stood on a boulder and looked out over a creek tumbling into a gully below. He whipped out the sketchbook he always carried with him and made a swift impression of the scene.

At Canticle Junction we took a right turn, then followed a dirt track called Bluehouse Road for a few hundred metres. When we came to the house, I stared at it and whistled.

'Didn't tell us it was a castle,' I commented as the girls trotted up.

'It's as draughty as one in winter,' said Possum.

The Bluehouse was perched on the edge of an escarpment looking out over the Windmark Valley. It was double storey, mudbrick, with recycled telegraph poles and beams and radially sawn boards. There was a small wooden cottage, painted bright blue, off to the east side of the house, and a corrugated iron workshop on the west. There were sculptures – stone, steel, glass – dotted around a tangled garden, with fruit trees to the north and a crazy playground to the south. A flying fox angled down from the upper level to a wattle in the yard.

The only anomaly was a chunky concrete blockhouse near the gate. It was half-buried in the slope, with a steel door out front and an observation port in the roof.

'What's that?' I asked Possum.

'Our fire bunker.'

I recalled Dad's comment about the country being ready to explode, decided that was a building I'd be keeping close to if ever the weather turned extreme.

Possum's parents were sitting out on the verandah. With them was a couple who were introduced to us as her brother, Nick, and his girlfriend, Nadia.

They seemed surprised to see us, but adjusted quickly and gave us a friendly welcome. Or at least, Lucy and Sam did. Possum's brother – half-brother, I found out later, with a different mother – was more guarded. He was a rangy young man in his late twenties, with scruffy dark hair and troubled eyes.

The source of the trouble, instinct told me, was the woman next to him. Nadia. He glanced at her and smiled, an attempt at reassurance that didn't get far. She was short and nervy, with cream-coloured hair and crow-coloured eyebrows. She was wearing a white silk dress and black boots. Attractive, in a way, but fragile. Her skin was like rice paper, her arms were heavily tattooed, stick-thin.

Was that a flicker of suspicion when she heard my name or was I being paranoid? She didn't say much, and what she did say was monosyllabic, mumbled. A minute or two after our arrival, she went over to the railing, lit up a smoke and stared at the scrub as if she expected zombies to come lurching out of it.

'Come in for a cup of something,' offered Lucy.

The interior of the house was an echo of the exterior. It had earthen walls, adzed centre poles, grey slate floors and a great stone fireplace. There were several distinctive Takada paintings on the walls. Soon we were sitting at the lounge room table sipping tea and eating fresh raspberry cake. Nadia came in last and sat next to Nick.

'Thank you for the hospitality, Lucy,' said Dad with a charm that surprised me. Where was the cantankerous old bastard I'd just seen arguing with the detective on Messmate Lane? He stretched back his seat and smiled congenially.

'A pleasure,' said Lucy.

'We were keen to see the country these paintings came from,' I said.

'Are you an artist yourself, Jess?' asked Lucy.

'Bullshit artist, sure. No, I just came along for the ride.'

'She's a cop,' said Possum.

Lucy's brow went up, Nadia's down. 'Don't know that that's a particularly polite way to put it, Possum.'

'I wouldn't worry,' I said. 'Plenty of worse ways where I come from.'

'She's investigating the murders,' Possum added, and I wished she hadn't.

There was a rattle of crockery. I looked around. Nadia was twisting in her chair, an upset expression on her face, an upset cup at her elbow. She fetched a cloth from the sink and busied herself clearing up the mess.

Nick gave me a hard stare. 'You're working for Homicide?'

'"In the general vicinity of" might be a better description.'

'"Getting up the nose of", from what I saw of the detective's reaction,' said Possum. 'He sure as hell didn't want you there.'

The comment was meant to be light relief, but the atmosphere in the room grew tense. I explained that I was officer in charge of the community Adam Lawson came from and we were not there in any official capacity – we just wanted to assure ourselves it happened the way they said it did.

'You have any reason to think it didn't?' pressed Nick.

'Not really – it just seemed out of character.'

The conversation drifted for a minute or two, then faded away.

'More tea anyone?' asked Sam, more in hope than expectation.

A glance between Nick and Nadia and they rose to their feet, saying they had to get back to work. I did my best to get a little more out of them before they left.

'What do you do?' I asked Nick.

'Try to make furniture.'

'Nice. Where do you do that?'

'I've got a workshop in Windmark. Nadi and I came here to pick up some timber. I keep a supply of it in the shed.'

'Nick does beautiful work,' added Lucy. 'Bush furniture, using waste material from the local logging operations.'

'Started out as an artist,' said Nick. 'Switched to woodwork a couple of years ago. Figured a small income's better than none.'

I turned to his partner. 'Do you work in the business, Nadia?'

I looked into her eyes – only for a moment, but that was enough to get a sense of her complexity and depth, her wariness. There was a history in those eyes, and it wasn't a pretty one.

'My god, no,' she replied. 'I'd just slow him down. I'm new in town, but I have picked up a few cleaning jobs.'

She glanced at her watch, and I couldn't help but notice that the undersides of her arms were a battleground of scratches and track marks. The last arms I'd seen that bad were on a hay-carter.

'One of which starts in ten minutes,' she said. 'Nick, we really have to make a move.'

We accompanied the couple to the front steps. They made their farewells, then climbed into an old blue jeep and rattled away in a haze of petrol smoke and a chorus of vibrating panels and chains.

Lucy gazed after them, then turned to me and Dad. 'I'm sorry about that. Nadia finds it distressing, all this talk of murder.'

'So do I,' I replied. 'Have they been together long?'

She exchanged a nano-glance with her husband, then Sam explained that they weren't sure. Nick had been spending most of his time down in the city, running round after Nadia, they gathered, but he'd only brought her home to meet the family a couple of weeks ago.

Lucy expressed her surprise that I was looking into Daisy's death. Tragic as it was, the local police had seemed so confident that Adam was responsible.

'I just thought they were too quick to pin it on him,' I said as we walked back into the house.

'That's what I've been saying,' Possum threw in. 'Not that anybody's listening. Plenty of other people might have wanted her out of the way.'

'Like who?' I asked.

'Loggers, yobs, rednecks,' she exclaimed. 'Take your pick. That's the way things work round here. One half of the town's got it in for the other. Drought's making things worse. They're at each other's throats.'

Her youthful enthusiasm was a worry.

'You seem to be taking a keen interest in all of this,' I said.

'Daisy was my friend.'

We went into the lounge room and resumed our seats. Lucy replenished the food and drinks.

Sam told us he'd attended the accident on the Grinwood road as captain of the local volunteer fire brigade. He'd spoken to the investigating officers, concerned that the community might have a killer in its midst, but they'd assured him that Adam was responsible.

'They're whistling,' I said. 'They couldn't know that for sure. He was with her on the night, doesn't necessarily mean he killed her. I can imagine a number of scenarios. Maybe he came across the body, freaked out – knew he'd get the blame.'

'Do you think he was capable of murder?' asked Lucy.

I gave the matter a moment's consideration.

'I start on the general principle that anybody's capable of anything and work my way down from there. Been a while since I saw him. Even when he was in the Territory, he was always in trouble. Partying way too hard, heavily into light drugs. But kill someone? That's in a different league. I never would have pegged him for a killer.'

'I only met him once,' said Possum. 'But neither would I. He seemed more like the kinda guy who saw the funny side of everything.'

I felt quietly pleased that she'd noticed that about Adam; at least somebody down here had seen him for what he was.

'Major hole in the investigator's case,' I said, 'is the lack of motive. Why would he want to kill her?'

'What did the police say about that?' asked Sam.

I thought back to the reports I'd read. 'Not much. Suggested it was a "crime of passion". Always seems a cop-out to me, empty box where they chuck the stuff that doesn't fit. I'm more of a materialist myself.'

'What's that mean?' asked Karly.

'I'm a low-level copper in a little outback town,' I said. 'Most of the deaths I get lumbered with involve a couple of drunks arguing over who's gonna buy the next round …'

I paused for a swig of tea then resumed my discourse on law enforcement, Territory-style.

'But when we do get something that stretches the brain cells,' I said, 'I follow the advice my sergeant gave me when I started out on this caper: it's all about the money, honey – even if that's barely enough for a bucket of chips.'

I must have spoken more forcefully than I meant to: when I paused for breath, the entire table was staring at me.

'Who are the vested interests round here?' I asked while I had their attention.

'The what?' asked Karly.

'The ones with something to lose,' I said. 'Up our way, they tend to be miners, cattlemen, pub owners. The operators.'

Possum glanced at her mother, who nodded her consent. She told me to wait a minute then went up to the mezzanine floor and came back with a box of books. She picked up the top one – a photo album – shuffled through it, found the page she was after and showed it to me.

'That's Daisy.'

She was looking a lot better than the last time I saw her. Bright silk hat, laughing eyes, hair as yellow as a sunflower. But being led away by a cop, her fingers in a cheeky V for the camera.

The officer looked familiar. It was the young constable who'd been with Wallace on Messmate Lane. There was a crowd of protestors waving banners in the background.

'Why was she being arrested?'

'It was an anti-logging protest,' said Lucy. 'Up at Echidna Creek, last spring. Daisy and a couple of others chained themselves up in the trees.'

Possum told me to take a closer look at the background of the scene, but I'd already spotted it: moving through the crowd was a B-double truck, on its door an unmistakable logo: a beaming tree, hands on hips. Below it, the words *A. Gaunt & Sons*. Glaring out from under a red cap was a padded claret face I'd seen before – the man on the road at Messmate Lane.

'That's Allan Gaunt,' said Lucy. 'He was there to log the area, they were trying to stop him.'

I put the album back on the table. 'Okay, so she had a run-in with Mister Gaunt. So did a hundred others. Why her?'

'They're Gaunts,' said Possum. 'They don't need much reason.'

This kid was as sharp as a butcher's blade, but I had to point out that a photo of a truck in a crowd wasn't exactly proof. I asked if she had anything else.

'The morning I found her,' she said, 'I spotted a ute coming down the road. Big black Ford with spotties, covered in mud. Looked a lot like Brock.'

'Brock?'

'Allan's oldest boy. See the other guy in the truck? That's him.'

I studied the photo. There was an offsider, but I couldn't discern much more than the family flat nose and a weak chin.

'You told this to the police?'

'Of course.'

I turned to Karly. 'Your dad's in charge of the police station? Sergeant …' I tried to recall the name from the notes. 'Tehlich?'

'That's us.'

'He at work today?'

'Far as I know.'

I checked my watch. Nearly four. I said I might drop in and have a word with him on the way home.

Sam commented that it was turning into a long day, said we were welcome to stay at the Bluehouse overnight.

I glanced at Dad. He was looking weary: tired eyes, mouth agape. Not surprising – he was getting on, and this southern stuff was proving harder work than the desert he was used to.

'What do you reckon, Dad?'

He nodded his agreement. 'Appreciate it, Sam, Lucy. Might take a little walk in the morning. See how Takada's paintings compare with the original.'

I thanked our hosts and drove back down to Windmark.

CHAPTER 11

The trip to the Windmark police station took me through the town's industrial zone. I was struck by the name of the road: Cinnamon Row. It was like the backstreets of small towns everywhere: panelbeater, tyre yard, stockfeed depot, mechanical workshop. There was a plasticated cafe with a bunch of young guys slurping chocolate milk and eating donuts in the forecourt. The general air was one of heat, grease and grime, with the windows barred, the fences and the faces barbed.

The vehicles were mostly built with a job of work in mind: greasy trucks, delivery vans, rough and tumble utes.

There were two exceptions. As I passed a service lane I caught sight of a Porsche and a Kia, pulled over, up close. The former was high-gloss blue and low-slung, power-packed, as smooth as molten metal. The latter was workaday white, with bubbles of rust and a broken tail-light – as cheap as the other was expensive. There was a man leaning over the Kia with an air of menace, arm on the roof, hip against the door.

I drove on. Not my business. A couple of blokes arguing over an unpaid bill. I was off-duty, plenty of other things on my plate.

Then the Kia driver looked around long enough for me to recognise her: a blaze of cream-coloured hair, a pale complexion. Nadia. The expression on her face was one of fear.

I pulled over in time to see the man thump the roof. I got out and came up behind him, reaching for my police badge.

'Is there a problem here?'

He glanced around. He had a chiselled nose and chin-beard, drug-fuelled pecs and guns. The tattoos on his forearms were like blueprints for a medieval torture instrument. I didn't rate more than the glance.

'Fuck off,' he grunted, returning to his task, which rapidly escalated into tearing off the car's aerial and using it to lash the roof. He seemed to find the exercise amusing.

I raised the badge. 'Sir, I'm a –'

He spun round and pushed me backwards. 'Told you to go away, you nosey little cunt.'

I have, I must admit, kicked a few testicles in my time – all in the line of duty, of course – but I doubt I've ever delivered a better kick than I did just then. Maybe it was the angle, or the heat, maybe it was the pointy-toed boots I was wearing.

My right foot automatically snapped out, hammered into whatever the steroids had left in his underpants. The bloke's eyes rolled, he groped his groin and his body buckled like an upturned centipede.

'Oops,' I said.

I reached down and removed the aerial from his shuddering hands, hoping I wouldn't have to use it as a whip when he got his shit together.

That was when things got complicated.

The doors of the Porsche opened and two men radiating hostile intent appeared. They were like walking mugshots. The driver was another goon, broad of body and skull, droopy of mo – Nick Cave on growth hormones.

The one in the back was somehow scarier: older, balder, fatter, but his eyes were as hard as ball-bearings. He was in charge – the others were just the help.

The driver took the lead, his gait threatening, his jacket leather gangster-chic, despite the heat. He came close. I was struck – not literally, thank Christ – by his fists: hairs on the back of his hairs. The aerial in my hands felt inadequate; he looked like the sort of feller who'd have a shooter under his coat.

Somebody somewhere yelled, 'What the hell's going on over there?'

The interjection came from another man, this one sitting at the wheel of a silver BMW that had just pulled up in front of an adjacent office.

Our little back-alley contretemps was becoming as crowded as a Bollywood dance number. The newcomer climbed out of the Beamer, strode across the road, clearly willing to get involved. He was tall, strongly built, with thinning dark hair.

The ball-bearing man looked around, sizing him up.

'What's going on is nothing.' He had a shifty smile and an accent I couldn't place – somewhere guttural. 'A misunderstanding.'

I glanced at Nadia. She wasn't misunderstanding anything. She was terrified. Her face was as pale as her hair.

The newcomer noticed as well. He pulled out a mobile. 'I'm calling the police.'

'Don't bother,' I said, showing my badge. 'I am the police.'

I thought about pursuing the matter, making an arrest – assault with an aerial? – but decided against it, not quite sure my footwork hadn't strayed into the realms of police brutality. Who knew how many CCTV cameras were in the vicinity?

'Perhaps,' said the older man from the Porsche, 'it would be best for us all if we went our separate ways.'

He frowned at the guy on the ground. 'Benny.' He enunciated the word like it was something he'd just scraped out of the grooves in the sole of his shoe. He snapped his fingers. 'Come.'

As Benny rose and hobbled away, the newcomer drew closer and I recognised him. It was the ex-footballer I'd met at the gallery.

'You're Dominic Talia,' I said, then regretted it – the man with the ball-bearing eyes was still within hearing distance. He glanced back with a look that hit like a fist. I had no idea who he was, but everything about him said the less he knew about you, the better.

Dominic looked puzzled.

'Jesse Redpath,' I said. 'We met at the gallery last night.'

'Ah, my god yes – Ben's daughter.'

The Porsche trio piled into the vehicle, flew down the road on silver rims, ballistic. I heard the V8 scream as they hit the highway.

Dominic leaned in towards Nadia. 'Are you right there, miss?'

'I'm fine,' she muttered, but she didn't look fine: forehead on the wheel, fingers white, clenching. Tears in the corner of her eyes.

She made to drive off, but Dominic suggested she give it a minute or two.

'Maybe wait'll you get your breath back,' he said. 'Don't want to drive when you're upset.'

He stepped away, realising, rightly, that another male was not what she needed right now.

'How'd you get involved in this?' he asked me.

'I saw them hassling her,' I said. 'Came over to help out.'

A fleeting smile. 'Saw the way you help out. Give you a run with the Windmark Reserves, right hoof like that.' He took another look at Nadia. 'This is Nick Kelly's girl.'

'Nadia,' I said.

He looked at me suspiciously. 'How do you know that?'

'I'm staying with the family. I just met her.'

He nodded and said he'd give Nick a call.

I stepped over to the Kia and did what I could to reassure Nadia while he rang the number. I was making small talk, she was making no talk, but at least her tears were drying. Nick was there in a couple of minutes, the blue jeep roaring down the road. He climbed in beside her and she buried herself in his arms.

Dominic and I repaired to the footpath to give them some space.

'You have any idea who those blokes were?' I asked.

'Sure as hell weren't locals. Old friends of Nadia's, I presume. Couldn't exactly say I know her, but I know the family well. Good people. Nick and his old man have both worked for me over the years.'

'What do you do?'

'I'm a builder. The girl's only been here for a few weeks, but I did hear she had a troubled past.'

'What sort of trouble?'

'Drugs.' His teeth crunched the word, like it was a bone. 'Those pus-bags must have been some sort of fallout from it.'

'Well, I'm grateful you came along when you did. Would have had my hands full with three of them.'

'Peaceful town, this – for the most part,' he added, recent events maybe taking the edge off his positive opinion.

'I got a rego,' I said. 'Might check it out in case there's complications.'

A sharp laugh. 'The one you kicked in the nuts'll have complications. And you say you're a cop?'

'From the Territory.'

'Bit out of your bailiwick, aren't you?'

'I knew the young man who died at Canticle Creek the other week. Wanted to make sure it went the way they said it did.'

He cocked an eye. 'There's doubt about that?'

'Can't argue with the evidence. Just seemed out of character. He was a good kid.'

Nick came over, shook Dominic's hand and thanked him for his assistance.

'Don't thank me,' Dom replied. 'Jesse Redpath here's the little tiger.'

When I asked Nick if he knew who the men were, he

glanced at the road down which the Porsche had disappeared. The city was a dirty smudge on the horizon.

'The devil and his fucking apprentices,' he muttered.

'What were their names?'

He shook his head. 'You wouldn't want to know.'

'Why were they harassing her?'

'She owes them money.' Dom had already told me why. Not that I was surprised – the track marks on her arms, the haunted echo in her eyes. She'd always owe something somewhere. 'That was a reminder.'

Then he turned away and said he'd better get Nadia back home.

'Mate, you oughta report this,' Dominic advised.

Nick shook his head and said Nadia wouldn't want anything to do with the cops.

I glanced at her, struck by the ring of sadness round her face; the drawn cheeks, the frazzled eyes.

'Want me to sort the Kia?' offered Dom. 'Get one of the boys to drop it round?'

'Appreciate that,' said Nick.

'Still on Connolly Street?'

'Yep.'

Nick had a word with Nadia, then handed over the keys. He picked up her bag and helped her into his jeep.

Dominic and I watched them leave.

'Poor kid,' he muttered.

I grunted some sort of agreement, but my mind was elsewhere, wondering if it was more than a coincidence, a trio of goons lurking in the vicinity of a murder.

I thanked Dominic again and headed for the station.

CHAPTER 12

There was a sergeant watching me from the counter. He'd been watching from the moment I parked the car. His arms were folded and deeply tanned, his eyes were hooded, hawk-like. He looked to be in his mid-forties, with copper hair and a burly build. The name tag said 'Vince Tehlich'.

'Afternoon,' I said. 'I'm –'

'Lemme guess.' He studied the ceiling. 'LSC Jesse Redpath? Queen of the Wild Frontier?'

Wallace had dobbed me in.

The sergeant's voice was rough around the edges, blunt, authoritative. His handshake was similar. Everything about him said solid country cop.

'You're well informed,' I said.

'My town. Like to know what's going on. Tom Vallence says to say hello and to be nice to your senior officers.'

Jesus. 'He said all that?'

'Last bit might have been wishful thinking.'

'On whose part?'

'Both of us.' He looked out into the car park. 'Where's the other half of the team?'

'My father? I thought he needed a rest. We're staying out with Lucy Takada.'

Whatever Tom had said about me couldn't have been all bad – Tehlich invited me into his office, seemed interested in a chat. Unless it was a spider–fly thing.

Five minutes later he was regaling me with tales of a trip he'd made to the Gulf a few years before. He enthused about the size of the barramundi, the speed of the summer storms. He'd passed through Willoughby River, stayed long enough to thank god he didn't have to work there.

I looked at the bookshelves. They were a change from the usual bureaucratic copper dross: plenty of policy and procedure, but also books on fishing, cricket, war – Rex Hunt, Big Max, Peter FitzSimons. The Good Ol' Boys.

The young constable I'd run into on Messmate Lane delivered the drinks, was introduced as Jace Gradey.

'Jace,' I said. 'Where's your mate?'

'Detective Senior Sergeant Wallace? Back in town. He was only up here for the day, checking witness statements for the inquest.'

'Learn anything new?'

'Not that he's shared with us,' said Vince. 'Must admit, Tom Vallence was a bit vague about what you're hoping to achieve down here.'

I told him about my concerns with the case: the inconsistencies in the drug results, my worry that somebody was jumping to conclusions, stranger-blaming. I said I'd seen

Adam affected by drugs – admittedly, only weed – and it just made him laugh.

Vince tapped the folder in front of him.

'We're not as slapdash as you seem to think,' he said. 'Evidence was strong, but it'll be an open case until the coroner says otherwise. You're welcome to look through the case notes.'

He really had been expecting me.

I checked the time. Getting on for five. The file was thick. I said I'd be back tomorrow.

I rose to leave, then decided I had time for a few quick questions. I've always gotten more out of people, face to face, than I do from paper files or liquid crystal screens.

'You've spoken to Possum Kelly?' I asked. 'She says she saw this Gaunt boy running around up at Messmate Lane the morning of the murder.'

He ran his tongue against the inside of his cheek. 'She saw a muddy ute, might have been Brock's, might have been one of a hundred others on the mountain. But we did interview the Gaunts – two brothers and the old man. They had alibis.'

'Solid?'

He shook his head. 'More your Ikea variety. Alibied each other. Say they were up shooting pigs at Bridnok.'

'Anybody verify that?'

'What were we supposed to do? Interview the pigs?'

I could imagine what some of my old customers would have said about that: pigs interviewing pigs.

When I told him Possum had suggested that somebody might have been gunning for Daisy because of the protest at

Echidna Creek he gave an exasperated shrug. 'There were a stack of other protesters up there. Why her?'

'Luck of the draw? Maybe they just came across her, got into an argument?'

'Maybe,' he said, but there wasn't much conviction in the word. I could guess what he was thinking: this woman is tossing darts, hoping one'll hit. Probably not that far from the truth.

'One more thing,' I continued. 'Do you know Nick Kelly's girl, Nadia?'

There was a spark of renewed interest in his eyes. 'Why do you ask?'

'Just came across her getting harassed in the street by a trio of evil-looking dudes in a blue Porsche.'

He glanced out through the glass, frowning. 'Where was this?'

'Cinnamon Row. Sent em on their way. Last I saw she was going home with Nick and the Porsche was heading for Melbourne.'

'Get a rego?'

I opened my notebook and read it out. He disappeared into a back room, returned a few minutes later with a print-out.

'This the lad?' he asked.

A familiar face scowled up at me: shadowy, hard-nosed.

'He was the one dishing out the orders.' That casual snap of the fingers, the way the bloke dragged himself out of the dirt.

'Eddie Razic,' said Vince. 'Not a man you'd want to meet in an underground car park, not without a squad of Soggies at your back.'

Soggies. Special Operations. Industrial-strength cops. 'What about his mates?'

He produced a second page, this one with half-a-dozen photos. Bottom left: aerial man. I touched his ugly head.

'That one,' I said.

'Benny Rork,' he said. 'One of the crew. Henchman, wannabe hard man. Bartender in his boss's club when he's talking to the tax man.'

I asked what they'd been doing to get onto the A-list but Vince just grunted with frustration.

'Convicted? Nothing much – yet. Suspected? You name it. Amphetamines, manufacture and import. Protection racketeering. Prostitution. Murder. Even bloody chop-chop.'

Out of my league, most of that. Out of your average country copper's league, too, I would have thought. Maybe not the chop-chop.

'Surely they didn't come all the way to Windmark to hassle a few bucks out of an old customer?'

He flicked a brow. 'Nadia? Investigators reckon she's more than a customer. They describe her as an employee.'

This forced me into a rapid mental recalibration. 'In which aspect of the enterprise? Sex? Drugs? Tobacco?'

'All of them. She's an addict. Multiple convictions: dealing, stealing, soliciting.'

I shifted uneasily in my chair, wondering if Nick's family knew what a mess of trouble he'd brought into their midst.

'Do we know anything more about her?' I asked. 'I didn't even get a surname.'

'Kovac. Nadia Kovac.'

'Is there anything more about her background?'

'Not much. She's described somewhere as "refugee".'

'From where? Broadmeadows?'

He ran a finger down the page and said she came from Yugoslavia.

'Yugoslavia? Doesn't even exist anymore.'

I thought about the altercation I'd just witnessed in Cinnamon Row, the air of reflex aggression about those men. I asked him if they'd considered whether Razic might have been connected to the deaths at Canticle Creek.

'Homicide have,' he assured me. 'But there's nothing to tie him to it, except Nadia. She was the one who brought Adam up here.'

'What!' There'd been nothing about that in the reports I'd read.

I once sat listening to a freshwater ecologist and old Elsie Napanangka swapping notes about the waterhole at Wattle Creek. I was bewildered, then, by the deepening levels of complexity, by the questions without answers and vice versa.

This case was going the same way. Every time I crested a hill, all I saw was more hill.

'The two of them knew each other in Melbourne,' Tehlich continued. 'Nadia drove him up here, day before the murder. Says she left him with the car and came back to Melbourne on a bus. They considered charging her as an accessory. Still haven't ruled that out, but the evidence is weak. That's why Wallace was keen to get up to Messmate Lane when he heard there was a strange woman poking around. Thought it might have been her, returning to the scene, tampering with the evidence.'

Hence Wallace's barnstorming entrance – unless he always arrived like that.

'Personally, I've got my doubts,' Vince added. 'I've spoken to Nick. He assured me Nadia's trying to get clean, get away from the life.'

I nodded at the window, out into the leafy thoroughfares and sizzling bitumen backstreets of Windmark.

'Not having much success, if what I saw out there's anything to go by. The life's coming after her.'

He looked again at the report on his desk and tapped it with a pen. The third man, I noticed, the one with the horseshoe tash, was nowhere to be seen.

'I just wish Nadia would open up,' said Vince. 'I'm sure she knows more than she's letting on.'

I thought about the expression on her face as she cowered in the car. 'She's terrified.'

He nodded at the print-out. 'Friends like that, can't say I blame her.'

He said he might do a run round town to make sure they'd pissed off. He rose from the desk and reached for his hat. 'Jace!'

A couple of minutes later I was standing at the door of the SUV watching them climb aboard a patrol car. Tehlich made a pistol of his hand and pointed it at me.

'You'll let me know if you find anything?'

More of an order than a question.

'Of course.'

CHAPTER 13

When I turned into the Bluehouse drive, the only person in sight was Possum, who was sitting on the steps oiling a bridle.

I walked towards her, then stopped, distracted by a middle-aged man flying through the air above me, hanging onto his hat and whooping with delight – until he crash-landed in the middle of the yard. A magpie on the verandah railing fluttered up in alarm.

Possum jumped to her feet. 'Dad! You've fixed the flying fox.'

'Still needs a bit of fine-tuning,' said Sam, picking himself out of the dirt and gingerly probing his backbone. He explained that the fox had been out of action for months – rusty pulley, rotten wood – and he'd only just got round to the repairs. 'Who wants to be guinea pig?'

I looked at the apparatus warily: a chain-leather seat suspended from a steel-strand cable stretching from the upper storey of the house down to the wattle near the front gate.

Possum was up for it, but I said I'd better see how my old man was going.

'He and Mum are in the studio,' she said.

'Getting on like a house on fire,' added Sam.

The studio – Takada's original cottage, I was to discover – was the little blue building off to the eastern side of the house. I opened a door and came across my father putting the finishing touches to a painting on the side of a ceramic bowl.

The studio was a sharp contrast to the one I'd visited the day before. Where Daisy's dwelling was an explosion of raw colour, this room was sparser, harder, dominated by strong lines, white light, a geometry of angles and glances. Even the mud seemed clean. Both locations were light years away from Dad's usual painting ground – a patch of red dirt at the bottom of a crater.

'Quite like this pot business,' he said. 'Never too late to learn. What do you reckon, Luce? Take a day or two to figure it out?'

'Ha!' she said. 'It's taken me forty years.'

'Okay – maybe a week.'

She threw a lump of mud at him. 'See if you can make anything out of that, ya smartarse.'

A lock of jet-black hair fell across her forehead, catching the afternoon light. I was struck by the lively expression in her eyes. She and Dad were like a pair of kids on an unexpected adventure. She'd lost some of her reserve, Dad, a little of his cantankerousness.

I left them to it and went out to join Sam and Possum on the fox. I made a few rough landings, but it turned out to be quite a rush. This family knew how to enjoy themselves.

We ate a simple meal that night – rice and beans, a tuna salad – and shared something of our stories. Sam Kelly was a mudbrick builder. He'd been a widower with a teenage son – Nick – when he came to do an extension on the Bluehouse and never left.

'Lucy owns the place,' he explained wryly. 'I'm just a kept man.'

Lucy told us about her father's arrival in the region. Norbert Looms, father of Christie and operator of a commercial pottery in town, went to Japan and came back with Kenji Takada in tow. The artist was a quiet, compact man who owned little other than the contents of the cardboard suitcase in his hands. He wore wooden sandals and his trousers were held up with string.

Takada was travelling on a specialist visa that said he would share with the local artisans his skill in painting on clay, but nobody – least of all, apparently, Takada himself – foresaw the creative explosion that emerged from the interaction between his traditional technique and his new environment. He'd been stunned by the Australian bush, and his wonderment manifested itself in a rush of landscape paintings that had redefined the genre.

After dinner Sam, at the request of his daughter, pulled out a weather-beaten steel guitar. He described himself as a part-time member of a part-time country band. He belted out a few old songs – 'The Days of Old Khancoban', 'Saturday Night at the Movies', 'Belle Starr' – in a deep, gravelly voice that had everybody joining in. Possum tootled along on a penny whistle, Lucy sang high harmony. Maybe in honour of the Territorian visitors, Sam finished with a rough-hewn rendition of Joe Geia's 'Yil Lull'.

My accommodation was a neat little room at the back of the house. I went to bed early, but had trouble getting to sleep, the day's dramas replaying in my head. Rambling gangsters, timber millers, drug addicts and coppers: how did they all fit together?

Finally the chorus of that last song floated up and carried me sleepwards.

CHAPTER 14

The next morning I was up early, a habit I've acquired since moving into the outback. It's a worthwhile habit for a community cop – lets you catch the world unawares, nip it in the bud.

Dad's room was just down the corridor. I checked it out. Empty, of course. If I was a first-light riser, he was a moonlight one. I come from a long line of insomniacs.

I glanced through the screen door. He'd be out there somewhere, checking out the lie of the land. 'Can't settle down,' he'd said to me one time, 'till I know where I am.'

'Why's that?' I asked.

'Stop em sneaking up on you,' he replied, although he never did explain who – or what – was doing the sneaking.

I suspected it was something he'd carried with him from his early days. He came to Australia as a thirteen-year-old migrant from Liverpool. He spent his first weeks creeping around the schoolyard waiting for somebody to jump him. It took a good couple of months before he realised that wasn't how things worked in his new country. If there was any jumping to be done here, it was of your more subtle variety.

I sat in an armchair up in the mezzanine, looked out through the panoramic triangular windows and listened to the dawn chorus. Currawongs whistled and rang, magpies chortled, willy wagtails chattered. A kookaburra call burst out from the ridge tops and cut through it all like a splitting axe.

I was impressed. They had some serious birdlife down here. The Kulara chorus was mostly roosters, blowflies and old blokes coughing in their swags.

Speaking of old blokes, Sam Kelly wandered out in a battery of groans and yawns, the odd fart, toasted a slab of bread, slathered it with Vegemite. He noticed me, gave a friendly wave, indicated that he had to be off to work. A minute after he went out the door I heard a set of diesel injectors kick into life and a car cruise out onto the road.

The sun made its appearance. The ridge above the house was ablaze with black and yellow skeleton trees, the high windows bending long red beams. It was going to be another hot, dry day.

There was a cardboard box on the table. Possum's books, from yesterday. I picked one up: *A Field Guide to the Flora of Xinjiang*. Scribbled on the title page: *Daisy Baker, Messmate Lane, Canticle Creek*. Another: *Western Himalayan Alpine Shrub and Meadows*. Same owner. A third: *The Orchids of Victoria*, Gary Backhouse and Jeffrey Jeans. A fourth: a sketchbook, also Daisy's, her intricate artwork leaping off every page.

I shuffled through the box. There were a dozen books, all related to botany, from field guides to dense textbooks. All Daisy Baker's.

The sketchbook looked promising. It was black-bound, quality paper, bamboo. The woman had obviously spent more on resources and materials than anything else in her life.

Scribbled on the first page, *W R 5*.

W R. Windmark Ranges?

And the five? Was this the fifth journal? If that was the case, where were one, two, three and four?

The sketches were all of flora. Below most images were handwritten notes. Common names, scientific names: Tiger orchid, *Diuris sulphurea*; Mountain Greenhood, *Pterostylis alpine*; Summer spider orchid, *Caladenia aestiva*. From time to time, there was additional information, apparently to aid location: *Canticle Creek, right side of the low ford. Crowcall verge, two hundred metres south of the messmate grove.*

I heard bare feet on the stairs behind me.

I turned around. It was Possum. She was wearing a pair of baggy blue pyjamas and a piercing stare. Her early-morning hair was a mass of black and silver.

'Gotta keep your eyes open in my line of work,' I said. 'And your mind. Where'd you get Daisy's books?'

'From her mum.'

'Even the sketchbook?'

She picked it up and flicked through the pages. 'Good, wasn't she?' There was a wisp of sadness in her eyes. 'I used to go out with her sometimes, do a bit of drawing. Mrs Baker gave it to me. Sort of a memento, I suppose.'

As she put the book down, one of the drawings caught my eye. It was an orchid – I'd come to recognise the curved petals and weird labella. Daisy had added more background than she usually did – the sketch was almost a miniature landscape. There were several large trees and a formation of wave-shaped rocks.

But it was the description at the bottom of the page that struck me: instead of the usual scientific or common names, Daisy had scribbled three letters – *wtf?* – in a quickfire, energetic hand.

'You know anything about this?' I asked Possum.

'Yeah, I noticed that. Obviously wasn't one she recognised.'

'More like something that surprised her.'

It was a tiny detail, but it left me unsettled. I'd seen major cases turn on tiny details. I remembered the Great Kulara Post Office Robbery – a B and E that netted seventy bucks – that was solved when Danny Jakamarra noticed Wilson Jukut wearing a new pair of old boots.

Lucy appeared at the top of the stairs, fresh-faced, curious. She was wearing a flowery shirt and white shorts, with a watering jug in hand. 'Morning. What's the mystery?'

I explained what had piqued my interest. She took a look at the picture.

'Strange,' she mused. 'I've never seen a spider orchid quite like that.' She went across and watered the japonicas and ferns on the windowsill. 'We could ask Wolf.'

Possum rolled her eyes.

'Wolf?' I asked.

'Wolf Gunther,' said Lucy. 'He's a botanist; lives down on the road to Windmark. He's German, but he knows the local flora as well as anyone. If you think it's important, I'll call him after breakfast.'

'I don't know that it's important at all,' I said. 'It's just one of those little things that bug me.'

'Can't have our guests being bugged. I'll call him.'

I joined Possum as she went outside. Honeyed fragrances drifted in from the bush: eucalyptol, peppermint, lemon myrtle. A flock of honeyeaters splashed about a birdbath making water whirls and fleeting rainbows. A silvereye flittered in, dangled upside down from a grapevine and pecked at the fruit.

A magpie – looking very much like the one that had been on the verandah yesterday – floated in and strutted across the ground, listening with its claws. It detected something: a slug, which it devoured with a savage toss of the beak. Then it looked up at Possum expectantly.

'Friend of yours?' I enquired.

'Name's Pendles.'

'He lives here?'

'Nick found him on the side of the road. Cat killed his mother. We try to persuade him he's a bird, not a person, but he likes it here. And I like having him here. He's taken over the paperbark near your room.'

The magpie followed from a distance as we went down to the horses. There were two of them: a pushy bay pony called Nutmeg and the stockhorse Possum had been riding yesterday, whose name was Atomica. We broke off a couple of slabs of hay, tossed them out, watched the animals munch and crunch and give each other little nips.

'So what's your problem with this Wolf Gunther?' I asked.

'He's just up himself. Nothing he likes better than seeing his own face on TV.'

'What's he do to get on TV?'

'He's boss of the Windmark Conservation Society.'

'That gets you on TV?'

'Does if you organise protests like the one at Echidna Creek.'

There was a movement to the south. 'Oy there!'

My father strode out of the scrub, the sunlight jangling in his silver stubble, his boots looking like he'd given them a serious workout.

'What have you been up to?' I asked.

'Just having a look around.'

He ruffled through his pockets and came out with some souvenirs: a snakeskin, a cicada shell, an iridescent crystal.

He glanced at the magpie, then looked again, cocked an eye.

'I'd watch out for that feller,' he said.

'Why's that?'

'He'd steal the watch out of your pocket.'

But he seemed more amused than concerned by the creature.

Dad was clearly invigorated by his morning walk. When we went in to join Lucy for breakfast, he ate heartily and leaned back in the chair. He pulled the crystal out of his pocket, gazed at it for a moment then up at the surrounding hills.

'Interesting country, this,' he said. 'You can almost see the tertiary band surfaces reflected in its ridges and valleys. I'd like to paint it. What do you reckon, Jess? We got time to hang around?'

'I dunno if we can impinge upon these good people's hospitality any longer. We'll get a B&B in town.'

'Nonsense,' said Lucy, who'd been listening closely. 'You're welcome to stay as long as you like – and to use the studio.'

'I'd like that,' said Dad. 'Might help me see the country the way your old man did.'

Lucy offered to show him round the Windmark Ranges, take him to the places where Takada used to work. When he agreed, she suggested they could begin by visiting Canticle Creek itself, the spot where her father had done the painting at the gallery. It was within walking distance, further along the escarpment.

'We could go this afternoon,' she offered. 'If you're interested.'

'I am,' he said. 'What are our chances of seeing that platypus?'

'If you're with me,' she smiled, 'they're good.'

Lucy was clearly keen to be involved in whatever Dad was planning, and I could understand why. Her own father's work was the product of an interaction between two cultures. Dad was proposing the interpolation of a third – the science which underlay everything he did. She was obviously curious to see what emerged from the collaboration. So was I.

The two of them spoke a little about the materials and equipment he'd need – Dad seemed to be planning something really large – then headed for the studio

Lucy paused at the doorway. 'By the way, Jess, I spoke to Wolf Gunther. He'll drop by later this morning.'

CHAPTER 15

An hour later a grey Nissan four-wheel drive cruised into the yard and the driver stepped out. He was a tall, lean fellow, maybe in his mid-thirties, wearing a green polo shirt, khaki shorts and beautifully weathered boots. He had burnished hair, thin lips and a square jaw.

Lucy popped out of the studio. 'Morning, Wolf,' she said. 'Thanks for coming.'

'No problem. I had to head up this way anyway.' Just a trace of an accent. Amazing how they do it, these Europeans – he spoke better English than I did. 'I have a meeting with a park ranger at eleven.'

'This won't take long,' she said. 'Wolf Gunther meet Jesse Redpath.'

He shook my hand firmly. He had a confident physical presence: piercing cerulean eyes and perfect teeth, the trace of a smile about his mouth. Bit of all right, I had to admit – Possum's objections notwithstanding.

'When Lucy said she had a police officer asking for information,' he said, 'you are not what I had in mind.'

'I'm from the Territory,' I said. 'We've got our own way of doing things.'

I asked him when he'd last seen Daisy, and he replied that he hadn't seen her for weeks but she'd called him a few days before she died, also wanting his help to identify some plants.

'Did she say which ones?'

'Not on the phone. I gather she was going over sketches she'd made in the field, trying to identify them. We promised to catch up, but, alas, we never did.'

We went inside and gathered around the lounge room table. Lucy made us all tea and put out a plate of oatmeal biscuits.

'Ah yes,' Wolf exclaimed when we showed him the image. He clicked his tongue and shook his head. 'I see the problem.'

'What's wrong with it?' I asked.

'It doesn't exist is what's wrong with it. I'm surprised. Daisy was no scientist, but she had an excellent eye.' He raised his head and addressed us all. 'That eye seems to have betrayed her here.'

Possum was offended on her late friend's behalf. 'How can you be sure?' she said. 'You can't know every plant on the mountain.'

A smile slid across his mouth, fell off the other side. This was a guy who suffered neither fools nor kids. 'I believe I do know just about every plant on the mountain. And I assure you, Daisy has made a mistake.'

He tapped the page forcefully. 'What she's drawn looks a little like *Caladenia cruciformis* – the red-cross spider

107

orchid – which is a problem in itself. They're not found in the Windmarks; they are more Central Victoria. But look at the clubs. They're lemon-coloured, distended. Impossible. And those sharp red spots on the petal. The green labellum. It's all wrong. There is no such plant.'

Possum wasn't giving up that easily. 'Maybe it's a new species? Daisy was always hoping to find one.'

Wolf looked again at the orchid, his brow smooth, unruffled by doubt. 'If it truly looked like that, it would indeed be a new species. A significant discovery. But I know the flora of these mountains – forgive me – better than anybody, and I've never seen such a plant. Daisy was an artist – maybe she was attempting to be creative, rather than scientifically accurate?'

Possum snorted and demolished one of her mother's biscuits.

'Couldn't we find this spot and the orchid?' I suggested. 'That should tell us, one way or the other.'

Wolf gestured out at the yard, where the sun was hitting everything with a blast of dazzling white light.

'It's the tail end of a brutal summer, Jesse, at the end – we can only hope – of a five-year drought. Most of the flowers are long faded, and there's nothing to specify where this sketch was done. No names, dates, locations.'

I took a closer look at the picture, suggested that the trees in the background might give us a clue.

Wolf examined them. 'Manna gums,' he said. 'And that's – what – between them? A black she-oak? Not a particularly unusual combination.'

'What about these?' I asked, pointing at the trio of curved boulders on the left side of the page.

'Ach, my bad.' He smiled archly. 'I spend so much energy concentrating upon the intricacies of the flora, I sometimes fail to pay sufficient attention to inanimate objects.'

I caught a glimpse of Possum's scowl and wondered if there was anything I could do to lighten her mood. I swept my gaze across the page and was struck by an unusual image – a face – which seemed to emerge from the texture of the foremost rock.

'That looks like an old man,' I said, touching the sketch. 'Shading his eyes and staring into the distance.'

Possum leaned forward. 'I see what you mean,' she said. 'It could almost be my grandpa.'

She was right. The face was angular, the eyes Asian, the fingers long and graceful. The overall effect was not unlike the faded photos I'd seen of Kenji Takada. It didn't mean much, surely: a trick of the light. If the drawing had been done moments before, the illusion would have vanished. But Daisy had chosen that particular point in time for a reason. I looked at the rock again and felt a shiver down my spine; it was almost as if she was speaking to me through the image.

Lucy stood up and stepped over to the window, a delicate furrow etched into her brow.

'A stand of manna gums and a black she-oak,' she said. 'An outcrop of rocks, one with a picture of my dad. Doesn't ring any bells for me, and I've lived here all my life. Rocks and trees all over the place. You could be scouring the hills for weeks trying to find something we don't even know exists.'

'I agree,' said Wolf.

'I don't,' snapped Possum. 'If Daisy drew them, they were there. She didn't make things up. That's not how she worked.'

She leaned back in her chair and took a peremptory swig of tea.

An awkward silence descended upon the room. Wolf glanced at his watch and said he had to go. 'I do know a stand of manna gums a little like these,' he said. 'Up near Johnson's Falls, on the Cody Creek.'

He said the trees were near a waterhole there, five or six k's to the south-east. His eyes locked onto mine. 'No promises,' he added, 'but it's the only location I can think of which is anything like the one in this picture. I could take you there if you wish.'

'I'd appreciate that,' I said.

I took a photo of the sketch with my phone, labelled it *wtf*, and added Wolf's number to my contacts. He said to give him a call whenever I wanted to go.

We walked out onto the verandah and watched Wolf drive away.

'What are you going to do now?' asked Lucy.

I looked down towards Windmark, curious to know how the Gaunts would react if somebody suggested they stop logging an area because there was an unclassified plant nearby.

'Think it's time I met these dreaded Gaunts,' I said. 'Where do I find them?'

Lucy was heading back to the studio but she said they had an office at the mill on Maddison's Road.

When her mother had gone, Possum stared at me, aghast. 'Why on earth do you want to meet them?'

'See if they can shed any light onto the matter.'

'Brock used to shed light onto me,' she grimaced, 'with matches.'

'What do you mean?'

She explained that at primary school he'd had a creepy fascination with fire. He'd been caught lighting fires in rubbish bins and the bike shed, and his favourite trick was flicking burning matches at preppies like her. Once he'd even set a kid's hair on fire.

'Classy,' I said.

'He was leaving about the time I was starting, thank god, so I didn't have to put up with him for long.' She smiled, clearly enjoying the prospect of a confrontation between me and the Gaunts. I knew what was coming next. 'Can I go with you?'

Bloody kid wanted a finger in every pie. 'Sorry, Possum. Police business.'

CHAPTER 16

I parked out the front of a large industrial block. There were maybe a dozen vehicles in the car park and an array of heavy equipment – log loaders, forklifts and trucks – in a yard out back. The mill itself was a corrugated-iron mausoleum with partially open sides, a ten-metre kiln and twenty-metre racks. To its left was a mountain of timber, neatly stacked, a sprinkler on top whirling arcs of cooling water.

A bunch of blokes with steel-capped boots and heads were unloading a B-double truck at a ramp near the entrance. They bounced around, chiacking each other, all beefsteak energy and blue jokes. An older fellow with fisherman's ears and skin like waterlogged cardboard licked his lips and leered as I walked past.

Somewhere a giant bandsaw screamed. Somewhere a hammer pounded with a metal-echo boom.

I headed for the office, past the row of cars. Hesitated when I noticed one of them was a black F250 with a bank of spotties on the roof. Was this the vehicle Possum had mentioned? The window was down. Never look a gift horse – I poked my nose in. Learnt little other than that the occupant's tools and diet had one thing in common – an abundance of grease.

'Help you, ma'am?'

I jumped up and bumped my head.

Standing behind me was the man I'd last seen peering out the window of a truck at Messmate Lane. Allan Gaunt. Hi-vis vest, in-vis neck. Power belly, spikey grey hair, battle scars on the back of his hands. Customer-service smile.

The smile vanished when I flashed my badge. He shook his head and waved his right hand. The hand, I couldn't help but notice, ended in a row of stumps – mementoes of a life among blades.

'Jesus,' he grumbled. 'Not again.'

'Again?'

He fixed me with a slow-burning stare. 'This is about the greenie woman, I presume? We had Vince bloody Tehlich nosing around, week or two back. Him and some dickhead from the city.'

'We just need to cross the t's –'

'I heard it was that ...' – accusatorial eyebrow descending – 'boyfriend who did her.'

Did her? Gross.

'There'll be an inquest,' I replied. 'We're going to look pretty silly if we haven't covered every angle. Did you know Ms Baker?'

Hands on hips. 'Nope.'

'Ever meet her?'

Hands off hips. 'Nope.'

'I heard you had some kind of run-in with her, last year.'

He frowned and said he'd never laid eyes on the woman.

'At Echidna Creek?' I pressed. 'I've seen you in a photograph.'

'The blockade?' He twisted his mouth into something between a smile and a sneer. 'She might have been there; I wouldn't know one of those ring-tailed idiots from another.'

I looked around the compound.

Gaunt came across as the sort of feller who'd never made it past primary school, but he was doing all right. Doing bloody well, if the top-of-the-range Rover in the manager's spot was anything to go by. Amazing what elbow grease, rat cunning and a limited imagination can do for you.

The unloaders had finished and were making their way back into the mill. The B-double was turning out onto the road. The sight of it reminded me of my first encounter with Gaunt.

'You normally drive the trucks yourself?' I asked.

'Only when there's a chance of squashing a few greenies.' A twisted smile; apparently that was meant to be a joke. 'In me dreams. Nah, might help out when things get hectic.'

'Like yesterday morning at Messmate Lane?'

'Ah, that was you, was it?'

Why did I have the feeling that he'd known that all along?

'Who was the old guy?' he asked.

'My bodyguard.'

He may have blinked. 'Like I said, I do the occasional job when one of these bludgers calls in sick, but normally running the show's enough to keep me –'

A shadow moved on the ground beside the shed. He followed my eyes and swung round. 'Brock!'

A young bloke in a truckie's cap and a camouflage vest came round the corner of the building. Brock? Possum's fearsome match-flicker. Had he been eavesdropping? He halted and hunched, raised his head. He had rip-curl lips and snake-infested forearms. Not much happening in the chin department. A dark forelock flopped onto his forehead.

'Dad?'

His eyes raked me with a swift, cold glance.

'Where you going?' asked Gaunt senior.

'Lunch run.'

'Boozer bloody run,' snapped his father. 'Not going anywhere until you've finished servicing the loader.'

For a moment, Brock looked like a man drowning in a septic tank, his face twisted with outraged disbelief. He opened his mouth to say something, then read the older man's mood. He thrust his fists into his pockets, snorted and stomped back to the plant yard.

'And make sure you lock her down,' Allan growled.

He turned to me. 'Slack bastard. Been all kinds of theft going on round here. Now, if you don't mind, I'm a busy man.'

Somewhere in the distance I heard a machine kick into life and do some heavy rumbling. Tracks rattled, metal rang. A puff of black smoke floated up from the plant yard. Allan Gaunt headed for the office.

Time for one last throw of the dice.

'Did Ms Baker ever talk to you about flowers?' I asked his back.

He stopped and made a half turn, his face clouding over. 'Flowers?' The word was as hard as hammered iron.

'Orchids. She was a botanical artist. Seems to me a botanical artist and a logger might have had a few things in common – or bones of contention.'

He stared out over the yard, the burning gravel reflected in his cheeks. 'That badge. What's a Territory cop doing down here anyway?'

I said I was from the young man's hometown and that we were assisting with the investigation.

He ran a truncated finger across his jaw.

'You knew him personally then?' he asked. 'This Adam Lawson character.'

He wasn't having any trouble remembering the name now.

'I did.'

'So you've come to show he didn't kill her. And to do that, you gotta find somebody to take the fall.'

'I came down here to –'

He raised his right hand like it was a stop sign. 'You got a warrant?'

'No. I just –'

'Well you can fuck off then.'

He turned away and disappeared into the mill.

I sighed. The blue-collar interview, one aspect of the job I'd never mastered. Tom Vallence would have had the truth out of this character in a couple of minutes, then joined him for a beer, possibly not in that order. All I seemed to do was make blokes like Allan Gaunt angry.

When I reached my vehicle, I looked back. Brock was sitting in a log loader, hands on the levers, head turned in my direction. His right arm moved and the vehicle shuddered and rang, metal on metal. The boom buckled and swung, the tongs crashed. The machine jumped forward.

He was forty yards away and swathed in hat-shadow, but even at that distance, you could feel the heat, the hostility. It had seeped into the machine.

Had I done something to piss him off, or did he always look like that? Was it because I was investigating the deaths at Canticle Creek? Maybe he just didn't like strangers. Or cops. Or women. Or all of the above. Whatever the reason, he was trouble. I could smell it, the way I'd learnt to smell smuggled booze on the Kulara evening breeze.

CHAPTER 17

At the station I said hello to Vince and spent a few hours wading through the files and talking to his team. I told them about the welcome I'd received at the timber mill. The sergeant wasn't surprised.

'You would have been keeping him from his work. Likes to keep the cash flow flowing, Allan.'

Then he gave me his version of the Canticle incident over a cup of tea.

It had been a bugger of a morning. They'd been racing out to a reported fatal accident on the Grinwood Road. Just as they arrived on scene, they received word of a frantic emergency call from Possum Kelly, who'd come across the body of her friend. Tehlich had left his leading senior in charge then carried on up to Messmate Lane. It hadn't taken them long to splice the deaths together.

I could see why everybody had assumed Adam was responsible. I'd have thought so too, if I hadn't known him. Local woman murdered, stranger fleeing in a stolen car. The evidence – forensics, criminal record, witness statements – all pointed in one direction. Adam's life was described as 'spiralling'. There'd been a warrant out for his arrest and he'd been spotted in Daisy's company the night before. His DNA was all over the crime scene: in her house, her bed, her body. The couple had had sex in the hours before their deaths – whether or not it was consensual, the pathologist couldn't say.

Vince assured me that they'd kept an open mind on the subject, were keeping one still. He'd reported my run-in with the Razics to his colleagues in Homicide, who were giving them renewed consideration. Fresh interviews had been conducted, evidence reassessed, but, to date, no links between the Razic outfit and the crime had been uncovered – apart from Nadia. If the Razics – or even the Gaunts – were involved, they were doing a good job of hiding it. The investigation was ongoing.

'Case that bad,' said Vince. 'Always ongoing, long as I'm in this chair.'

My first instinct had been correct: a solid country copper.

But one likely to solve a crime like this? I had my doubts. At heart, he still thought Adam was the perp-most-likely. That'd slow him down. Officer in charge of a busy country station, other things would come along, interfere, take priority: sui/homicidal young men, hot-car chases, pub brawls. Adam and Daisy would be gradually shunted off to the backblocks.

I returned to the files. An hour into my reading I came across a note I hadn't picked up anywhere else. Maybe a late addition? I checked the date. Yes, it was a print-out of an email received a few days ago.

I showed it to Vince. 'Forensics don't think she was murdered where she was found?'

'Apparently not,' he replied, explaining that the opinion was based upon a more detailed analysis of the blood: flow pattern, oxygen levels, the lack of splatter marks. Daisy was already dead when she was dumped in the ditch.

'Do they have any idea where she *was* killed?' I asked.

'Nothing definite yet. Somewhere on the property, they're assuming.'

I met his gaze. 'Assuming?'

He looked away.

'Not in the cabin?' I pressed.

'No evidence of that,' he admitted.

'And yet they found the murder weapon near the body.'

'Homicide's theory is that he dragged her into the ditch to conceal her, give himself time to get away.'

I thought back to my mental image of the crime scene: there was no indication that Adam had gone anywhere near the ditch.

'What about the rock?' I asked. 'Why did he leave that near the body? Just to incriminate himself? And if he was going to all the trouble of dumping her in a ditch, why not bury her in the bush? That would have given him even more time.'

Vince's fingernails drummed a heavy tattoo on the table.

'Looks to me,' I said, 'like somebody was trying to set him up.'

He stood up and pushed his chair back.

'Jesus, Jesse,' he said, 'you start thinking like that, you'll turn yourself inside out. Every case has got inconsistencies, if you look hard enough. Every mongrel in the Acacia Unit swears he's been fitted up, the witnesses lying, the evidence planted.'

He said he needed a coffee and disappeared into the kitchen.

I returned to the files, made more notes, asked more questions. Didn't get many useful answers. There was nothing to suggest that Tehlich and his team had stuffed up or were holding anything back. They seemed like a decent enough crew.

They just didn't know.

If I was going to find out what really happened at Canticle Creek, I was going to have to do it by myself.

CHAPTER 18

It was late afternoon when I left the station, but the sun still had plenty of bite. Dazzling white light punched through the air, recoiled from metal and glass, and seemed to end up mostly in my eyes. The hairs on the back of my neck wilted, my shirt clung, my bra itched. Bloody heat: would it never end? I thought Victoria was meant to be cool.

I needed a drink. A quick search on my phone led me to Springhills, a brewery-cum-bakery at the southern end of town.

I settled into a honeysuckle-shrouded nook on the back balcony and ordered a cider. The setting looked out over the river. I'd struck paydirt. Springhills was charming: bubbling waters, bobbing ferns, funky bread. An eclectic soundtrack, from Johnny Cash to Justin Townes-Earle. Just what I needed.

The only sour note came from the thrash metal racket blasting out of the grungy pub next door. The two establishments seemed to be embroiled in a battle of the bands. When Springhills played Gram Parsons, the neighbours countered with Megadeth. Poor Nina Simone found herself going head-to-head with Judas Priest.

The server smiled sympathetically as she delivered my drink.

'Sorry about the ruckus. Knock-off time for the tradies. They love pumping up the jukebox. Do it just to piss us off.'

'No probs.'

I picked up a magazine and flicked through it. A kingfisher drifted in and sat on the railing, looked at me, angling for a feed. When that was unsuccessful, it shat on the deck and took off.

I'd been there for half an hour when Wolf Gunther entered the room, spotted me and came over.

'Ms Redpath,' he said. 'How goes the investigation?'

'Slowly but slowly.'

'Do you mind if I join you?'

I gestured at the seat opposite.

He sat down, draped an arm across the back of the bench and crossed his legs. There was a sheen of sweat across his forehead, a golden glow in the stubble on his chin. His eyes had grown electric blue in the heat.

He winked at a shapely blonde behind the bar, who promptly came over.

'What's the time, Mister Wolf?' she purred with a batting-eyed intimacy that told you they'd slept together, or soon would.

'I believe it's beer-time.'

She disappeared, came back with a honey-coloured schooner beaded with condensation, then minced away.

'You're a regular here,' I commented.

'Ah, yes – these bloody Australian summers.' He gestured at the hot copper sky glowering over the trees. 'You have to be a regular somewhere.'

'All that ice and snow in Germany wouldn't do much to equip you for weather like this. Which part of the country are you from?'

'Frankfurt am Main.'

'And what brought you to Australia?'

He explained that this country was still a newfoundland for somebody in his line of work. Much of the flora here was still undocumented, species diversity was contentious, the pollination systems still under debate.

'Europe,' he concluded, 'is, by comparison, a suburban lawn.'

He'd studied at the Goethe Institute of Higher Learning and completed a doctorate in orchid morphology, the study of the form and structure of the organism. 'My research,' he added with a smile that came perilously close to a smirk, 'was in pseudocopulation.'

I raised a brow. 'Sounds like a tautology – it's mostly pretty pseudo up where I come from.'

'It's when a wasp or bee attempts to fuck a flower.'

'Why on earth does it – actually, I don't want to know.'

He raised his glass and took a long pull. 'It's all about self-interest and deception.'

'Sounds like Tinder.'

He licked a sliver of foam from his upper lip. Pseudocopulation. Something about the way he said the word and licked that lip suggested this wasn't the first time he'd used the term as the opening gambit in a game whose ultimate goal was copulation of the non-pseudo variety.

Lucinda Williams came over the sound system: 'Crescent City'. She was immediately countered by something Guns n' Rosy next door. Small birds flew for cover.

I asked Wolf what he was working on now, and he said that, in addition to his voluntary conservation work, he ran a small – mostly one-man – botanical survey company. The Department of Environment had engaged him to carry out a survey of the southern section of the Windmark Ranges, the results of which would eventually be incorporated into a master plan.

'Master plan?' I queried. 'That'll decide who does what where?'

'More or less. Farmers, hunters, hikers and riders ...'

'Loggers?'

'Yes, of course. They are all watching with interest.'

Some hoon in a bright blue Commodore ute came fanging down the road, swung into the car park, sent an arc of gravel flying as he hit the anchors. The driver jumped out and headed for pub next door, a thirsty look in his gait.

'I met Allan Gaunt today,' I said. 'He must have been thrilled to hear it was you who got the contract.'

'Given that I was out there protesting against him a little while ago?' He laughed. 'I run a business, just like him. All is fair ...'

I pulled a flower from the vine, sucked the nectar from it and asked what the protest at Echidna Creek was about. He was happy to fill me in.

'The government granted a logging permit which was inimical to the ecosystem of a critically endangered marsupial: the Leadbeater's possum.'

'How did it turn out?'

'We took them to the appeals tribunal and – amazingly – we won. The permit was rescinded.' He flashed a glimmering tribute to German dentistry. 'Maybe there is a God.'

'That must have left the loggers pissed off.'

'Pissed off and out of pocket, if what they say is true. But that is of little significance for our current contract. We are simply studying and recording what is there: species, genera, the biophysical data and its level of degradation.'

I thought about the implications of that. Was there a motive for murder in there?

'Have you found anything worth killing for?' I asked.

'I imagine that would depend upon the mindset of the killer, but if you're wondering whether the Gaunts are breaking the law – logging in water catchment areas, felling protected species – then no, I've come across no evidence of such behaviour. Not lately. Maybe they know we're watching them.'

A flock of cockatoos wheeled across the western sky, creaking and screeching, a white storm.

An idea drifted in upon their wake. I asked him how he thought Daisy would have reacted if she came across somebody breaking the rules, and he said she would have spoken her mind.

'She was passionate about her flora,' he said. 'She was always the first into the treetops, the last to be dragged down.'

I wondered whether she'd spoken her mind too rashly, paid for it with her life?

I thought about those hot-under-the-collar Gaunts – the defensive Allan, the offensive Brock. It didn't look like it would take much to make either of them lash out. They'd already lost business because of Echidna Creek, wouldn't want to repeat the experience.

There was a burst of belly laughter and a scream of twisted power chords from the dump next door. The buildings were so close I could see into the dimly lit back bar. Definitely the boozer of choice for your rowdier man about town – sweat everywhere, boots and balls, pool table, dartboard. A mob of sozzled, gaping faces. I was relieved not to be in uniform – red rag to a bull, that'd be.

'What's that joint called?' I asked.

'Ah, the Burns. I've never been in there. It's dirty and rough.'

'Blood in the sawdust?'

'Exactly. A remnant of the days when Windmark was just a timber town. I get a much more congenial welcome here at Springhills – as, I suspect, would you.'

One of the men around the pool table next door was staring at me; his eyes were like searchlights on a prison wall. He was wearing a singlet and shorts, with a cap on backwards and a swarm of blue tattoos. He took a swig, raised a cue and smashed the rack. One of the balls jumped the head rail and rattled an angry passage across the floor.

A mobile rang. Wolf and I reached for our phones simultaneously. It was his. He apologised, took the call.

But where was my own phone? Not in my bag. I must have left it in the car. Not a smart move. I should be keeping it handy, the number of things going on round here.

I gestured to Wolf that I'd be back and went out to the car park.

There was a burst of noise from the Burns. The door jumped and two men, one big, one not, whirled out swinging punches at each other. They hit the gravel and rolled in my direction. The big one got up, the little one knocked him down. A boisterous crowd gathered and cheered them on.

Almost on cue, a black-shirted gorilla stomped out of the pub, tore the combatants apart and threw them in opposite directions. The brawlers shuffled away, dripping sweat and spitting blood, flicking backward glances.

'A week for the pair of you,' growled the bouncer.

The spectators dispersed and I spotted a trio of malingerers near my car. One of them was leaning against the bonnet and looking in my direction. It was Brock Gaunt. I realised he was the pool player who'd been giving me the evil eye from the back bar a few minutes earlier. He was giving it still. The other two were sniggering.

They moved away as I approached and then re-joined the stragglers heading back to the Burns. Brock left me with his trademark glare.

Closer to the car, I noticed the back left tyre was flat. There was a slash in the sidewall that must have been deliberately inflicted.

'Fuck,' I muttered.

'Are you right there?' said a voice behind me. I looked back to see Sheree Talia standing there. 'Oh, hi Jesse,' she added when she recognised me.

'You've got a good memory,' I replied.

'Dom mentioned you were in town. Bad luck,' she added, nodding at the tyre.

'Dunno if luck's got much to do with it.'

Wolf appeared, frowned when he saw the puncture.

'Deliberate?' he asked.

'Looks it,' said Dom Talia, coming over from his BMW, keys in hand. He and Sheree were out for a night on the town by the look of them. 'The Gaunt boys were just here. Did they know you were a police officer?'

'I was out at the mill this morning, interviewing their father.'

Dom raised a brow. 'Yeah, that would have done it.'

'I did warn you,' said Wolf. 'That's just the locals' way of saying hello.'

I noticed, for the first time, a familiar black F250 squatting like a toad a few spaces away.

'Bastards,' I grunted. 'Tempted to slash a few tyres myself.'

'Don't let them get to you,' said Wolf. 'Do you still want to go to Johnson's Falls?'

I shrugged. Why not? I'd just seen the dark underbelly of Windmark. A little spell in a revitalising natural environment might do me good.

Dom and Sheree headed into Springhills, where they were meeting friends for dinner. Wolf suggested we leave my car at the tyre shop on Cinnamon Row and collect it when we got back. He picked up some food and wine while I changed the tyre and in ten minutes we were on our way.

CHAPTER 19

We headed out of town, turned onto Robinwood Road, drove past the new estate. The dozers and graders there were still at work, beeping and backing, flashing orange lights. An excavator was gouging out ditches and shaping mounds of mineral earth. Men in hard hats and blue singlets were wielding sledgehammers and shovels.

On the opposite side of the road a posse of baseball-capped kids were flinging BMXs over jumps they'd made on the verges. Hobby horses gazed at us from hobby farms, tawny cows chewed their cud and swished their tails.

We climbed up into the hills: Canticle Junction, Crowcall Road, long, anonymous stretches where the undergrowth came creeping out onto the verges. My ears began to pop. As we topped a rise, I glanced back. There was nobody behind us. Or was there? A wave of cockies further down the hill suggested we weren't alone.

I asked Wolf if Daisy had ever said anything to him about Johnson's Falls.

'Not that I recall,' he replied. 'Your theory, if I read you correctly, is that she came across what she thought was a new species of orchid, then threatened to halt a nearby logging operation.'

'More or less,' I said. 'It's just an idea, but that's the only way I know to work – look for anomalies. That orchid's an anomaly.'

'Or a figment of her imagination.'

'Maybe.'

Up near the end of the bitumen, the road ran past a steep cliff that afforded an excellent view of the Windmark Valley. There was even a lookout, with a telescope, a seat and a sign that read *Demon's Leap*.

'What's with the name?' I asked.

'Legend has it that's where your more desperate locals go to escape their demons.'

'By jumping off?'

'So they say. I've never felt inclined to see if it works.'

At a place called Tanglewood Junction – plenty of wood, most of it tangled, a junction, not much else – we turned right and ploughed along a narrow dirt track. Gravel crunched under-wheel. Dust tumbled in our wake then lingered in the air; the plants along the verge were smothered in it, their leaves a pallid yellow camouflage. The road glowed like a ribbon of magnesium.

'This is as dry as the bloody Centre,' I commented.

'Don't worry – we have an oasis up ahead.'

He wasn't wrong. A final rise and the track descended into a shallow gorge. Dirty trees gave way to iridescent fronds and ferns, creepers and greenery, cinnabar crags. A minute or two's drive and we pulled up at a little waterhole, maybe ten metres in diameter. Above it a creek – the Cordy – tumbled over pitted mudstone, formed little falls and runnels, transparent pools.

We got out and walked down to the water's edge, took off our shoes. Tiny shadow fish darted around our toes. A whipbird cracked the silence, its languid call echoing through the valley. Dragon and damsel flies inscribed drifting figures of eight on rainbow wings, skimmed the surface then made touchdown.

'Those are the manna gums I was thinking of,' said Wolf, indicating a stand of grey-limbed eucalypts looming out of a patch of Prickly Moses scrub on the opposite slope.

I took out my phone, compared Daisy's image to what lay before me. The site didn't look promising: the gums were too small, the rocks along the creek too distant, with little suggestion of an old man's face among them. There was a black she-oak, but it was on the wrong side of the stand. Still, I'd better check it out. I popped my shoes back on and worked my way down the gully and up through the wallaby grass. I stood on the opposite slope, looking over the gully. No, I decided, this isn't the place. Daisy was too precise an artist to have misrepresented the scene to that extent.

I glanced back at the vehicle. Wolf must have been feeling the heat; he'd stripped down to a pair of shorts and was sitting on a rock at the water's edge. He dived in smoothly, then he rose and shook the spray from his hair.

'Ach, frrreezing.' He laughed, clutching his ribs and climbing out of the water.

By the time I got back he was perched on the rocks. Trickles of water ran down his torso, catching the rays of the setting sun and lending his body a golden glow. A bottle of wine and a basket of bread and cheese sat beside him.

'What did you find?' he asked.

'Nothing. Don't think it's the place.'

'My apologies.' He shrugged. 'It was only a hunch. I remembered the manna gums and the she-oak.'

'They're here, but in the wrong arrangement.'

'Well, at least it hasn't been a wasted trip.' He swept an arm out at the scene. 'You get an opportunity to enjoy the natural beauty of our Windmark Ranges.' He tapped the rock. 'Have a seat.'

I sat and chewed a blade of onion grass. Tasty. 'Can you think of any other place that might fit the bill?'

'I'm sure something will come to me,' he said. 'Would you like some wine?'

He poured me a glass. I took a sip.

'Nice,' I said.

'It's Goldengrove Estate,' he said, pouring one for himself. 'One of our five-star locals.'

I cast my gaze onto the surrounding bush. It was so thick, you could barely see a hundred metres. I was beginning to think I was doing this exercise arse-about. I'd be better off looking at current logging jobs and examining their surrounds, searching for any sign of the scene in Daisy's sketch.

'Are there any other active coupes nearby?' I asked him.

'There are a couple further along Johnson's Road.'

'Gaunts?'

'One of them.'

He stretched back against the boulder and ran his hands through his hair.

'Anyway,' he said, 'they will still be there tomorrow. For now, let's just relax and enjoy this beautiful evening.'

He put a hand on my knee.

I raised my brows and put the hand back where it belonged. 'Not today, thanks.'

'Come now, there's no need to let your inhibitions ruin what —'

I frowned. 'It isn't inhibition.'

He looked into my eyes and gave me the dazzling smile that had no doubt melted Madchens' hearts from Frankfurt am Main to Melbourne. The hand returned with a little more vigour, started to feel like a claw, gave my leg a squeeze. Moved up my thigh.

'I said no!'

I pushed him away and made to stand. He stood up and threw an arm around me, dragging me into an embrace. When I tried to shake him off he pressed his lips against mine and his tongue into my mouth.

I stepped back and punched him in the face.

'You crazy bitch,' he rasped, transformed, teeth bared, nose bleeding. He sprang at me, so I caught him on the fly — the energy of momentum running all one way — and diverted him into the water.

I've no idea what they taught at the Goethe Institute of Higher Learning, but five years at the Outback Institute of Lower Learning — gutters, pubs and camps from Alice to Darwin — had sharpened my reflexes to such a degree that I didn't even have to use my feet.

'Cold bath,' I called as I walked away. 'Help you cool down.'

He scrambled onto the rocks and huddled there, catching his breath and nursing his nose. His upper lip was covered with blood. He snarled at me, blue eyes ablaze. Shook his body like a wet dog.

I set off down the track, heart pounding, then decided a little more impediment wouldn't go astray. As I passed the car, I grabbed my bag then whipped the keys out of the ignition and threw them away.

'Keys are in the scrub,' I called – generously, I thought, given the circumstances.

'Fuck you!' he yelled. 'Enjoy the walk back to town.'

I began to wonder if I'd done the right thing. No regrets about thumping the horny bugger, but it was getting late and I wasn't quite sure where I was. I reached the road in ten minutes and headed downhill, hoping to get to Windmark before the snakes came out.

I strode a little faster and began to feel wheezy. I reached for my ventolin. Damn, not there. Best to take it easy. No desire to cark it on this lonely road because of a randy German.

You idiot, I admonished myself. You should have been on your guard. Distracted by the investigation – not to mention the damage to my car – I'd let myself be lured into a potentially dangerous situation. But, Jesus, could you blame me? What did it say about a place when you couldn't even trust the greenies? It would be a relief to get back to Kulara – people there might have had their problems, but deviousness wasn't among them. You mostly knew what you were going to get.

I'd covered maybe half a kilometre when I heard a vehicle behind me.

'Wolf?' I thought warily, figuring I might have to go bush if his hormones were still running amok. I'd got the better of him once but I'd had the element of surprise.

A white SUV cruised past, then drew to a halt. Somebody must have recognised me. Or wondered what a woman was doing up here on her own. The passenger's window slid down and a familiar head popped out.

'Looking for something, Jess?'

Sam Kelly. Talk about luck.

I jogged forward. 'Yeah, a lift back to town.'

He told me to climb aboard and I jumped into the back seat. The driver turned round.

'This part of the investigation is it, lass? Rambling about the Ranges on your ownsome?'

It was a knobby-nosed Scotsman I'd met before – the building supervisor in the ute at the Robinwood Lakes Estate. What was his name? Geordie North.

'What on earth were you doing up here without a car?' asked Sam.

'Had a car. Also had some company I didn't want.'

He frowned. 'Who would that have been?'

'Your Wolf bloody Gunther.'

Sam looked aghast. 'Mine! I don't own him. Lemme guess: tried to chat you up?'

'And the rest.'

'Wolf by name, wolf by nature, that lad.'

'Aye, *Deutschland uber alles*,' threw in Geordie. 'And *unter*! Feller's got a reputation.'

Sam told me Wolf had worked his way through all the eligible women in Windmark and a good percentage of the ineligible. Said somebody should have warned me.

The comment rang a bell. I thought about my recent conversations.

'I think somebody did,' I said. 'Your dear daughter.'

'Ah, Possum. Yes, she's not a fan.'

Sam glanced through the dusty rear window. 'Where's the wolf now?'

'Probably looking for his keys,' I said. 'Or nursing his wounds.'

'Not the goolies again?' crooned Geordie, highly amused.

Again? What sort of reputation was I getting around this town?

He read my puzzled expression and explained that Dom Talia had told him about my run-in with the Razics on Cinnamon Row.

'I see,' I said. 'No, I spared him that. What were you two gentlemen doing up here so conveniently anyway?'

Geordie explained that he was the construction manager at the new Estate and that Sam was doing a little job for them.

'Little!' protested Sam.

'Maybe not that little.'

'Big!' riposted Sam. 'Very big. I'll have a broken bloody back by the time you've had your way with me.'

He explained that they were going for the rustic look in the new clubhouse; they'd gone to check out an old quarry above Johnson's Falls to see if the rocks were suitable for the fireplace.

'And were they?' I asked.

'Close,' said Geordie.

'Fuckin obsessive compulsive,' growled Sam. 'Had to lift a ton of the buggers before he decided that.'

Geordie countered that he'd learnt his craft in Aberdeen, and that the first thing they taught you was how to build a fireplace; he said you could shape the house around it.

The luminous mountain scenery whirled by my window: a honeycombed rockface, a hillside carpeted with purple pincushions. A white cat being harassed by a flock of stroppy wattlebirds. A wallaby cruised alongside the vehicle, then decided we weren't worth the effort and peeled off.

Geordie asked me what I was doing at the Johnson's Falls in the first place. When I said I was up there looking for orchids, he scratched around his skull, maybe trying to find some hair.

'Why on earth would you put yourself at risk wi' a prick like Wolf just to find a flower?'

'I'm a naturally curious person.'

He gave me a puzzled stare. 'Aye, that you are ... Curiouser and curiouser.'

They dropped me back at the tyre shop, where my car was ready and waiting.

'Appreciate it if you didn't mention this to the rest of the family,' I said to Sam. 'I feel like an idiot.'

He put a finger to his lips and gave me a sardonic smile. 'Mum's the word.'

CHAPTER 20

I arrived back at the Bluehouse in time to join the household for dinner. It was all friendly enough – we had pasta smothered in veggies fresh from the garden and an apple pie with fruit just off the tree – but the atmosphere didn't reach the convivial heights of the night before.

Lucy and Dad bailed early, adjourning to the lounge room, where they had a topographical map of the region laid out on the table. Dad had been out all day, driving around the district in Lucy's car. From what I could pick up from their conversation, he was trying to align his field observations with their cartographic representation.

He peppered Lucy with questions about the country and its inhabitants: who was new, who was old, who fitted in, who didn't, how they fitted together. When Sam joined them, Dad asked about the local businesses: farming, logging, building, the odd gold mine or water plant. He asked them both about the environment: changing water courses and weather events, floods and fires, the direction and depth of the thunderstorms, the severity of droughts.

I was too tired to take it all in and went to bed. My head and heart were still thumping after my encounter with Wolf Gunther. I wondered whether the bastard had ever really thought that Johnson's Falls was a viable candidate for the orchid's location, or if it had all been a ploy to set me up for a little waterside tryst?

Where did that leave my investigation?

Getting nowhere fast, still up to its knees in *merde*.

I tried to sleep, but this investigation was playing havoc with what little was left of my circadian rhythms. I stared at the timber ceiling, studied the shapes in the grain. Figures emerged: various gangsters and Gaunts, Benny and Brock, Eddie Razic, that muscle-bound Nick Cave.

Even the bit players came out of the woodwork. Everybody was a suspect until proven innocent. Wolf. Nadia. Geordie and Dom, Nick, Sam. I tried to imagine if any of them had motive, means or inclination.

I got nowhere. I had a mountain of suspicions, but proof of nothing.

Eventually I closed my eyes and let the frustration carry me sleepwards.

When I awoke, I found myself lying in the debris of a dream about cleaning houses.

It took a moment or two to work out why.

The dream was inspired by the memory of my first day at Kulara. As I pulled up in front of the station, I spotted a mob of youngsters scampering out the back of the residence. I walked into the house, then stopped and stared, aghast. There were chunks of kangaroo carcass on the kitchen floor, maggoty nappies in the sink, dust, dirt and dogshit everywhere.

The station had been vacant for weeks. The locals, knowing how nature abhorred a vacuum, had broken in and made themselves at home. A couple of them were still snickering at me from the front gate.

'Piss off!' I screamed.

I gazed at the room and just about fell over with the hopelessness of it all.

Get a grip, I told myself. There's only one place to begin: the beginning. Nobody's going to do this for you.

I found an empty bin, backed the ute up to the verandah, put on some pumpy music – 'Born to Run' – and ran. The first thing that caught my eye was a stray sock in a teapot in the middle of the lounge-room floor. A teabag of last resort? I hurled it into the bin. Then I threw the pot in as well; I couldn't see myself enjoying any cups of tea from that particular piece of kitchenware.

My next port of call was the pile of takeaway containers on and around the kitchen table, a lot of their contents still there, half-eaten and breeding god-knows-what. Into the bin they went. I caught the rhythm of the song, picked up the pace and the rubbish. Food scraps, dresses, empty flagons, empty underpants, everything found a home. The bigger stuff went straight into the back of the ute, ready for a tip run – if there was a tip.

Eventually, I paused, exhausted, out of breath. I gave myself some ventolin and looked out over the chaos. The odd floorboard had begun to appear, but the task still seemed gargantuan. Then I realised I wasn't alone. I swung round.

Two teenage boys – the pair who'd been laughing at me from the front gate – were standing in the doorway. With them was another youth, tall, with long hair and a stockman's hat. I thought they'd come back to gloat, but then the young man spoke.

'Morning, Sarge. Heard you had a rough welcome, so the boys have come to help you clean up.'

This was my first encounter with Adam Lawson.

The four of us got stuck into the job and in an hour the place was as good as it was going to get.

Okay, I said to myself as I lay listening to the early birds of Canticle Creek work up a storm. That was then, this is now. But the principle's the same: when you're faced with overwhelming chaos, all you can do is get off your arse. Find somewhere, anywhere, to begin, then go for broke. And if you're lucky, fate might lend a hand and an Adam Lawson will turn up.

Where to begin? What was the sock-in-the-teapot in this affair?

Daisy Baker's mysterious orchid.

It wasn't much, but it was all I had. Everything else was just whispers and suspicion, airy nothingness. That little sketch was a solid fact.

The thing I missed most – something I'd become accustomed to, even in my fledgling career in the Territory – was authority. Down here, I was nobody, an outsider, an afterthought. People brushed me aside, told me to fuck off. I couldn't harass the Razics over their morning espressos or rouse the loggers from their beds. I couldn't threaten anybody, or interrogate them; I couldn't even shoot them.

All I could do was pick at the loose threads, keep going until I found one that went all the way home.

Right now, Daisy's sketch was the nearest thing I had to a thread. Why I thought so, I couldn't say – hunch, hunter's instinct, the most fleeting of scents.

So how could I extract its secrets?

The artwork back at Messmate Lane.

If the plant had puzzled Daisy as much as the scratchy energy of those scribbled letters suggested it had, maybe she'd recorded more detail in some of her other sketches or notes, something that would give me a clue to the orchid's location.

If I had that, I could investigate any logging or other activities nearby. And if nothing came of that, I could put it aside and head off in more profitable directions.

I grabbed an early breakfast – a slice of cheese and a chunk of bread – and drove up to Messmate on my own, not wanting to involve anybody else in the spot of breaking and entering I knew was coming.

CHAPTER 21

I pulled up at the entrance to the lane, wondering if this was a wise move. The local stickybeaks had dobbed me in once; how many lives did you get round here? Neville Wallace was already looking at me askance.

I decided to play it safe and check out the lay of the land. I left the car off-road and took to the animal trails, staying low, stepping over cubes of wombat shit on logs and moving around a watchful tiger snake. A few minutes later I was picking leaves out of my hair and crouching on top of a slope that ran down to the side of the house.

All seemed quiet. The only thing that had changed since my last visit was the sense of desolation that shrouded the cabin. It had grown heavier. Weeds were springing up around the steps. There were vines creeping over the windows, piles of dirt at the door, leaves in the guttering. The crime-scene tape was still in place.

I walked down to the building slowly, cautiously. I went up onto the verandah, stepped round to the side of the house.

Then I jumped in surprise.

There was a man sitting there. Tall, in a blue shirt and battered overalls, with shaggy black hair and a scraggy beard. He was leaning forward, his face buried in a pool of purple material, his glasses pushed back on his forehead.

I began to back away, but a board creaked and his head swung round.

'What the hell!'

He leapt to his feet, rattled. Not that I could blame him for that – I'd be rattled myself if somebody had crept up on me while I was sitting in what I assumed to be the solitude of the bush.

The material – a scarf – fluttered to the ground.

It took a second to recognise him. It was Christie Looms, the sculptor I'd met at the exhibition – and the water carter who'd come across Adam's wreck.

'Sorry, mate,' I said.

He adjusted his spectacles and peered at me so hard I felt like an insect under a microscope.

'Jesse Redpath,' I said. 'I met you at the gallery.'

He seemed to gain a measure of control.

'You were Ben Redpath's daughter ...'

'Still am, I hope.'

'What the hell are you doing here?'

'Just having a look around,' I said. 'We're staying with Lucy Takada. What about you?'

He turned his gaze towards the scrub. 'I'm waiting.'

I noticed a rifle at his side, thought for a weird moment he was going to use it on himself. Or on me. I tensed.

'For what?'

'Feral fucking feline.'

He explained that the last time he saw Daisy, she'd asked him to help get rid of a pair of wild cats that had been prowling round her block. He'd shot one last week, was hoping to get the other this morning.

I glanced at the scarf on the ground, and he scooped it up and buried it in his pocket.

What he'd just told me wasn't the truth. Not the whole truth, anyway. There was more going on here than cats.

Or was there? He froze, studied the distant vegetation and raised the rifle.

'Mind shutting up?' he whispered. 'Other little fucker's there now.'

'Where?'

'In that tree.' He nodded in the general direction of north.

'Which tree?'

'The yellow box at the end. Second branch over the fork.'

I focused as best I could, but I couldn't see anything resembling a cat.

'Don't move,' he warned. 'Cunning bastards. They can feel you watching them.'

He squinted into the sights, hunched a shoulder and eased his finger into the trigger. A sharp crack rang out and something tumbled fuzzily from the branches.

'Damn,' I was surprised to hear him say.

'But I think you got it.'

'Too late.'

We walked down to the foot of the tree and came across a fat cat, tiger-striped, razor-clawed. It had a bird in its mouth and a bullet in its brain.

'That,' I said, 'was one hell of a shot.'

'Bit like sculpture. All you need's a good eye and a steady hand.'

He studied the sad tableau of predator and prey at our feet. 'That's one for the blue wrens,' he commented.

'And for Daisy Baker,' I threw in, curious to see what sort of a reaction I got.

He shot a piercing glance in my direction, as if he was wondering what I was getting at. Then, seemingly deciding I wasn't getting at much, he shook his head.

'Ah, poor Daisy.'

Nothing ventured. 'Mind if I ask you something, Christie?'

He arched a brow, waiting.

'I hear it was you came across the fatal on the Grinwood Road.'

He nodded warily. 'It was.'

'Did you go down to look at the wreck?'

'Of course. I'm in the fire brigade. We deal with accidents all the time, especially up here in the hills. Dickheads drive too fast, dunno how to take the turns and the gravel. I knew nothing about Daisy at that stage; just came across the vehicle, went and checked it out. Wish I hadn't,' he added. 'The guy was way past anything I could do for him.'

The story had a ring of truth about it. It fitted in with what I already knew.

His studied me for a moment then his eyes narrowed. 'Why all the questions?'

I decided there was no point in dissembling. Everybody else round here seemed to know what I was up to, so he might as well hear it from me. I told him about my background, gave an edited version of my purpose in coming here.

He listened carefully then shook his head. 'If this Adam did what they're saying he did, fuck him. I'm supposed to be sympathetic? I liked Daisy – liked her a lot.'

'Yeah but what if he didn't?' I replied.

Christie said he hadn't seen anybody else but Possum on her horse that morning, had no idea who'd want to harm Daisy or Adam.

I asked if he knew of any particular areas Daisy had been working in of late, but he said she tended to wander all over the ranges. She had a random, erratic way of working, striking out in whatever direction took her fancy. I showed him the image on my phone and asked if he recognised the setting, but he didn't.

'What about the orchid in the foreground?' I asked. 'I showed it to Wolf Gunther and he –'

'That prick?' he snapped.

'Not a fan, then?'

The curl in his upper lip was visible through the beard.

'Hardly.'

'Don't suppose you know if he and Daisy were ever an item?'

A flicker of emotion in his eyes. What was it? Jealousy?

'Briefly. Months ago. Didn't last, of course.' He turned back to me, his expression set like three-day concrete. 'He's a user, that guy: causes, ideas, people. Finish with em, throw em away. I know for a fact he was having it off with a couple of other women while he was with Daisy.'

There was a bitter edge to his voice. More than an edge – the bitterness was a double white line, straight down the middle of the bitumen.

'I see,' I said.

And I could. Wolf had done his best to use me and had also shown he was capable of turning nasty when things didn't go his way. Had he put the hard word on Daisy, wanted a fuck for old- or good-time's sake and been rebuffed?

As far as suspects went, Mister Wolf was on the charts and rising. Mind you, Christie himself had just entered the top forty with a bullet. I hoped – given what I'd seen of his marksmanship – that he wouldn't be sending it in my direction. He said he hadn't been into the shack, but that scarf he'd been burying his face in looked exactly like one I'd seen in Daisy's room.

I thought about the vehemence of Christie's reaction to the mention of Wolf, the way he'd hit the booze at the gallery, the air of solitude he wore like an old coat. Had he been in love with Daisy? Maybe it was him who'd been rejected? Love and hate: flip sides of the same coin.

The first flies were beginning to settle on the splattered cat below.

'Speaking of creeps,' said Christie, nodding at the creature, 'might bury this one.'

He found a mattock in a lean-to behind the cottage, got to work and had the cat in the ground in two minutes flat. Christie might have been overweight and a drinker, but he was powerful.

'Won't be wasting any prayers on that,' he said as he wiped his hands. He glanced at the eastern sky and said he'd better be on his way before it got too hot.

'Where's your car?'

'Came on foot.' He patted his paunch. 'Exercise.'

His home, he explained, was a kilometre to the west.

He accompanied me to the road, the rifle slung across his shoulder.

'Why'd you park out here?' he asked when he saw my vehicle.

'Didn't want to disturb anybody,' I mumbled, which made even less sense at second glance than it did at first.

As he marched away, I crouched down and studied his boot print.

No sign of any spiders.

'Hey, Christie?' He stopped and turned. 'You always wear those boots?'

He crimpled his brow. 'That's a weird question.'

'I'm a weird person.'

He raised his right foot and tilted it to one side, inspecting the sole. 'Blunnies. Indestructible. Been wearing the same pair for ten years.'

I gave him a thumbs up. 'They look good for another ten.'

I sat in the SUV and watched him walk downhill.

CHAPTER 22

When Christie had gone I went back to the shack, retrieved the key – might as well be hung for a sheep as for a lamb – and spent an hour or two searching the building. There were dozens of works at various stages of completion, from quick sketches to finished paintings, but I found nothing that shed any light upon the *wtf* orchid.

I dug deeper, rummaging through drawers and cupboards, boxes and bookshelves, the tins and canisters in the kitchen. Still nothing. I was on the point of giving up when I noticed, in a bowl beside the bed, a fat little plastic flower that didn't look like the sort of thing Daisy would have owned.

When I picked it up and examined it, it came apart; the bottom section was a USB.

I had no means of looking at it just then, so I slipped it into my pocket and trailed back to the car. I leaned against the bonnet and considered my options. There weren't many. 'Keep looking' was the best of a bad bunch. The cottage had given me nothing, with the possible exception of the USB.

I spent the rest of the day driving around the Windmark Ranges, trying to get a feel for the region and its secrets. Mostly what I got was a sense of my own inadequacy, my otherness. I was an outsider down here and it wasn't making my task any easier.

I followed the road to Grinwood, which turned out to be little more than a cluster of abandoned buildings and overgrown bush blocks. There were scattered farms, rusty cars and a weatherboard church that had gone to meet its maker. This was where Adam was supposedly headed after killing Daisy, but I couldn't imagine him having any reason to come here.

From time to time, I'd get out and scout around for anything that resembled the location in Daisy's sketch. Nothing presented itself. I'd learnt to recognise manna gums and she-oaks by now, and there were a few to be seen, but I saw none in the right configuration.

Just after sunset I found myself driving down past Demon's Leap.

I pulled over and walked back to the lookout, which afforded a stunning view of the Windmark Valley, especially at this time of day. I leaned onto the low wire fence and lost myself in contemplation of the lightshow blazing before me: salmon-pink rays radiated out from below the horizon like the blades of a giant fan. Golden filaments of cirrus cloud floated overhead.

I felt as if I were standing in the middle of a hologram. More than that, I felt like I was part of the hologram, a photo-image of laser light diffracted. I raised a hand in front of me and it seemed luminescent, the focal point of the sky's energy.

I turned away and walked back towards the car, my head still swimming with all that lustre. So distracted was I, the approaching sound took a moment to register. A moment too long – by the time I was aware it had morphed from a distant mechanical rumble into the roar of a vehicle racing up behind me, too close.

Then, at the last moment, the resonators roared and it swerved in at me. I felt its metal mass convulse the air, the whoosh and suck of supersonic winds. It was everywhere at once, like a swarm of black bees.

I threw everything I had – every ounce of energy, every reactive instinct – into a flying cartwheel kick that sent me sailing over the ledge and into the abyss.

CHAPTER 23

I began that dreadful descent in what felt like glacial slow motion.

I threw a hand out at the fence but failed to find it. I crashed into rocks and bushes, grasping for a hold, gasping for breath, flailing wildly.

The wind rushed around my head. My body twisted and turned, powerless. Finally my left hand snatched at a root that held. I clung there, stunned, terrified.

Somewhere above me I heard the mystery vehicle pause – long enough for its driver to assess the situation – then take off.

I looked down.

Jesus. Not a wise move. Fifty, sixty metres of airy nothing then a rocky floor. I looked up. How far had I fallen? Maybe ten, twenty metres.

How was I going to get out of this? I'd done a bit of rock-climbing at uni, but that was with the comforting presence of ropes, carabiners and partners who knew what they were doing.

The root in my left hand was looking dangerously loose so I groped around for something better. Found it. I climbed a few centimetres, steadied myself, tried a branch. It held. The rock I was on didn't. As it crumbled and fell away, I swung my left leg out and found refuge on a chunk of granite. I huddled there, spread-eagled across the rockface, trembling. Gravel trickled into my eyes, my mouth, my shirt.

Focus, I told myself. Think about this bloody cliff. Feel your way into it. Become it. Your arms and legs are weapons; so is your head. Use them all. Assess every millimetre, give yourself an anchor point, a retreat, a launch pad. A pathway.

I pushed off. Upwards. Sometimes sideways, sometimes back. One metre gained, then two, three. Waves of pain rocketed along nerve fibres I didn't know I had. My muscles were screaming, my hands were going numb, but the distance diminished. I kept going, one micro-step, one fingerhold at a time. Finally, I reached the last obstacle: a fat overhang. No choice but to traverse it. I put everything I had left into the best grip I could find then swivelled out and around; as I flew in from the deadpoint of my trajectory, I flung my right hand up and over the ledge.

Was that metal? A rail? It was. I grabbed hold of it, rested a moment then dragged myself over the fence and collapsed into the gravel.

I lay there, face down, panting furiously. Was the bastard who sent me over the cliff still within striking distance? I looked around. Nothing. My own car was still there, fifty metres down the road, like a relic from an older, quieter world.

I got to my feet, looked around, braced for action. There was none.

Who was my attacker? God only knew. Where? On the way to Windmark, presumably. Why? Just bad driving – apparently an epidemic round here – or something more? The latter: the vehicle had veered into me, then the driver stopped to make sure I'd gone over. That was no accident.

I walked back to my car, watching every direction at once. The keys were still in the ignition. I climbed aboard and drove back to the Bluehouse.

I sat in the driveway for a few minutes, tidying myself up and wondering what to tell them. What could I tell them? A car had veered at me, I'd jumped out of the way. I hadn't seen who was driving or what make it was. I knew nothing about it except that it had a bull-bar and it came close to killing me.

I decided to keep the incident to myself. I didn't want to worry Dad, and I was reluctant to let the others know how stupid I'd been. They were sitting down to dinner when I walked in.

'What happened to you?' Possum asked.

I caught a glimpse of myself in a glass cabinet. My clean-up in the car hadn't achieved much; I was still bloodied, bruised, dishevelled.

'Been out bush-bashing,' I answered. 'The bush hit back.'

Dad was gaping. 'Are you okay?'

'I'm fine. Just had a bit of a tumble.'

'You look like you tumbled off a cliff!'

I swallowed and said I'd be right back.

I went to my room, washed myself and changed my clothes. Re-joined the gathering. Did my best to head off any discussion of my day.

A couple of hours later I was standing next to Possum over a sudsy sink. I was doing the washing and drying, she was directing operations. A squadron of moths fluttered against the kitchen window. A huntsman shifted in the corner, sending a wave of anxiety through them. The spider waited until they settled down, then pounced, seizing a moth and dragging it away.

'So what really happened?' she asked.

No point trying to pull the wool over this one's eyes.

'I was walking along the road up near Demon's Leap. Car came too close. I had to jump out of the way.'

'Jesus! The Demon! You didn't go over the edge?'

'Managed to grab a bush on the way down.'

'Deliberate, wasn't it?'

I shrugged.

'And you didn't recognise the car?' she continued.

'Had a bull-bar. Might have been black. That's about it.'

One thing I did know was that if anybody knew the ins and outs of what was going on round here, it was this sharp-eyed teenager. I figured I could benefit from her insights.

'You seem to know more about Daisy than anybody else,' I said. 'What did she think of Wolf Gunther?'

'God's gift? She was wary of him.'

'Afraid?'

'Dunno about afraid. They had a bit of a fling, but Wolf has flings with everyone. Or tries to.'

I could vouch for that, I thought uncomfortably.

She shot a glance at me. 'No!'

'No what?'

'Put the hard word on you, didn't he?'

I may have blushed. 'Word wasn't all that was hard,' I grunted.

She stared at me, aghast. 'Oh yuck, you didn't go along with him?'

I shook my head.

'No,' she said. 'Course you didn't. You're tough. But Daisy wasn't. She got sucked in. Didn't last, of course. Always greener pastures for old Wolf. Last I heard, he was shagging Katie Fisher's big sister.'

'She doesn't work at Springhills?'

'Nah, that's Bree Goward. He's doing her too.'

'Jesus. Energetic, these Germans.'

Could it have been Wolf behind the wheel at Demon's Leap? Maybe, but the list of locals with a grudge against me was growing by the hour.

Possum put away a saucepan, did her best to catch half-a-dozen others that crashed out of the cupboard, threw them back in oddly shaped piles and slammed the door.

I gazed out the window, wondering how to work this latest piece into the puzzle. I didn't get far. At my current rate of progress, all of the suspects would be in their graves before I figured it out. There were too many fragments, dead ends, non sequiturs.

One more thing – I'd forgotten about the USB. I retrieved it from my jeans and asked if I could borrow a computer.

She led me into the office but looked suspiciously at the device.

'Wasn't that Daisy's?'

When I fessed up to my little burglary, she shook her head but looked on with interest as I opened the drive and scanned its contents.

The USB was full of photos. Most of them were of flora. Possum identified them: nodding greenhoods, leopard orchids, trigger plants.

But there were a few of people. A dangerous lot, by the look of them: knitting nannas, mothers nursing babies, a hobbit-footed hippie being coaxed out of a tree. There was one of Wolf, sitting by a campfire nursing a beer, another of Daisy painting a flower onto a bulldozer blade.

'Is this Echidna Creek?' I asked.

'It is.'

We'd gone through most of the images when I came across a long shot of a woody thicket dominated by a pair of trees and a rectangle of white that might have been a boulder or a body of water. It was the trees that caught my eye. They were manna gums.

'Can you tell where this was taken?' I asked.

She scrutinised it carefully.

'No, but I know who might. Look at this.'

She took the mouse and zeroed in on the thicket. What I'd taken to be rock or water was the door of a vehicle. She zoomed it to the max and a figure emerged: a beaming gum tree, hands on hips.

Daisy had been snapping the Gaunts.

Was that surprising? Maybe not, but it was yet another ingredient to be thrown into the mix.

'Do you reckon this is Echidna Creek?' I asked.

'Don't think so,' said Possum. 'Not at the protest anyway. There's nobody around. I was up there – whenever the trucks tried to get through, they were mobbed.'

I returned to the index and looked for more detail; the photo had been saved to the device three days before she died.

CHAPTER 24

I opened my eyes, puzzled. Something was wrong. I sat up. Silver moonlight slanted across the room. Shadow-paintings on the wall, mirror on the dresser, bookshelves, pot plants. I shifted my gaze, then hesitated, returned to the mirror.

Something had moved. A flicker of reflected gold.

I dragged myself out of bed and across to the window. In the hills above the house, up in the direction of Messmate Lane, was a glow that could only mean one thing.

Confirmation – I spotted a set of red-and-blue lights climbing Crowcall Road, heard a siren yowling on the still night air. I looked at the carport. Sam's Prado was gone. He'd said he was captain of the local fire brigade. He must have been on the truck. Maybe it was his departure that first stirred me.

I threw on some clothes and found my keys. The fire was probably none of my business, but this case was turning into a complicated web, with threads running in every direction. Anything out of the ordinary warranted a closer look.

When I stepped out into the yard, I noticed the door of the tack room was open. Even more suspicious, there was a small horse with a big head leaning over the fence. Nutmeg. Where was Atomica? I jumped into the SUV, and had almost reached Messmate Lane when I came across what I'd been expecting: Possum riding swiftly up the road.

I pulled over in front of her.

'Your folks know you're out?'

She reined in, the horse frisking about, champing. 'They're slack like that. I heard Dad running out the door. Thought I'd come and have a geek.'

'House fire, isn't it?'

'Looks like Daisy's.'

We resumed our journey. The small crowd gathered at the entrance to Messmate Lane – a firey holding a stop sign, a handful of neighbours, a cop I didn't recognise – told us what we didn't want to know. It was definitely Daisy's place. The smoke and flames were visible through the trees. Another tanker – this one from Windmark – came racing up the road and the cop waved it through.

'Close as we're gonna get,' I said.

'We could sneak round the west side,' suggested Possum.

I was tempted.

What was the point of temptation if not to be given in to once in a while?

A few minutes later we were on a rise just above the cabin. Possum dismounted.

The scene below was one of furious activity, the cabin engulfed, ringed by red tankers. Flames leapt a dozen metres into the air, blue smoke billowed and pulsed into the trees.

We sheltered in a wattle copse, but Possum inched forward, the fire a magnet.

Fat figures in padded yellow jackets rushed about, bowling out hoses, blasting the fire with jets of water, knocking it down.

'Get around back,' somebody boomed. I knew the voice: Geordie North.

There were other firefighters I recognised: Christie Looms untangled a hose and connected it to the newly arrived Windmark tanker. Dom Talia fitted a branch to a line then moved towards the cabin, directing a jet of water through what was left of the front door.

Through the blackened skeleton of the building I saw shelves, tables and other furniture amid spitting and spinning waves of flame. The blaze had more colours than a flock of rainbow lorikeets. An adjoining ghost gum had ignited, lighting up the night like a giant chandelier. Shapes intersected and collided, flew off and made new shapes: parabolas and lances, crosscut saws, circles and whirls.

Possum and I stood there, mesmerised, until a particularly vicious explosion sent a blast of magnesium light through the atmosphere. One of the fireys was looking directly at Possum.

He trotted across to a cluster of men in yellow, tapped a red-helmeted one on the elbow and pointed in our direction.

Sprung.

Red Helmet turned round and raised his visor. The burst of light had faded, and he probably couldn't see us, but he didn't need to.

It was Sam Kelly.

'Possum!' he roared.

Normally his voice was one of those 'settle-into-your-chair-and-take-it-easy' affairs, but he was clearly capable of breaking the sound barrier when the need arose.

'You get on back home!' he bellowed. 'This isn't a show put on for your entertainment.'

'We better go,' she said. 'Dad hates rubberneckers and he's got his radar going. There's no escape.'

But then there was another flare-up. I happened to glance to my right, and realised there was a figure on the rise, barely a dozen metres away. Had they followed us, or had they been there all along? Whatever the answer, I needed to check it out.

'Hey there,' I called.

No response, so I moved closer. Our fellow watcher was a solid, weak-chinned man with a dark hoodie and big boots. He was staring at the blaze, entranced, his mouth open, his eyes glowing, excited.

'Think we're not wanted,' I said.

He turned and faced us.

I heard Possum inhale sharply.

It was Brock Gaunt.

'You can't always get what you want,' he said. His eyes flickered and burned; was that just reflected fire, or the expression of a deeper disturbance?

'I'm outta here,' said Possum.

She mounted up and urged Atomica away.

I took a last look at Brock. A thin smile played upon his lips. He'd returned his attention to the conflagration, losing interest in us. Or had he? His right hand gravitated down to the bulge in his pants and slipped into a pocket. Was that for my benefit?

'Weird,' I muttered to myself. I remembered Possum telling me how, even as a kid, Brock had been fascinated by fire, that he'd set a kid's hair alight.

I trod back through the bush and out onto the road, alert, listening for sounds of movement in the scrub behind me.

There were none that I could hear, but I locked the car doors and followed Possum closely until we got home.

CHAPTER 25

I was dragged out of a spidery dream by a chorus of door knocks and deep voices. I forced my eyes open and the room swam into focus.

I heard a door creak, a big voice boom.

'Need to speak to your house guest, Ms Takada.'

'House guest?' asked Lucy.

'Jesse Redpath.'

Jesus, was I ever gonna get any sleep? I pulled on a pair of shorts and wandered out. As I went past Dad's door, I glanced into his room. No sign of him. He'd be out on the dawn patrol.

I pulled back a curtain to suss out the visitors. Bloody hell – the mountain had come to Mohammed. Both mountains: Nev Wallace and Vince Tehlich. There was even a little hill – Jace Gradey, sneaking off in the direction of the back door. I came and stood next to Lucy.

'Morning, Sarge. Sarges. What's up?'

Wallace stepped inside. 'How do you know something's up?'

'Don't imagine you guys are banging on the door this early to shoot the breeze. And what's Jace doing covering the escape routes? Think I'm gonna make a run for it?'

Wallace pulled a notebook out of his pocket. 'Need you to tell me where you were the day before yesterday.'

I braced myself. The looks on these men's faces. Whatever this was about, it wouldn't be good.

'Wednesday? I was all over the place. Here. In town. That Springhills brewery. In your office, if you recall,' I said to Vince.

'Were you up at Johnson's Falls?' pressed Wallace, his cheeks puffed. He looked like he was playing an invisible wind instrument.

'Sounds like you know I was.'

'Were you alone?' Wallace continued.

'I wish I had been.'

'Who were you with?'

'Wolf Gunther.'

What might have been a smile in other circumstances cracked the natural slab of Wallace's face.

'What was he doing the last time you saw him?'

'Nursing a sore nose.'

'How did he get that?'

'Ran into a door.'

Vince lowered an eyebrow. Just the one. Tom Vallence had a similar habit when he smelled a rat. It must have been a trick they taught at the academy back in the Stone Age. No point in bullshitting them.

'Okay,' I admitted. 'I may have had a little something to do with it.'

'What sort of little something?'

'He made a pass. More than a pass – an assault. I defended myself … Wait a minute – he's not laying bloody charges, is he?'

Wallace leaned in so close I could smell his breakfast: Big Mac, mayonnaise, chips with sauce, the greedy bastard.

'He's laying, but not charges,' he said. 'He's in the morgue.'

I swear my chin touched my throat. 'Jesus, what's he doing there?'

'Not a huge amount.' Vince sighed, as if it was getting a bit much for him, all this mayhem reverberating through his quiet little country town.

'They found his body in the water at Johnson's Falls,' said Wallace.

I stepped back, went and sat at the kitchen table, dropped my head into my hands. Tried to settle my pounding heart.

They followed me in, managed to make a half-circle around me.

I swallowed hard, fearful of the answer to the question I was about to ask. 'How did he die?'

Vince replied that the initial forensics examination suggested he'd been bashed and drowned.

'Fuckin hell,' I muttered at the tabletop. Had I smacked him harder than I realised? Did he have a glass nose? Had he lost consciousness – delayed concussion, perhaps – and fallen in?

'Doesn't make sense,' I said. 'He looked fine last time I saw him. A bit pissed off, but his pride was hurting more than his head. Who found him?'

'Family of tourists,' said Wallace. 'Pulled in for a picnic, spotted a body among the rocks. Pleasant surprise for the kids.'

The questions were pouring out of my brain faster than I could get them out of my mouth. 'How did you know I'd been there?'

'Set of prints on the keys. Amazed when Livescan told us they were yours.' He grunted and harumphed. 'Maybe not that amazed. Last of the Badlands up there, is it? The Territory? Kill people who rub you the wrong way? Travellin Outback Sisterhood? Feller makes a pass and he's dead meat?'

Still trying to reel in my racing head, I wasn't paying much attention to what he was saying.

'Where were the keys?' I asked.

'In the ignition. Did you drive the vehicle?'

'No.'

'What were your prints doing on the keys?'

'I threw them into the bushes.'

A swift, hungry glance. 'Why did you do that?'

'I was trying to slow him down. He was getting cranky. And the fact that they were in the ignition reassures me that I didn't kill him; he must have been sufficiently with it to retrieve them.'

'Don't suppose you've got anything as convenient as a witness?' asked Vince. 'Back you up on any of this?'

I stared into the apple tree on the other side of the window: green leaf-light, luminous, the touch of an early breeze. I thought about the sequence of events up at Johnson's Falls, told them how Sam Kelly and Geordie North had picked me up.

Vince turned to Lucy, who'd been leaning against the kitchen bench, her mouth widening as the conversation progressed. 'Where is Sam?'

'Still not back from the fire.'

He stepped outside and spoke into his phone. A few minutes later he came back and said, yes, Sam had picked me up but couldn't say what I'd been doing before that. He asked me why I'd gone up there with Wolf in the first place.

'He said he'd show me the sights,' I replied. 'He did, but they weren't the sights I had in mind.'

Vince shot a piercing look at me. Years of being a country cop would have fine-tuned his bullshit-detector.

'Okay,' I said. Time to come clean.

I'd been reluctant to give them the reason for my trip to Johnson's Falls. They thought I was half-mad already, and when I did tell them, my reluctance proved to be well-founded. I told them how I'd come across the orchid in Daisy's sketchbooks and wondered if it was connected to her death. I showed them the picture on my phone. I took them to the computer and brought up the photo of the timber truck on the USB.

'Where did you get this device?' Wallace asked, frowning.

I swallowed. The answer was obvious.

'And that's your big insight?' he continued, apparently not too concerned about my break-in. 'A flower?'

'I've been looking at motive,' I said. 'Daisy was passionate about plants. I figured that might put her on a collision course for somebody who chopped them down for a living. You saw the photo. She was keeping an eye on the Gaunts. What it's got to do with Wolf, I've no idea.'

'I've got some ideas,' said Wallace. 'Mostly to do with you muddying the waters.'

He told me to make myself decent and come down to the Windmark station.

So it was that I found myself in a setting with which I'd become familiar – a police interview room – but on the wrong side of the desk, with the digital recorders rolling and the interrogators drilling.

Wallace took the lead and hit me with a battery of questions designed to find holes in my story. By the time he switched the machine off, he had a record of everything I'd done over the past couple of days, from when I left the station to when Possum and I went to look at the fire the night before.

When I told them how I'd been run off the road yesterday evening, neither seemed convinced.

'You're telling me you went over Demon's Leap and survived?' asked Vince.

'Convenient bush on the way down.'

'And this vehicle,' asked Wallace. 'Anything at all on it? Make? Model? Was it a Panzer tank or a go-kart?'

'It was all so quick,' I explained. 'One second I'm walking down the road, the next I'm flying through the air and fighting for my life.'

The sergeants exchanged a glance then left the room.

'Stay there,' snapped Wallace when I made to follow.

I sat at the table speculating furiously about what could have happened to Wolf, going over everything I'd said, seen or done that afternoon. Twenty minutes of that and all I figured out was that I was hungry. I knocked on the door. Jace Gradey opened it.

'You gonna let me starve to death here?'

He disappeared into the kitchen, came back with a watery coffee and a stale donut.

I took a sip. 'Hmmm, maybe I'll take starvation.'

'Sorry, Jesse – I never liked the guy anyway.'

'Wallace?'

'Wolf.'

I grunted and dunked the donut, ate a sizeable chunk, just to get something into my stomach. 'I didn't like him much either; doesn't mean I killed him. Mind you, I'd be tempted to now if he wasn't already dead.'

Wallace returned with a stocky blonde he introduced as a forensics officer. 'This is Marilyn. She's going to examine you.'

I raised my hands in frustration. This guy was really getting my goat. There was a killer out there somewhere, and I'd never find out who it was if they kept me cooped up in here. 'Be my guest,' I said. 'Anything else you'd like? Drug test? Blood alcohol? Blow job?'

Wallace tutted and left me to her.

'You're a member?' she enquired.

'That guy's a fucking member.'

She was amused. Easy for her – she wasn't the one being set up.

She took my DNA, examined my hands and feet, gathered samples from my fingernails and clothing. When she was finished, the sergeants returned.

'Feel free to fuck off,' said Wallace. 'We'll be taking a close look at the evidence when it's all in.'

'Terrific,' I said. 'Now can we go to Johnson's Falls?'

'What's this "we"?'

I'd had enough of this dickhead's stonewalling. 'I was thinking I might be able to help sort out what happened. I am a police officer, you know. A colleague. Respected, if I say so myself, where I come from.'

I stood up, did my best to come up to their chins, gain some leverage.

'There's some awful shit going down round here,' I continued. 'If you guys can't see that it's connected, maybe it's time you brought in somebody who can.'

'Somebody who's a suspect?' asked Wallace.

'Jesus, Sarge, use your brains. Can't you see what it is these deaths have got in common?'

'And what would that be?' asked Vince.

'The bush!' I snorted. 'The first victim was a botanical artist, the last a botanist.'

'And Adam Lawson?'

'He was a witness.'

I told them about the damage to the lemon tree at the cottage, the pattern of the footprints – what the evidence suggested.

Wallace seemed uncharacteristically discomfited. 'Forensics didn't pick up any of that.'

'Were they even looking?' I replied. 'You'd already told them what happened.'

'You learnt all this from looking at a tree?'

'I've been working with the best trackers in the world,' I said. 'Do the arson guys know if the fire was deliberate?'

'They haven't decided yet,' said Vince.

'Whoever lit it was trying to get rid of something,' I mused. 'Did you know Brock Gaunt was there last night? He was staring at the blaze with an intoxicated look in his eyes.'

'Everybody stares at a blaze with an intoxicated look in their eyes,' commented Vince.

'Brock had an intoxicated look in his pants as well,' I replied. 'So are we going up to Johnson's Falls? I know I didn't kill Wolf, and I might be able to help you figure out who did.'

Wallace pondered the question for a moment or two, then stood up.

'You can come with us,' he agreed. 'Long as you stay where we can keep an eye on you.'

'While we're at it,' added Vince, 'You might show us where you had this accident at Demon's Leap.'

'Wasn't an accident,' I said.

CHAPTER 26

Twenty minutes later we were standing on the edge of the road at Demon's Leap. I did what I could to make sense of the tyre tracks, but the ground was packed so hard, it wasn't giving much away. There were scratch marks on the fence that might have come from a bull-bar, the odd torn wire. My attacker had obviously clipped it on the way through.

'And this bush you're saying saved your life?' asked Vince.

I peered over the ledge. There were a few shrubs on the way down, but they looked awfully insignificant in the light of day. I'd been luckier than I realised.

'I'll bring forensics here when they're finished at the Falls,' said Wallace.

We left, and ten minutes later we were rolling into Johnson's Falls, now transformed from leafy green idyll into grim familiar crime scene: cop cars, clipboards, methodical officers in blue overalls and rubber gloves, cameras round their necks.

We climbed under the tape and made our way to the waterhole. Wolf's Nissan stood there forlornly, a grey ghost, patches of print-dust scattered across its panels, leaves building up on its wipers.

'When did they remove the body?'

'Few hours ago,' said Wallace.

I wasn't complaining. I didn't want to look at it. The man had been a bloody nuisance when he was alive and was proving even more of one now that he wasn't.

I retraced my movements from a couple of days ago, walking the banks of the waterhole, kicking divots, tearing off a leaf or two. I came back and leaned against the car, trying to come up with an explanation for what had happened here – preferably one that didn't involve me going to jail. If you thump somebody and they drop dead days – even weeks – later, an enthusiastic prosecutor could still do you for murder, especially if they had an equally enthusiastic investigator arranging the evidence.

Surely the silly bugger hadn't gone back to the car, found the keys, then returned to the creek, fallen in and drowned? He must have had some assistance.

Why would anybody want to kill Wolf? And how was his death connected to those of Adam and Daisy? Surely it must be, somehow. An unpleasant idea floated to the surface, bobbed about like a Polly Waffle in a public pool. Could it have been me they were after? I thought about Brock Gaunt staring at me from the Burns, or jerking off at the fire. What had he been up to – aside from the obvious? Was he trying to scare me off?

When Vince came back I shared my concerns about Brock Gaunt and his ongoing attempts to creep me out.

'He's weird,' I concluded.

Vince folded his arms, listening carefully.

'Brock's got this way of looking at you,' he said. 'Somebody must have dropped him on his head when he was a baby. That's just his manner. But aside from a few bar-room brawls and the odd DUI – all rites of passage round here – he hasn't got a record to speak of. You didn't actually spot him out here, did you? Any specific reason to think he followed you?'

'Nothing solid,' I admitted. 'I remember thinking we weren't alone – saw a flock of birds rising ...'

Vince gazed into the northern sky, as if he hoped they'd still be there, that they'd give him something useful. He turned back and asked if I'd ever had an actual conversation with Brock.

'Nothing you'd call deep and meaningful.'

'How about shallow and meaningless?'

I shifted uncomfortably. Vince had a home-ground advantage here. I told him about Brock's comment at the fire: You can't always get what you want.

'So maybe he's a Stones fan,' said Vince. 'Lemme get this straight. You're suggesting the guy's a triple killer and you've barely said a word to him?'

I floundered, trying to find a justification for what he seemed to regard as more prejudice and guesswork on my part than serious investigation.

'He was eavesdropping when I was talking to his old man. Didn't look happy about it.'

'Brock wouldn't look happy if you put him on a drip and fed him Foster's for the rest of his life. That's just the way he looks. But he's as thick as a Besser block. You're suggesting he's killed three people. That's possible, God knows. Anything's *possible*. But having the wits to plan it, shift the blame, cover his tracks like that ...' He shook his head.

I thought about Allan Gaunt's aggressive reaction to my questions at the mill and asked Vince if they'd ever seriously considered him as a suspect. He could have been working with his son, or at least covering for him.

The sergeant kicked at the dirt with his heel and stared into the tumbling waters.

'He'd have the smarts, Allan,' he said. 'I'll grant you that. Knows how to swing a deal, work out the profit margins. Maybe that's my problem with what you're suggesting. He's a businessman. Likes to balance the books. Have to have some pretty heavy numbers in the credit column to make a debit like that. He'd need a motive, and I'm buggered if I can see one. Sure, he lost a bit of work at Echidna Creek, but he's got half-a-dozen other coupes across the ranges; he'd have just moved on. He might have yelled at you but I suspect he'd have forgotten about it by the time the next load of logs came in.'

One of the forensics called him over. He clicked his tongue, annoyed, and left.

Birds fluttered up from the trees, unsettled.

I stood there, thinking about what he'd told me. I started walking, kept walking, and found myself retracing the path I'd taken when I was stomping away from Wolf. I came across the odd little print that might have been mine. I'd gone maybe a hundred yards when I noticed there was a rough trail – wallaby track? – running through the scrub parallel to the road. I turned and followed it back towards the waterhole.

I was halfway there when I caught a glimpse of a boot print that gave me pause. I knelt down to examine it. It was fading, faint, windblown – but at its centre, I made out the remnants of a spider with a crack in its abdomen.

I stood staring at the impression. It had been headed away from the waterhole. There was just a single print visible – whoever made it had kept to the grassy verges, maybe trying to conceal their presence.

'Found something?' Vince Tehlich was beside me.

I showed him the print, explaining that I'd seen something similar at the crash scene on the Grinwood Road.

He crouched down. 'Looks like a Redback boot. They're not exactly unique in this part of the world. And they all crack sooner or later.'

'Bit of a coincidence, isn't it? Been around at least two of the deaths, this Spider-Man.'

Wallace came up behind us. 'Captain America here too?' he enquired. He'd caught the wrong end of the conversation. 'Batman?'

Vince explained the print and its possible connection to Adam's crash.

Wallace tilted his big head, thinking. 'There's other explanations. The bloke who found the body.'

'Christie Looms,' I said.

'He's the local water man. Maybe he refills here, popped into the bushes for a piss.'

'He says he always wears Blunnies.'

Wallace glanced across at his colleagues, still working their way around the waterhole.

'I'll get forensics onto it,' he said. 'Make a cast. Add it to the evidence.' He said it like his main hope for the evidence was that it would incriminate me.

'Where's that leave me?' I asked.

He gave me a wilting stare. 'Staying where we can find you.'

Vince drove me back to the Bluehouse, dropped me at the front gate, and warned me to keep out of trouble, if I could manage it. I went inside. The house was empty. There was a note from Lucy on the kitchen table: *kid run – back by 5.*

The only one home was Pendles, who was eyeing me suspiciously from his perch in the paperbark near my room. I went and sat up in what was fast becoming my favourite place round here: the armchair in the mezzanine. A skink was sitting in a lozenge of light on the carpet, staring at me. It licked its big dish eyes. I blinked; by the time I finished blinking it had disappeared.

'What's your secret?' I asked its vanishing imprint.

Daisy's sketchbook was still on the table. I picked it up, turned to the mystery orchid, asked the same question of it and received as useful an answer. I flicked through the book for a while, then leaned back and closed my eyes. Floral images continued to haunt my vision, especially those spider orchids; they were fascinating plants with their wickedly curved labella, their blood-tipped clubs and waspish seductions.

My mobile buzzed.

Vince Tehlich.

'There's been a development,' he said.

'Yes?'

'Investigators have been reviewing CCTV footage of servos between here and Melbourne, Wednesday evening.'

The day of Wolf's death.

'Big job,' he continued. 'Normally take weeks.'

'I can imagine.'

'They got lucky.'

He told me they'd picked up a blue BMW E46 at Greendale Shell, 9.20 pm, heading for Melbourne in a hurry. The number was registered to a Dubica Holdings.

'Dubica?' I repeated. 'Name means nothing to me.'

'Meant something to the investigator. Driver looked like a pal of yours.'

'Miniscule group, that'd be.'

'One Benjamin Rork.'

Ah. Eddie Razic's mate, last seen holding his nuts and hobbling towards the Porsche on Cinnamon Row.

'Hommies are questioning him as we speak. Meantime, I'd suggest you lie low.'

'Why me in particular?'

'I've heard a little more about your run-in with Benny the other day. Oughta keep your boots to yourself. Save a lot of trouble in the long run.'

I shouldn't have been surprised. Small towns, loose lips. Even Geordie North had heard about it.

'He might have a bone to pick, don't you think?' Vince continued. 'Bout the only bone he'd be capable of, what I heard.'

'So you're suggesting — what? He couldn't find me so he went and picked it with Wolf instead?'

'It's a possibility.'

This case is rife with bloody possibility, I thought as I finished the call. It reeks of the stuff.

What it lacks is proof. Certainty. Conviction. Convictions.

Lie low?

Not yet.

CHAPTER 27

I drove to Windmark early the next day and found the Kia in the driveway of a tiny weatherboard cottage in Connolly Street. In the front yard was a spreading elm tree, a hedge and a bench, a wooden gate falling off at the hinge. The grass was dead, but that wasn't unusual; a lot of things were dead here at the business end of summer. One thing that wasn't dead was the cicadas: they were screaming shrilly up and down the street.

I'd been putting this off for long enough. I didn't want to do it, but the latest development told me I had no choice. There were too many black holes in this little chunk of spacetime, and everything I'd seen thus far suggested that Nadia knew enough to send some light into at least a few of them.

No jeep to be seen. Good. I wanted her on her own.

I walked up the path and rang the bell. No response. I rang again. I heard a shuffling noise within, then the door creaked open.

She was barefoot, yawning, wearing a nightie with a shawl spread like a net of silk across her shoulders. She gaped, blinked, began to close the door.

'Can't talk to you, Jess.'

I raised a hand. 'Nadia –'

'You're dangerous.'

I put a foot in the door.

'There's been another death.'

She startled. 'Who?'

'Wolf Gunther.'

'The greenie? What happened?'

'Dead in the water at Johnson's Falls.'

Her brow crimpled. 'Dead how?'

'Bashed, drowned.'

She seemed to shrink before my eyes. 'Johnson's Falls?' she mumbled. 'I don't even know where that is.'

She gave the door another push. I stood my ground.

'I'm not going away, Nadia.'

She cast an anxious glance up and down the street then let me in.

I found myself in a room adorned with torn curtains, threadbare chairs and a moth- or, on closer inspection, possibly rat-eaten couch. The furniture was op-shop musty. The bare boards were covered, in places, by washed-out rugs.

'Excuse the humble abode,' she said. 'Nick and a bunch of his mates used to live here.'

'You're talking to somebody who spends her life living out of a swag. This is luxury.'

We sat on the couch. Her smile was as convincing as a McDonald's apple. 'Suppose I should thank you for your help the other day,' she said.

'Not needed. Fellers like that need an occasional boot in the balls. Keep em from breeding.'

'You can joke – you don't know them.'

'But I do – Eddie Razic and associates. Purveyors of overpriced drugs and underpriced tobacco.' And working girls, but discretion was the better part of bluntness right now. 'Gimme some credit, Nadia. I'm a cop – I have come across a few villains in my time.'

Somewhere the hands of a clock unseen worked their way around its face. She glanced out the kitchen window, over the back fence.

Then she cleared her throat.

'You're the one who took Adam out to Nickel Creek, aren't you?'

'Great move that turned out to be.'

'He liked you. Told me about your predecessors. Said they were a bunch of thugs. Then you came along and listened to people. He said you were amazing – so amazing I knew it'd be safer to steer clear of you.'

'Why?'

'Like I said at the door – you're trouble.'

'That feller giving you grief in the street the other day,' I said. 'He was trouble. Why was he doing that?'

'Mind your own business.'

'Nick said you owe em money.'

'Nick talks too bloody much.'

I wish I could get you to talk too bloody much, I thought. The heavy approach wouldn't work; she'd crumble, like a cicada shell.

Her face hardened. I could read the frustration in her eyes. 'What are you doing here, Jess?'

I hesitated, not quite sure where to begin. I asked if she realised Homicide suspected her of aiding and abetting in Daisy's murder.

'They tried that bullshit on me,' she said, her hands waving around as if she were trying to spin answers from the air. 'It was Daisy's car. Adam had borrowed it to bring his stuff up from Melbourne. He was moving in with her.'

'Why did he ask you to do the driving?'

'He was worried about being pulled over. There was a warrant out for his arrest. We drove to Daisy's place. She gave us a cup of tea, but I had to get back to Melbourne.'

'Why the urgency?'

She trailed a finger across a scarred arm. One of the deepest lines ran along a thick blue vein. I thought about those scars, the stories they could tell. She touched a medallion on a chain around her neck, seemed to draw a measure of comfort from it.

'I was doing rehab at Harrison House. Only allowed out for the day, so Adam dropped me down at the bus station in Windmark. That was the last I saw of him.'

She caught my eye, as if challenging me to find fault with her explanation. I couldn't, so I decided to pump her for more information.

'And you've got no idea if the Razics were involved in their deaths?'

She fumbled around her pockets, found a packet of smokes and flipped the lid.

'You mind?' she asked.

'It's your home, Nadia. Why do I have this feeling you're not telling me everything?'

She cupped her hands, as if trying to conceal herself in the act of lighting up. She inhaled then blew out a wisp of lonely smoke.

'These people,' she said, a little jittery with nicotine, or worse. 'You don't know what they're like.'

'They're a bunch of outer-suburban lowlifes. I've seen worse.'

For some reason, the comment pushed her over a ledge. She rounded on me, lips taut, teeth bared. Maybe I'd be getting something out of her after all.

'Seen worse, have you?' Her eyes were spitting sparks. 'Jesus, Jess, you have no idea. The world's a fucking bubble. One prick and it explodes, leaves you drenched in blood.'

It was the strongest outburst I'd heard from her, but the bitter imagery of her language left me puzzled. Pricked bubbles? Showers of blood?

'Not sure what you're getting at, Nadia.'

'If you'd seen what I have …'

She went at the fag like a feral kitten going for the teat.

What was she referring to? The gangland violence? The heroin hunger games? The years of selling her body to feed that hunger?

'What have you seen?' I asked.

'You don't want to know,' she snapped.

'Try me.'

She put the cigarette in an ashtray, watched it wither and die. She closed her eyes and breathed deeply. Then she did something that surprised me: she put her head on my shoulder. She seemed exhausted. Beyond exhausted – she was the ultra-marathon runner struggling to reach the top of the hill. Whatever secrets she was keeping inside were tearing her heart out.

I put an arm around her shoulders. She didn't object. I kissed the top of her head, tried to breathe healing into it, the way I'd seen the old ladies at Kulara do for the kids – even the young men – when they were flipping out.

I felt her pulse slow down, her muscles relax. She leaned back into the couch, gazing at the ceiling.

'Adam was right,' she said.

'In what way?'

'You. You're fucking quicksand.' Her voice was like a wisp of smoke. 'You've heard of Bosnia–Herzegovina?'

'Of course,' I said, remembering what Vince had told me about her background. Yugoslavia. He hadn't known which bit.

'Why "of course"? Who in this country notices anything other than beaches and barbies and who's won the fucking footy?'

'There's a few,' I replied. 'What's Bosnia got to do with it?'

'I was born there. In a town called Luka.'

She touched the ornament at her neck. 'This is all that's left of Luka to me now – not much, but it saved my life.'

I took a closer look at it: a blue and yellow star in a white metal setting.

'How did it do that?' I asked.

'There was a time – months ago – I was about as low as a person could get without being six feet under. I'd taken a shot, must have been a hot one – I came to in a pool of vomit, my head screaming, my body on fire. The physical pain was bad, but it was just a shadow of the pain inside my head; the shame, the disgust. I hated myself. *Hated*. All I wanted was escape. I ran a bath, went scrabbling through the cabinet looking for something sharp. Instead I found this medal. How it got there, God knows – the last time I saw it, it was in my mother's jewel box. It's as close to an heirloom as you get in a family like mine. When I picked it up, it seemed to speak to me – and what it said was that I had another option: go. Get away from these people. From the person I'd become. From the things I'd carried with me since … since Bosnia, really.'

I sensed she wanted to keep going.

'What happened in Bosnia?'

She gazed at the medallion, then spoke in a whispered monotone that gained colour and strength as the words fell out of her mouth.

'When I was a little girl,' she said, 'there were these enormous fields of barley, next to our house. I'd lie there at night listening to the wind rustle through the grain. And I'd hear voices. Dangerous, threatening voices. They terrified me, those midnight whispers. The Barleymen, I called them. I told my mother, my father, anybody who would listen. Tried to warn them. It's nothing, they assured me. Fairy tales, nightmares. Grow up little girl. Until there came a day when men did come charging through the barley; real men, with blood on their hands and fury in their hearts.'

She raised her head and caught my eye. 'They shot the men, raped the women. Loaded what was left of us onto a truck and drove us out of town. That was the last I saw of Luka.'

I took her hands in mine, held them for a long time. Felt the loss, the anger, understood the despair that had driven her into the gutter.

We needed a circuit-breaker. I stood up and went into the kitchen.

'Mind if I make us a cuppa?'

'There's no milk.'

'Black's fine.'

The breathing space helped. Some vestigial instinct for hospitality stirred inside her. She got up and filled the kettle, found some crockery.

Soon we were leaning against the kitchen bench, cups in hand, gazing out into the backyard. I spotted a chicken scratching about. Then another. Dust tumbled and fluffed.

'Good you got chooks,' I said.

A little more life stole into her face. 'I like chooks. More than I like people.'

I took a closer look at the birds. They were scrawny specimens, their feathers flecked with dirt, their necks thin. That was okay – it wasn't a beauty contest.

'Did Adam ever tell you about Kulara?' I asked.

'Of course. When he got going, you couldn't shut him up.'

I had to laugh at that.

'I remember one time,' I told her, 'there was this new magistrate. All the boys were worried, wondering what he'd be like. Adam's up on a B and E, said he'd go first. Somehow, in the middle of proceedings, he's telling the judge about the local fishing spots, paints such an impressive picture that, come lunchtime, Adam's acquitted and the judge is out at the waterhole with him, tossing in a line.'

She smiled. 'I can imagine.'

The smile was an invitation.

'Not much in the way of books or writing up there,' I said, 'but they've got a lot of stories.'

I told about the time my father and I were out bush with a man called Magpie, a Warluju desert painter. We came upon a stand of ghost gums and Magpie went quiet; there were tears in his eyes and he asked if we could leave that place. Later on, he explained: when he was a little boy, he and his family were camping there. A police party came along, rounded them up and put them in chains. His mother hid him in a hollow log. He was still there when the shooting started. Come dark he crawled out and found his entire family massacred.

Nadia said nothing, but her breathing slowed and long hollows were forming in her cheeks.

'What I'm getting at,' I said, 'is there's terrible things everywhere. But the only way you're ever going to confront them is by speaking out. That old Magpie spent his life telling his story, painting pictures. Speaking out. He knew you can only keep things bottled up for so long – eventually they'll explode.'

She wandered into the lounge room, clutching her elbows.

'My god,' she said. 'You make it hard.'

'It manages that all by itself.'

She sat back down and leaned into the cushions.

'I can't give evidence in court. If they find out I've spoken to you …'

'They won't.'

She pulled out another cigarette and lit up.

'It's Benny Rork,' she said. She'd seen him here, in Windmark, around the time Daisy and Adam died. It was when she was getting on the bus to Melbourne. She'd spotted a group of men in the McDonald's car park. One of them was Benny.

'What was he doing?'

'Sitting in his BMW. The others were talking to him through the window.'

'Did he see you?' I asked.

'Yes. I was waving goodbye to Adam. Benny glanced in my direction and spotted me. He jumped out of the car, but the bus took off and I lost sight of him.'

She exhaled, waved away the smoke.

'Did Benny know Adam?'

She nodded. 'Adam was an occasional customer. When we were driving up here he told me he'd scored some dope – trouble was he'd stolen it from his dealer – ultimately, from the Razics. He thought it was the greatest joke ever. I tried to tell him how dangerous they were, but he didn't get it.'

She said she'd stayed on the bus, thought she'd got away, but when she got to Southern Cross Station she spotted one of the gang – a man called Lev – waiting for her.

'This Lev,' I said. 'He wouldn't be a sizeable character with a head like a stubbed cigar, horseshoe moustache? Balding. Likes a leather jacket?'

'That's him.'

The third guy in the car on Cinnamon Row. Nick Cave.

'He's only been in Melbourne a little while,' she said. 'Some sort of gangland import from Western Sydney. But the way they talked about him …' She shuddered, made a slicing gesture with her forefinger. 'Cut your throat, casual as he'd cut a piece of bread.'

From what I'd seen of him, I wasn't surprised. He hadn't actually done anything, but some people don't need to.

'So what happened?'

'I told the bus driver I was in trouble. He offered to call the cops, but I didn't want that, so he dropped me back up the road and I called Nick. We spent the night lying low at a squat in Footscray. Then I heard about Adam and Daisy.'

She paused, emitted a gentle sigh.

'Yes?'

'I felt like the bus had run me over. Figured Benny and his mates must have followed Adam up to Canticle, tried to teach him a lesson.'

I thought about the story. The timeline. It made sense. It definitely added weight to the case against the Razics. Even if Nadia wouldn't testify, there could be other ways of verifying the information: CCTV, witnesses, forensics. I wondered if there was anything more to be squeezed out of it. I asked if she knew any of the men with Benny that day and she shook her head.

'And you've got no idea what they were up to?'

'Most of what they're up to involves drugs, but Benny doesn't usually get out and do the dirty work himself. Thinks he's some kind of fucking executive, with his fancy cars and gold watches.'

I stood up, walked to the window, my thumbs hooked into the belt of my jeans. I gazed at a gnarled peppercorn tree draping its branches over the fence.

I felt like an odd-job guy trying to piece together a shattered plate of glass. What Nadia had given me hadn't exactly solved the puzzle, but it had joined a few fragments. I could only pray that, if ever I did succeed, the glass wouldn't turn out to be a mirror, that I'd be looking at something more than a mangled reflection of my own bewilderment.

Nadia was studying me. 'What are you going to do now, Jess?'

'Not quite sure, but whatever it is, I'll make sure you're kept out of it.'

'If only it were that easy.'

She understood that better than I did, knew what a risk she was taking. There was a mountain of courage behind those words. Behind this entire conversation, even if I'd had to bully her into it.

The shawl slipped from her shoulders. She didn't strike me as a person who slept much. I could relate to that.

I stood up and said I'd be on my way.

She stirred herself. 'I'm glad we had this talk. I feel like a weight's been lifted from my neck.'

That's nice, I thought. As long as nobody tries to break it.

CHAPTER 28

I rested a hand on the gatepost, a little overwhelmed by the conversation I'd just had and wondering how to follow up on the information Nadia had given me.

When I looked up there was a man leaning against the bonnet of my car, his expression clouded, his arms folded. Nick.

'What have you been up to?' he growled.

'Just having a word with Nadia.'

'About what?' His eyes were thin slits of suspicion.

'You've heard about Wolf Gunther?'

'I have. You told her?'

'I did.'

He appeared to ease off. 'I wasn't sure how to. Knew it'd freak her out. What the fuck's happening round here?'

'That's what I'm trying to find out.'

'You better not do anything that'll put her in danger.'

'I won't.'

He straightened up. 'I bloody hope not. We haven't trusted the cops in this from the get-go. That's why she was so wary of you when we met. They've been trying to rope her into it; we thought you'd be doing the same.'

'All I want is the truth.'

'Truth?' he spat. 'That's a bloody complicated thing in Nadia's world.'

I moved closer and quietly gave him a rundown of what she'd told me: the rehab, the Barleymen, Benny at the bus stop.

He glanced at the house. 'She must have connected with you. We need to talk. Not here. You got a few minutes?'

'I've got as long as you want.'

I followed his car down to a backstreet shopping strip, a quiet cafe run by and for little old ladies. It was called The Pioneer, appropriately enough. Most of its customers looked like they'd been around in the pioneering days.

'What'll you have?' he asked.

'Tea. Strong, black.' I surveyed the bountiful display cabinet. Those little old ladies knew their stuff. 'Muffins look good. Blueberry? My shout.'

We placed our orders and found a table. Sat quietly until the food and drinks arrived and the waitress wobbled away.

'Nadia,' he said. 'Jesus, Jess, you gotta tread lightly there. Where do I begin?'

'The beginning?'

He took a bite out of his muffin.

'She came here when she was six years old. Milena – that was her mother – was half-mad by then, still suffering from the shock of seeing her husband and brothers murdered by Serbian militia. She spent months in bed. Years, from what I can gather. Doped to the eyeballs.'

'With what?' I asked.

'Whatever her doctors or dealers gave her. Sounds like she was slowly cracking up. Then one day she jumped up and began painting the room black, didn't stop until she'd covered the walls and windows. Landlord threw them out and Razic stepped in.'

I watched a fat black fly dodging the fan blades in the upper reaches of the room.

'What happened to Milena?'

'She killed herself.'

'Jesus.'

He shrugged. 'Prescription drugs. Whether it was deliberate or not, they never did decide.'

'And Nadia?'

'That was when Eddie Razic started feeding her to the wolves.'

'How old was she?'

'Fifteen.'

The fly crashed into a high window and tumbled to the floor.

'How did you and Nadia meet?' I asked. 'I imagine you moved in different circles.'

'The bush-furniture maker and the junkie?'

'Your words, not mine.'

He said he had friends living at a house in Reservoir; one afternoon he came across Benny Rork smacking Nadia round in a car in the driveway.

'Why was he doing that?' I asked.

'She'd said she wanted to leave the life.' He rolled his eyes, then continued. 'I dragged him out of the car and sent him on his way.'

'Sounds dangerous.'

He shook his head. 'All puff, no pastry that guy. I heard he came back with reinforcements, but we were gone by then. I took her to a women's refuge, then the rehab place. Kept in touch. Somewhere along the way, keeping in touch turned into falling in love.'

Great way to start a relationship. Running from a pack of vengeful drug dealers. What a mess.

He must have read my mind. 'You don't choose it, you know.'

'What?'

'Who you love,' he said. 'It's not a nice orderly process; not like ...' He fumbled for a metaphor, then settled on one from his trade. 'Making a dove-tail joint. It's got a life of its own. Been chaos since we hooked up but she's paid me back. Don't ask me how, but she has.' The defensiveness had faded from his voice, almost without my noticing. He cradled his cup like it was fine china. 'A hundred times over.'

A hundred times? I wondered if anybody would ever say that about me. I doubted it. The lonely desert air was seeping into my bones. I was twenty-nine years old and I'd grown accustomed to the single bed, the solitary punching bag. There were plenty of men in my circle, but most of them were about as useful as the bag – probably less so. Maybe it's the job, I reflected. Puts up a wall between you and the world. Or maybe that was why I chose the job in the first place.

'So you brought her to Windmark,' I said. 'Razic found you. What happens now? You keep running?'

'I think I've got it sorted. I went and saw him.'

'What's he got, an office? Sign out the front? Thugs and Drugs Unlimited?'

'He owns a bar in Preston. The Dubica.'

I narrowed my eyes. It was the second time I'd heard that word recently.

Nick said he'd gone to see Razic and come to an arrangement. He was paying off her debts.

I frowned. 'I've seen the Razics at work. All you're doing is feeding their own addictions. The debt'll never end.'

He picked up his cup and took a sip. He had harsh, outdoor skin, calloused hands, cracked nails.

'Not a huge amount of choice,' he replied. 'Least they're off our backs.'

'For now.'

He finished his drink and rose to his feet, said he'd better be getting back.

Outside, when he opened the car door, he turned to me. 'She's an extraordinary woman. Imagine how much guts it must take, trying to rebuild your life out of nothing. Worse than nothing: Bosnia, her mother, the Razics. The smack. She comes across as fragile, but I had this feeling, the moment I saw Benny punch her in the face. She didn't even blink.' He climbed into the car. 'Shit ever does hit the fan, she'll be the last one standing.'

I watched him drive away.

Love, I mused. I hoped to God that that treacherous emotion would be enough to carry the two of them through the storms that I feared lay just off the radar.

CHAPTER 29

I was doing well to get a parking place of any description, but the one I scored was fully exposed to the raw blast of the late afternoon sun. A minute or two of that and I was sweating like a pig in a microwave.

I was fifty metres down from the club, on the opposite side of the road. Close enough to get a feel for the place without having it jump up and smack me in the teeth.

I studied the building: a brutalist monument of tinted glass and polished black pillars, with pebbledash walls and scarlet awnings, concrete everywhere. Over the door, a gold-plated sign: *Dubica*.

This was Eddie Razic's kingdom. Or at least his castle. The kingdom, I assumed, was elsewhere, or everywhere – a shadow-fabric of lost souls and hungry bones, of fire, thirst and loneliness.

My plan, for what it was worth, was to check the place out. Try to get a feel for these people and see if I could slot them into any of the scenarios rolling through my head. Maybe even pick up something that might be described as evidence, or at least evidence of evidence. Find links, anomalies. Recognise someone, something. Anything that could tie the Razics to Canticle Creek.

If I had more faith in the locals' investigation, I'd be happy to leave it to them, but I could see it petering out for lack of attention, being buried in the cold case box. The official unofficial line was still that Adam had killed Daisy, and then himself, that Wolf had fallen into the water and drowned – possibly with a little help from yours truly.

I didn't have enough solid evidence to disprove either of these scenarios, Spider-Man and CCTV from Greendale notwithstanding. I knew now that the Razics had been in the vicinity around the time of all three deaths, but the gap between a knowledge of their presence and proof of their guilt was still a chasm.

The conversations with Nadia and Nick had put a match to the fuse inside my head. God knows what would happen when it hit the dynamite. I was still simmering at the thought of fifteen-year-old Nadia being preyed upon by the likes of Eddie Razic.

How many others had there been? How much grief had the Razics inflicted on the world?

I'd spruced myself up: bright blue dress, bangles and bracelet, upgrade in the make-up department. Not exactly incognito, but sufficiently removed from my previous appearance, I hoped, to reduce the likelihood of their recognising me from a distance.

I watched from my car as the crowd heading into Dubica continued to build. Odd bods – plenty of bod, mostly male, with pumped guns and strutting gaits – drifted into the venue. Bodybuilding was apparently a growth industry round here, peptides part of the staple diet. Fast bright cars disgorged slow dull men.

I was wondering what to do next when a tap on the passenger's window settled the question for me. There was a woman there, heavy-set, big-busted and blowsy, lashes like tropical fronds, tattoos peeping out from under her dress. I opened the door and she held a phone out at me.

'Message for you, love.' Her voice was as cutting as an angle grinder.

From the speaker: 'No point sweating outside when you can come in for a cold one.'

Eddie Razic.

Somebody was on the ball. They must have had cameras covering every angle. Maybe they'd got my rego when I was getting theirs.

I pulled out my phone and called Vince Tehlich.

'Vince.'

'Jesse?'

'I'm sitting outside the Dubica,' I said, raising my voice so that all concerned could hear.

'The what?'

'Eddie Razic's bar.'

He hesitated and asked what the fuck I was doing there.

'I'm about to go in.'

'Hang on –'

I hung up.

'Cautious,' commented the woman.

'Kept me alive so far.'

I followed her across the road and through the front door. A wave of chilled air and big-bass music washed over me.

There was a decent crowd inside: forty, maybe fifty people sprawling on lounges and chairs or propping up the bar. A group of moustachioed veterans were playing cards in the corner and casually flouting every anti-smoking regulation ever introduced. One old-timer had his face down in a bowl of stew, meaty bubbles slipping from the corners of his mouth. Ropey young men in tight pants prowled around a pool table brandishing cues and taking shots. Women in lofty heels and tiny dresses slapped their buttocks, slurped colourful drinks, whinnied in waves.

The bartender – not Benny, thank Christ – was shovelling ice into a bucket with a vicious, kinetic energy. He was a bug-eyed, chunky, pumped-up man. He nodded at my escort, who led me down a long, dark corridor and into an office.

Eddie Razic was rising from his chair. He came round, hand extended. I couldn't quite refuse to shake it.

'And I didn't even catch your name.'

'Redpath.'

He gestured at a well-stocked fridge and bar. 'What would you like, Ms Redpath?'

'Some answers.'

He seemed to find this amusing. He poured himself a Chivas Regal, added ice and coke. He seemed relaxed, but his eyes were following every move I made. As he returned to his seat, I ran a quick eye across the paperwork on his desk. The glance revealed little more than a handful of logos. Westpac, Elgas, Paramount Liquor. Others weren't so readily identifiable: a blue cube, an ear of golden wheat. What did you expect? I asked myself. Packets of smack in the out-tray, labelled and weighed, ready for dispatch?

'If you've come to apologise for your behaviour the other day,' he began.

'Yeah, right.'

'These situations, they can so easily take on a life of their own, escalate in a way which helps nobody, achieves nothing. I was pleased your friend, Mr Talia, intervened when he did.'

'Dom?' I asked, then straightaway regretted it. This guy was as watchful as a fox. I'd barely mentioned Dom's name on Cinnamon Row, but that was enough. You wouldn't want a creature like Razic knowing of your existence, much less your name. 'Not exactly a friend,' I said, 'but I was glad he came along when he did.'

He took a sip from his glass.

'As was I,' he said. 'But if it was not to resolve any lingering negativity, what is it that brings you here today?'

This conversation was turning into a game of blitz chess, full of traps and threats, but also opportunities I might not get again. 'I'm wondering what you and your goons are up to in Windmark.'

He looked offended. 'We need an excuse to take a drive up into the hills?' he asked. 'Get a little exercise? Enjoy a Windmark pinot noir with some friends?'

His mouth was fixed in a shallow smile, but his eyes were preternaturally alert.

'Nice type of exercise,' I said. 'Terrifying women in the street.'

He waved a dismissive hand.

'Nadia is a disgruntled ex-employee; disgruntled ex-everything, truth be told. Benny does get a little enthusiastic – I've spoken to him about it. But if I might answer a question with a question, what were you doing in Windmark yourself? I understand you to be a police officer, but one far from home.'

Razic knew a lot about me for somebody who hadn't known my name a minute earlier. Why had he invited me inside? Was it just to annoy or intimidate me, or did he want to find out what I knew?

'I don't like loose ends,' I said.

'That much, at least, we have in common.'

'You didn't answer my question,' I said. 'I don't imagine you went all that way to wipe a few dollars off a drug debt.'

'Drug?' He smiled. 'You've been misinformed.'

'So what were you doing up there?'

'I have interests in the area.'

'What interests?'

'I'm afraid I cannot say,' he said. 'Commercial in confidence.'

I gave the phrase the sneer it deserved. Decided to change tack – maybe I could catch him off-guard.

'Somebody else died last Wednesday,' I said. 'Feller bashed and drowned in a nearby creek. I hear Benny was in the vicinity.'

A frown rippled across his placid features.

'Your colleagues were here earlier, making similar accusations. Most annoying. Benny was behind the bar here until the early hours of the morning.'

He gazed at me, his eyelids dark and heavy.

Off-guard? Forget it. This guy was playing with me. I wanted to jump across the desk and punch him in the mouth, depose a few of his crowns.

'I don't know exactly what happened at Canticle Creek,' I said. 'But I'll find out.'

'I'm sure you will.' He slipped a hand under the desk. Did he have a buzzer under there? 'I was curious to know what such an amusingly assertive young woman was doing parked in front of my establishment, but what she was doing, it seems, was very little.' He glanced at the door. 'Now, if you don't mind, I'm a busy man.'

I heard a latch click, felt a gentle zephyr against my skin.

Benny Rork was in the doorway. He had a smile on him like a cat's arsehole.

'Benny will accompany you to the exit,' said Razic.

'I can find my own way.'

His voice grew icicles. 'There are those out there who would not take kindly to the presence of a police officer on the premises.'

I stood up. As I approached the door, I glanced at a noticeboard on the wall. I saw planning approvals, licences, certificates, schedules of inspection. And a calendar: a galloping horse, an ear of golden wheat. The company name was Palomino Stockfeeds.

I walked out into the corridor with Benny breathing down my neck.

Just before we came into the open area, he leaned forward and whispered hotly: 'I'll be coming for you, cunt.'

I took a deep breath. This wasn't the time. He'd keep. 'That's about all the coming you'll be doing, I hear. How are the testicles recuperating?'

'Better than you will be,' he said.

I looked ahead.

The jittery bartender was in the doorframe, stance wide, a set of knuckledusters on his right fist.

'Have you met my brother?' Benny asked. 'Matty, this is the little bitch I was telling you about.'

Matty smiled in a manner that had me calculating the kicking distance between us. There wasn't enough of it. I braced myself, made ready to jump at him. I wasn't going down without a fight.

He took a step forward, his expression lascivious – then falling apart as a hand from beyond the frame grabbed him by the throat and jerked him into a meaty fist that came flying forward in a perfect counterthrust. He slammed into the wall, fell to the floor and stayed there. His mouth was making odd little shapes, like a goldfish nibbling flakes.

A man stepped into the wake of the violence.

Neville Wallace.

'Wallace,' said Benny.

The copper's eyes crackled. 'That's Detective Senior Sergeant Wallace, you puffed-up little sack of gym juice. What do you think you're doing?'

'Just escorting the lady from the premises.'

'With knuckledusters?' he snarled. 'She's a police officer. Somebody whose boots you aren't fit to lick. Now get back into whatever slime you crawled out of and take your junkie brother with you.'

I had to hand it to him. He had a way with words, Nev. There wasn't a huge amount of them, but what there was, he had a way with.

'This is a misunderstanding,' said Benny. 'We were –'

'I'm counting to three.'

'But ...'

Wallace crinkled his nose and curled his upper lip. 'Starting at two.'

The Rorks were gone before he said another word, Matty groaning from the bottom of his guts as his brother dragged him onto his feet and poured him into an adjoining room.

Wallace led me out through a crowd of pop-eyed patrons – cigarettes were stubbed, wads of cash covered – and marched me to my car.

'Thanks for that, Sarge.'

He propped his hands on his hips.

'What were you doing in there, Redpath?'

'Gathering information.'

He exhaled so heavily his moustache fluttered. He told me that this was a major criminal investigation, not an episode of *CSI Outback*, and that if I had any insights into the case, I was to share them with my senior officers – starting with him, now.

He glanced back at the club. A curtain flickered at a side window. A man in a black suit and mirrored aviator glasses came and stood by the front door, flexed his shoulders and squared his feet.

'I want you to tell me everything that happened in there,' said Wallace. 'Starting with what inspired you to go there in the first place.'

I said I wanted to get a look at the Razics in their own lair. 'Why?'

'I've picked up information, adds weight to the case that they were involved in the deaths at Canticle Creek.'

'We know about that; the Greendale CCTV.'

'I said deaths – plural. I've got a witness puts Benny Rork in Windmark around the time of Daisy and Adam's deaths.'

He shot a suspicious glance at me.

'Who is this witness?'

'Said I'd keep it confidential.'

He looked like an ocean swimmer who'd just hit the sewerage outlet. '"Confidential" doesn't include me, you idiot. I get to do confidential. You get to follow orders.'

I stiffened. 'I gave my word.'

He sniffed the air, as if something in it was troubling him. There were things in it troubling me, too, but I doubted they were the same things. 'Tell me about this supposed sighting?'

I told him my witness knew Benny, had spotted him at the Windmark McDonald's around the time of the deaths. I explained that Adam had stolen drugs from the Razics and how payback could have been a motive.

Wallace pulled out a notebook and scribbled some jottings as I spoke. When I was finished he looked over his notes for a moment then turned back to me.

'What else did you and Razic talk about?'

I took a deep breath, wondering how much shit I'd be in if I gave him all the details of the conversation in the Dubica. I swallowed, decided I'd better risk it.

'Our previous encounter,' I said.

'Where was that?'

'In Cinnamon Row.'

'Ah yeah – I heard you have a tendency to kick first and ask questions later.'

You can talk, I thought.

'What did he want to know?'

'Whether I was going to apologise.'

He glanced across the road. 'Arrogant prick. Anything else?'

'Not really ...' I hesitated over the last word. He noticed, of course.

'That didn't sound as reassuring as I'd like, Redpath.'

I swallowed. I had to fill him in, or I'd be compromising Dom's safety. 'There's one thing worrying me – when Benny and me were having our little disagreement, a local bloke came over to lend a hand.'

'Very civic-minded of him.'

'I may have – er – inadvertently dropped his name at the time.'

'What! To Razic?'

'Possibly. He mentioned it again just now.'

Wallace rolled his eyes. 'Brilliant. And you wonder why we get pissed off with amateurs. Are you willing to mention his name to me, or is that confidential too?'

'It was Dom Talia.'

'The footballer?'

'He lives in Windmark.'

'I've met him. Mate of Vince's. Used to do a seventy-metre torpedo; should be able to look after himself – but I'll tell Vince to warn him. We've been investigating the Razics for months now. Years. Joint op. One thing I've learnt – you don't want to get on their wrong side.' He looked at me wearily. 'Bit late for you, of course. You're already so far on their wrong side, you're coming up for more.'

He retrieved the notebook, made more scribbles and scratches. Cars hooted and roared, a tram trundled past. He breathed deeply and exhaled, invigorated. This was a guy who thrived on petrol fumes and rattling trams.

'Anything else you want to fess up to while you're at it?' he asked. 'No state secrets you let slip? Classified information you passed on? Safe house addresses? Passwords?'

'If I remember anything I'll let you know.'

He shook his head and walked away muttering.

'Thanks again,' I called.

As I headed up to the ring road, I found myself thinking about something I'd spotted in Razic's office.

The document on his desk, the calendar on the board. Palomino Stockfeeds.

Was there a lot of call for horse food in Preston? I pulled into the first watering hole I came to, got myself a cool cider and a quiet corner. Spent a few minutes on the net.

Palomino Stockfeeds. From the look of the website, the company catered for everything from ants to elephants, but they specialised in horses. There were half-a-dozen outlets scattered across the state.

I scrolled through the list of store locations.

Windmark, 141 Cinnamon Row.

Bingo.

I checked my watch. Bit late. I'd visit them tomorrow. I downed the drink and headed for the hills.

CHAPTER 30

Morning found me cruising back down Cinnamon Row looking at what it had to offer: a welder's flash, a diesel haze, a team of rowdy panelbeaters playing swing-and-a-miss cricket on a forecourt.

I sniffed the air. Still hot, and the bushfire smog was back. Or was it? Maybe that was just the miasma that seemed to be perpetually floating over this town.

Number 141 turned out to be a three-acre block at the northern end of the row. It had a shop out front and an array of metal sheds – some open to the elements, others not – out back. There were a couple of delivery vans and a white truck, all of them with the company logo – an ear of wheat, a galloping horse – on the door.

I saw more security than I would have expected: heavy gates and chains, fat bolts, barbed wire. A pair of big ugly dogs prowled about a metal cage. Horse food must have been a hot commodity round here.

As I drove in, a voluminous woman with tight white pants, fake blonde hair and a baked blonde child was heaving herself into a cavernous four-wheel drive. She rattled down the drive, a horse float bouncing around on the towbar, hay-dust drifting in her wake.

I parked and went inside. Behind the counter was a squat, bald man with a head like a turnip and a body like a bag of wheat. He was reading a magazine. *Bacon Busters*. He licked a finger and turned a page.

A gawky boy stacking shelves picked at a pimple and asked if I was right there, ma'am. He had ears like Christmas baubles and a sprig of russet-coloured hair.

'Just having a look,' I said.

Bacon Busters looked up from his magazine. His mouth, already small, puckered and pursed.

'At what?' Customer-service skills to die for.

'Horse food.'

He closed the mag, hauled himself up onto his haunches and gazed at me with thin eyes. He had a bunch of keys and a bucket of lard hanging off his belt. 'Can you be more specific? What sort of horse are we looking to feed?'

'Biggish black one.'

There was a perturbation among his bristly brows.

'I'm looking after it for a friend,' I explained. 'Not an expert. Maybe I'll just have some hay.'

'Lucerne?' he said. 'Oaten? Grass?'

'Grass sounds good.' I'd seen Atomica eating grass.

'How many do you want?'

'Just the one,' I said, hoping that it wasn't a ridiculous request, that I hadn't ordered a cupful or a truckload.

A few minutes later, and twenty-five bucks lighter, I watched the boy manhandle a floppy bale into the boot of the car. The gold-star service continued unabated: the binding broke and the manhandle degenerated into your full Greco-Roman wrestle. One slab got away, ended up in the gravel. He picked it up, dusted it off and lost another.

I stepped away, making a slower inspection of the premises: hay sheds, loading ramp, gas bottles and drums – and the turnip-headed man emerging from a side door and showing more animation than he had thus far. He'd been keeping an eye on me through the window.

'Was there something else?' he asked in a manner that said he hoped there wouldn't be.

I assured him there wasn't and left. I was heading out onto the main road when my phone rang. I checked the screen and pulled over.

'Morning, Vince.'

He wasn't messing about with formalities. 'Nev Wallace told me about your conversation with Eddie Razic.' The anger in his voice was palpable – and worrisome.

'Wasn't a huge amount of it,' I said.

'There was enough. You gave them Dom Talia's name?'

My chest felt like a muddy swamp into which my heart was sinking.

'I did.'

'Well done. Somebody tried to kill him last night.'

Fuckin hell, they hadn't mucked around. I found myself gasping for breath. 'Tried?'

'Didn't succeed. No thanks to you.'

I ran a hand through my hair. The chaos was spreading like fissures in a megaquake. How much of it was my fault?

'What happened?'

'They ran him off the road.'

'Was he badly injured?'

'He's in the Windmark Hospital. Had a lucky escape.'

I heard a truck revving in the background, blokes talking rough. 'You're certain it was deliberate?'

'Yeah, sure – they just accidentally drove him over a cliff and accidentally torched his car, thinking he was in it.'

'Shit. Did he recognise anybody?'

'Nope. Back it up!' he yelled at somebody offstage. 'I'm out at the scene now,' he explained. 'Gotta go.'

I sat there mulling it over and feeling awful. Maybe I should do everybody a favour and just keep driving. Go to the airport, the Territory, back to Kulara.

I decided to go to the hospital. At the very least, I owed the poor bastard an apology, maybe some flowers.

When I pulled into the hospital car park I spotted Geordie North coming out of the revolving doors and headed him off.

'Geordie.'

'Lass.'

'How's Dom?'

'Agh, he'll be fine. Just a little banged about, nothin a stiff drink won't fix.'

I asked what ward he was in, and was relieved to hear that he'd already gone home. 'There's a feller doesn't like to let the dust settle on him.'

'Mind telling me where he lives?' I asked. 'I wouldn't mind a word.'

His sharp little Celtic eyes narrowed and he told me to hang on. He stepped away and spoke into his phone, then returned. 'Dom says to come on out.'

'Where's he live?'

'Clayton Road, half a mile down, big stone house on the left.'

Either Geordie was losing his accent or I was learning the lingo: I followed his directions and found the place roughly where he said it was. Out the front was a set of ornate gates with bare-bummed cherubim dancing on stone pillars. The house was crafted from chiselled pink granite and blue slate. It had wide verandahs, sweeping arches and a beautifully coiffed garden.

I rang the bell and Sheree appeared.

'Come in, Jesse.' She smiled. 'Dom told me you were coming.'

Even at this hour of the morning, she was looking good: full-figured, trim, with tight white jeans, ash-winged eyes and a peach blush. I wondered if she'd be as welcoming if she knew the part I'd played in what had happened to her husband.

'Don't want to disturb him if he's resting.'

'Rest?' she huffed. 'Dom wouldn't know the meaning of the word.'

She led me through to a well-appointed office. Dominic Talia was sitting on a couch wearing pyjamas and a dressing-gown, a pile of papers at his side, a laptop on his knees. He had a heavily bandaged leg up on a pouffe, another bandage around his head, florid bruises across the side of his face.

'Jesus,' I said. 'You look like you've done ten rounds with Barry Hall.'

He smiled grimly. 'Got out of it lightly, all things considered. Nothing broken; just a few scratches and bruises and a bump on the nut.'

'Better the nut than the nuts.' Bit locker room, but the guy was a footballer. 'You up to talking about it?'

He glanced at Sheree, who was standing beside me.

'Maybe we could do with a cup o' something, hon?'

She got the message. 'Coffee or tea, Jesse?'

I asked for the former, black and strong. Figured with a name like Talia, they'd know a thing or two about coffee.

'She doesn't want to hear this,' Dom explained when Sheree had gone.

'What can you tell me?' I asked.

'You've spoken to Vince Tehlich?'

'Only briefly,' I replied. 'Didn't tell me much. But I owe you an apology.'

A quick look. 'How's that?'

'I was talking to Eddie Razic yesterday.'

'Why on earth would you want to talk to that creep?'

'Been wondering that myself. I was interviewing him about the deaths at Canticle Creek. God knows, I didn't get anything useful out of him. Thing is' – I swallowed – 'I may have given them your name.'

A flicker of concern. 'Vince warned me they knew who I was – didn't say how. But what on earth was he saying about me?'

'He said he was glad you intervened when you did.'

He seemed puzzled. 'And you believed him?'

'No, but guys like that, you don't want to be in their line of fire.'

He grunted and waved a dismissive hand. 'Fuck em. It's a free country. Don't blame yourself.'

I breathed a sigh of relief, boosted by his confidence. I figured it must have been an attitude he'd picked up on the footy field, a suspicion he confirmed with his next words.

'One thing I've learnt over the years about thugs: stand up to them and they crumble. Like the guys last night.'

I asked for more details about the incident, happy to steer the conversation away from my own incompetence.

He said he'd been driving back from the building site on Robinwood Road when a car came racing up behind and ran him off the road. There was a steep drop there; he would have rolled if he hadn't hit a tree. He'd been thrown clear, was lying there wondering what day of the week it was when two men came down and put a match to the fuel spilled on the ground. When he roared at them they scuttled back up the slope.

'And you've no idea who they were?' I asked.

He shook his head then grimaced. Whiplash? 'They were wearing hoodies. It was dark – until the car went up and all I saw then was the colour of their backs.'

'You didn't get a look at their vehicle?'

'Nah, it was up over the ledge, thirty, forty metres down the road. Sound of the motor, big diesel's about all I could say. Decent set of spotlights.'

Spotlights. Diesel. Brock Gaunt? Him and every other bogan round here. I pressed Dom for more information, wondering if he knew more than he realised.

'How well could you hear them?'

'My head was spinning, but I certainly heard the bastard who said: "Torch the fuckin car."'

'Would you be able to describe their accents?'

He looked surprised. 'I dunno that they had accents.'

'Everybody's got an accent. Think back to when you were playing footy, the guys you knew, the way they talked. There's two ends of the spectrum: the boom recruit from the bush, the bloke who could kick a wheat bag over the silo, or the boy from the northern suburbs, the clever goal sneak. One's got a lazy drawl, bit of a lift at the end of a sentence, the other twists his upper lip. First guy barely opens his mouth, the second juts his jaw and shouts.'

He stared at the ceiling. 'You may be right.'

'Yes?'

'I'd say there was one of each.'

Great. If I was trying to decide between the Gaunts and the Razics, Dom had just added a layer of complexity. My visit to the Dubica yesterday had me more inclined towards the Razics, but I was still in no position to eliminate other suspects. Maybe the incident was nothing to do with either family. Perhaps it was just a couple of iced-up revheads looking for kicks. Or somebody with a grudge.

'Anybody else who might want to have a go at you?' I asked. 'Disgruntled ex-employee? Business disputes? Deals gone bad?'

'I'm in the building game,' he said. 'There's always disputes, deals going bad – even the current employees aren't exactly gruntled all the time. But they don't end up killing you for it.'

He leaned back and adjusted his injured leg.

I wondered if he could add anything else to my understanding of the case.

'You know Allan Gaunt, I presume?' I asked.

'Al? Been dealing with him for years. Sons are a couple of dropkicks, but Al's okay.'

'No problems between the two of you?'

'Tough bastard,' he said. 'Drives a hard bargain, but so do I. We've had our arguments.'

'About?'

'There've been supply issues. Especially last year, when he was being held up by the greenies at Echidna Creek. We were forced to use other providers. He was pissed off, said we had a contract. I said we had a deadline. There was a bit of a yelling match, but it was nothing we couldn't settle over a cold beer and a hot steak.' He peered at me. 'Why are you asking about Al?'

'Just ticking all the boxes,' I replied. As gormless an answer as I could come up with, but I was learning to keep my cards close to my chest. This community had more twists than a triple helix – I didn't know who to trust.

Sheree came back with the coffee and garibaldi biscuits, both excellent. The three of us chatted. Dom asked about my work, I asked about his. When he'd hung up the boots he'd returned to his hometown and put his savings into the family business.

Back then, his father and brother were building granny flats. Now the company was branching out into apartment complexes and commercial buildings across the outer east. The Robinwood Lakes Estate was their biggest venture yet – a hundred hectares of prestige housing on fully serviced bush blocks.

'You've done well,' I commented, gesturing at the house.

'Been lucky,' he replied. 'Boom came along at the right time and we rode the wave. And worked bloody hard.'

He was still working hard. He reached for a biscuit, grunted and clutched his back. The poor bastard had been through the wringer. And it was my fault.

'Better let you get some rest,' I said. 'Appreciate your time. And your coffee.'

'No probs. Sorry it wasn't under more pleasant circumstances.'

Sheree walked me to the car, paused at the end of the pathway.

'This accident,' she said, the corners of her mouth drawn. 'Wasn't an accident, was it?'

'Sorry, Sheree, I can't talk about it.' If Dom didn't want to tell her, I certainly wasn't going to. My big mouth had got me into enough trouble already.

'Is Dom in danger?'

'He looks like he knows how to take care of himself.'

She stared at the ground. I gave her my number. 'Any problems, call me.'

'Vince Tehlich said the same thing. That's what got me worrying.'

'Probably best to call him first; I'm sure he'd be a lot more use than me.'

I glanced in the mirror as I drove away. She was standing on the walkway, arms folded, shrouded eyes frowning.

CHAPTER 31

I pulled into the Bluehouse yard and sat there wondering how to fit this latest piece into the puzzle. The bloody thing was exploding in every direction, like a redshift galaxy, or a Queensland mining magnate. It had wheels within wheels, complications, invisible rips and whirlpools.

The attack on Dom Talia might have shifted the dial towards the Razics, but I'd need more than speculation and guesswork to link them to the murders.

Was it really just payback for the altercation on Cinnamon Row, or did he have some other connection to his assailants? Had he witnessed something they didn't want him to, maybe inadvertently? His construction manager, Geordie North, was sourcing building materials from the bush – had he stumbled across something illegal? Was he involved in something? Was Dom himself? He'd had disputes with the Gaunts in the past, even if he claimed they were nothing that couldn't be settled over a cold beer. Would that have been enough to make them attack him?

Young Brock was an explosion waiting to happen. What the hell was he on?

Palomino certainly warranted further investigation. A stockfeed business would be the ideal cover for a drug or illegal tobacco operation. Had Daisy – or Wolf – spotted some illicit activity? A clandestine laboratory or marijuana plantation out bush? I'd be having a closer look at the company. But where to begin? That puddingy manager was clearly on his guard, and I had no authority to put the squeeze on him.

Maybe I'd return after dark, do a little surveillance, try to find out what those vans got up to when they weren't delivering horse food.

A xenica butterfly bumped into the windscreen and jittered away. Its movements were as smooth as an arrow's flight compared to the maze of speculation in my mind.

Through the leadlight window of the studio, I caught a glimpse of a familiar rabbit-skin hat moving forward.

My father was never a man to let the fragments overwhelm him. He just pushed on, piecing them together, never losing sight of the big picture. He'd oscillate between flinging paint at the canvas and laser-like brushwork, but when he was on a roll he just didn't stop. He never had.

That was why none of his marriages stuck. There was little room for people in his world when the Muses got their claws into him.

I stood in the doorway and watched him work. He was crouched low, leaning in close, brush in hand. The painting was turning into a sprawling mosaic, two metres high, four wide, mounted on a pair of easels and secured to a lintel.

It was different from anything else I'd seen him do. It was lighter, more fluid.

His sketchbooks were all over the table, an array of sheets torn out and lined up in a manner that suggested he was attempting to string the scattered particles into a single narrative.

I could see it was a map of the Canticle Creek region, of the variegated slopes of the ranges as they ran down to the Windmark Valley. I made out hills and gullies, reservoirs and waterholes, sparks of gold, swathes and waves of emerald green. Coursing through them were meandering indigo lines that might have been creeks or aquifers, flowing down towards a sizeable body of water. There were places and features I recognised: Grinwood, Messmate, Tanglewood, the Cordy Creek. There was an array of local businesses: quarries and mines, timber coupes, orchards and wineries.

In the upper left-hand corner, a luminous bird peered down from its perch like an avatar from another world, or time.

Unusually, for Dad, he'd inserted human figures into the landscape: loggers, botanists, plant operators, truck drivers. I spotted the Bluehouse, with Lucy and Sam on the porch and Possum on a horse.

'Morning, Jess,' he said without stopping.

'Dunno how you do it.'

'Do what?'

'Keep painting.'

He paused, still facing the canvas. 'I like painting.'

'Yeah, but all the death and destruction happening round here – how can you ignore it?'

He swung round, a penetrating light in his eyes.

'Who says I'm ignoring it?'

Fair enough: art was his way of making sense of the world, of understanding the forces at work on it. His paint brush was a lightning rod.

My gaze kept returning to the painting.

'How do you handle so many different things at once?' I asked.

He pulled a cloth from his pocket and wiped his hands.

'You just chip away,' he said. 'That's all I've been doing – trying to make sense of the place. Making a landscape's like doing a search.'

'For what?'

He hesitated. 'Hate to sound like a wanker.'

'Everybody needs a wank sometimes.'

He shot me a look then shook his head, maybe wondering if he was paying the price for neglecting my upbringing.

'You're looking for the source of a country's energy. There's always two, twisting in and out of each other.'

'And they are…?'

'Fire and water,' he said casually.

That sounded like a double helix. Or a cliché. 'Isn't it like that everywhere?'

'Yeah, but you have to work out where you are on the spectrum – then pull it apart. Up in the Centre, we're at the fire end. The earth's burnt by the sun; water's like a ghost, sucked up by bloodwoods and bottle-trees. That's what interests me about the meteorite crater; all those shatter cones and shale balls, the melted laterites. You're looking at fire *in extremis*. Energy stripped back, laid bare.'

I waved a hand at the surrounding hills. 'So down here it's … water?'

He gestured at one of the indigo lines in his painting. 'Yep. It's what blasts the topography into being. Carves out valleys and ranges, fuels the rivers and springs.'

He put his hands on his hips and gave the matter some thought.

'The fire doesn't go away, mind you,' he reflected. 'It builds up. Jesus, it builds up. Worse now with climate change stoking the boilers. You can *feel* it. When it's ready, it'll jump up and charge like a scrub bull, crush everything in its path.' He shook his head. 'We don't wanna be here when that happens.'

He leaned forward and added a slick of white to what might have been a leaf, might have been a snake's head.

I got the message. Piss off. He'd given me all he was going to and the rest was up to me.

I walked away, thinking about what he said. Find the source. The key. The legend to the map.

What was the source of the crime – crimes – I was investigating? The controlling influence. Did any of the characters on my list look like they could wield such a thing?

Not that I could see.

I needed to stretch my legs so I went for a wander along one of the little trails that criss-crossed the scrub around the house. I'd gone a couple of hundred yards when I came across a dead wattlebird on the side of the track. I stopped to look at it, struck by the maggoty-roiling guts, the worm coming out of its upward eye.

That bird seemed to sum up the way things were going around here: eat your dead, writhe, slither, destroy.

I kept walking and came to a rocky outcrop. I clambered up and found a cavity that had been carved into what was almost a chair. I tried it out. Not bad. I stretched, wriggled, settled back. Quite snug, in fact. How could stone be so comfortable?

I wondered who'd carved it, and received a partial answer when I noticed a few lines of kanji chiselled into the rockface.

Kenji Takada – dead for forty years, but he hovered over this place like a ghost.

The outcrop afforded an excellent view of the Windmark Valley below. Cars cruised, washing lines rippled, black birds – crows, choughs – floated over paddocks and wineries. The river glittered. Kilometres overhead a plane trailed smoke and thunder across the sky.

Looking at the world from this angle made me wonder if I could bring a similar breadth of vision to the case. Immediately below the outcrop was a patch of sand, a couple of metres in diameter. I climbed down, picked up a stick and scratched out a circle, in the middle of which I drew Daisy's orchid. Alongside it, I placed a couple of stick figures: Adam and Daisy.

I worked my way around the circumference, adding symbols to represent the various characters connected to the investigation. Why symbols, I couldn't say. Maybe it was something I'd picked up from the artists I'd been running into lately – they did have a way of getting straight to the heart of the matter. I remembered Danny Jakamarra doing something similar with his drawing in the sand at Kalaringi.

For the Gaunts I put in a timber truck, for the Razics a knuckleduster. Wolf was represented by a dog, Christie by a dead cat, Geordie North, a ute. Dominic Talia was there in the form of a football; Vince Tehlich and Jace Grady, a set of handcuffs.

I stared long and hard at the resulting image. How did it all fit together?

Was I leaving anybody out?

Maybe I should expand it to include people I thought I knew. Sam, Nick, Lucy, Nadia.

I heard a flutter of wings above me. 'What is *that*?'

Possum was standing on the outcrop eating a piece of toast. Pendles was watching from a nearby branch.

'Just working out a few ideas.'

She stared at it, her tongue gliding across her upper lip, her brow furrowed.

'About the murders?' she asked.

'Thought if I laid everything out in a pattern, I might be able to see it more clearly. Get some perspective.'

She looked out at the panorama before us.

'Mum tells me that's what my grandpa used to come here for,' she said. 'Perspective. He'd sit here for hours and watch the birds circle over the valley. Then he'd go down and paint Canticle Creek for the hundredth time.'

I nodded at the inscription on the rock. 'The writing there, that's his?'

'Yep.'

I climbed up beside her. 'Any idea what it says?'

She touched the characters, enunciating them slowly and clearly.

'*Yado ni aki ga nai, dakara makura gawari ni ishi o, futon gawari ni hoshi o.*'

'I'm impressed.'

'I wouldn't be too impressed,' she said. 'That's about the only Japanese I know.'

'What's it mean?'

'No room at the inn, so for a pillow I took a stone, for a blanket, the wheel of stars.'

I was looking at my sketch in the dirt while she spoke. By the time she finished I was seeing something I hadn't seen before.

Like Takada's stars, the events were definitely connected. There was a single, shape-shifting intelligence at work behind the disparate events represented in that wheel. There was a pattern, a logic.

I thought about Wolf. I couldn't say why he'd been killed, but whoever was responsible had made it look like it was me who killed him.

It was the same with Daisy. Her killer had arranged the evidence so that her death appeared to be the result of an assault by a drugged-up boyfriend. Adam's own death was staged to look like a panic-driven accident.

Misdirection – that was the link between these scattered events. It had been there from the beginning. It was there still. Look at the attack on Dom Talia. They'd tried to disguise it as an ordinary car crash, and would have succeeded if he hadn't been thrown clear and fought back.

Would somebody intelligent and quick-witted enough to carry out mayhem on this scale go to all this trouble over a minor drug deal or an orchid in a logging coupe?

Possum interrupted my ruminations when she rose to her feet.

'So where exactly is this Canticle Creek?' I asked.

'Few hundred metres further along the track. Come and I'll show you.'

We made our way along the trail as it descended into a gully. Fallen fronds crunched underfoot. A lyrebird darted into the undergrowth ahead.

The ground grew softer and darker, the air became cool and damp. Wiregrass and blackwoods gave way to ferns, moss-covered logs and mountain ash. We heard the creek before we saw it: the gully had created a natural amphitheatre from which sounds echoed and reflected. The burble and plash of water blended with the calls of golden whistlers, red wattlebirds and honeyeaters; the result was a sonic wave you could almost see.

Possum must have read my mind.

'That's why they call it Canticle,' she said. 'From here it runs down the escarpment and into the river.'

She led me out onto a little promontory that jutted into the creek and explained that this was where her grandpa used to sit and paint. Water dragons hovered and watched from the rocks.

'My god,' I murmured. 'It's beautiful.'

I thought of Takada's paintings and understood how much this place – with its movement and grace, its natural harmonies – had informed his work.

We stood there quietly for a few minutes, then she caught my eye, nodded and we left.

The track looped back to the Bluehouse. In the yard, Possum noticed my recent purchase, still in the boot of the car.

'Nice hay,' she commented.

I snorted. I knew sarcasm when I heard it.

While she was helping me drag it into the shed, she tore out a handful and sniffed it.

'Bit musty. How much they slug you?'

'Twenty-five bucks.'

'Jeez, they saw you coming. You got it at Dalgetty's?'

'Palomino's.'

She raised her eyebrows. 'Ah yeah, on Cinnamon Row. The new joint.'

'How new?'

She said the business opened about a year ago. She'd never been into the shop but, from what she'd seen of their vans, they really got off the beaten track.

I stopped.

'How far off?'

She tilted her head towards the ranges. 'Have you come across Orm Wilson?'

'Not that I've noticed.'

She filled me in. Mr Wilson lived in the hills to the south. She'd overheard him talking to her father a few weeks earlier and he said he'd seen Palomino trucks way up on Michaelmas Road.

'Maybe they're drumming up some trade?' I suggested.

'There isn't any trade up there to drum.'

I gave that a moment's consideration, then said I might go and have a word with this Mr Wilson. I should have known what was coming next.

'Can I come?'

'Not this —'

She threw up her hands. 'Not this time! Not this time! That's all you ever say. You'll never find Orm's place without me. Come on, Jess. I won't get in the way. Besides, Orm's thoroughbred's had a new filly. He asked me to come up and see it.'

I was about to knock her back, but hesitated. She was right. I'd be poking around the bush for ages trying to find an isolated property on my own. And, I had to admit, she was only sixteen but she did have a way of asking the right questions.

'Okay then – if your parents agree. But only to Orm's place. Any follow-up, I'm doing on my own.'

Possum went into the house and came back with Lucy, who had her doubts about the expedition but gave her approval, as long as her daughter stayed where I could keep an eye on her.

Possum winked at me. 'Fresh air, new foal, maybe some of Mrs Wilson's scones. What's not to like?'

CHAPTER 32

We set out after lunch. At Crowcall Road, we turned south, drove through heavy forest until we came to what could only have been a logging area. There was no equipment in sight, but a sign on the high side of the road read: *Echidna Creek. Timber Harvesting Safety Zone. Unauthorised access prohibited.*

A glance at the slopes beyond and nobody in their right mind would have wanted access of any description. Fifty hectares of scorched earth, the sole remaining plant a lonely fern, a couple of metres tall. All of my senses warned me that this place was a chemical inferno: there was a sharp sting in the air and an evil, green powder on the ground. Numerous piles of wood – the slash – lay waiting to be burnt.

'This was the Gaunts'?'

'Yep,' Possum said. 'Make a mess, don't they?'

'More than a mess.'

'All to make Japanese woodchips.'

I scanned the site. 'Where was the protest?'

'They set up camp round the edge of the forest there.'

I followed her outstretched hand. There were still signs of the event: colourful wood and paper sculptures of birds, butterflies and possums, rain-washed and fading, were scattered through the trees.

'You said you were with them?' I asked.

'Only for a day or two. Never camped here. Mum and Dad didn't want me getting arrested.'

I took out my phone and had another look at Daisy's sketch.

'And you can't recall anything like this nearby?'

She shook her head.

We drove to the edge of the forest, parked and checked the perimeter of the clearing. We found nothing resembling the arrangement of rocks and trees I was searching for. I hadn't really expected there to be. The protest at Echidna Creek had been months ago. I suspected that whatever led to Daisy's and Adam's deaths had been more recent.

We returned to the car and took off, rolling down the windows in an attempt to wash the creepy feeling from our skin.

Eventually we turned into a winding track called Michaelmas Road, then followed it until we came to a weatherboard cottage in the middle of a network of beautifully maintained fences and paddocks. The sign on the gate said *Elwyn*.

'What's this Orm feller do up here?' I asked.

'Not much – runs a few cows, grows a few apples. Loves his horses. Always says hello when he sees us riding past. He's a nice old man.'

She wasn't wrong. The dogs came first, a trio of border collies rushing the car, tongues and tails everywhere, whirls of slobber, delicate scratchy paws. A man followed them out onto the verandah, hands on hips, feet squared. He was short, sun-scarred, with a broad hat and a broader smile.

'Why it's young Poss!' he exclaimed.

'Hey, Orm.'

'Come to see the new foal, have we?'

'Sure have. Orm, this is my friend, Jess.'

He pulled a pair of glasses out of his pocket and looked at me, his nose twisted and pitted. 'Jess. Nice to meet you.'

An elderly woman came out of the house brushing flour from her apron. She was introduced as Nancy Wilson. 'Just in time for scones.'

Possum's eyes lit up, but she asked if we could see the foal first.

Orm took us round to the house paddock. The filly was a newborn beauty, satiny black, still working out angles and wondering what to do with all that leg.

'Storm is what I'm thinking of calling her,' said the old man. 'On account of it was storming when she arrived.'

Orm Wilson quickly turned out to be one of those people whose bodies seem too small to accommodate the wellspring of good humour within them. After watching the horses gambol for a minute or two he pulled a mouth organ out of his pocket.

'See if we can teach the filly to sing.'

'Sing?' queried Possum.

'Sure. Catch em when they're young enough, anything's possible.'

He launched into a jaunty rendition of 'When the Rain Tumbles Down in July'. The foal was oblivious, but the border collie at Orm's heel began to howl along.

The show reached its climax when Orm sneezed – a flamboyant 'kerthump!' – and the dog dragged a handkerchief out of his pocket and passed it to him. Possum just about laughed her head off and I couldn't help but give a round of applause.

When we were walking back to the house, Possum said: 'Orm, Jess here's a policewoman.'

If he was surprised, he managed not to show it. 'Very good,' he said.

'She wanted to ask you a few questions.'

'Yes?' He stopped and ran a hand through the fur of the hanky-thief.

'Possum tells me,' I said, 'you spotted a stockfeed van running around up where there aren't any stock to feed.'

'That's right. The new mob.'

'Palomino's?'

'That's the one. Didn't think much about it at the time. Lotta game up there – pigs, deer. Figured somebody's into hunting or fishing.'

Probably is, I reflected. What was the manager's magazine? *Bacon Busters*. Maybe he busted his own.

Orm told me his most recent sighting had been at a place called Turner's Yard, up on the High Line.

'High Line?' I queried.

He gestured to the south-east. 'Track that runs along the top of the ranges.'

'I'll take you there,' said Possum.

I considered her offer. 'Okay. You show me where it is. I'll do the looking.'

We ate some melt-in-the-mouth scones with blackberry jam and cream, then made our farewells and drove up Michaelmas Road. Ten minutes later we came to a left turn and a bullet-riddled sign that read High Line Road.

'Turner's Yard's just down there,' said Possum. 'Let's have a look.'

It was against my better judgement, but what the hell? Things had been as quiet as the tomb so far. There was nobody around but us and the wildlife.

We turned and drove on until we came to a clearing on the right-hand side of the road.

'Turner's Yard,' announced Possum.

I saw the remnants of an old structure: fallen girders and corrugated-iron sheets eaten out by time's fire. There were scraps of machinery, paddles and pans, and fragments of a concrete slab, overgrown.

'What was this place?' I asked.

'Used to be a gold mine – back about when Orm was a boy.'

I grabbed the binoculars and we walked to the middle of the clearing, the sunlight dazzling our eyes. A pair of parrots swivelled on the wind and whizzed by, a green flash, gravity zero. Smaller birds tinkled in the ti-tree, blue blades, red sparks.

To the immediate south was a craggy hill, its dark, rocky summit towering over the trees. Why it caught my eye, I couldn't say. Maybe the fact that it was the highest spot in the immediate vicinity and would offer the best vantage point.

I gestured at it.

'What do you call that?'

'Black Dog Rock.'

I raised the binoculars and studied it. As the crow flies it was seven, maybe eight hundred metres away. As the road wound, god knows. I could see no road. No crows either, for that matter.

There was something ominously compelling about that peak. The ridgetops were like a row of eyes, sun-shot, glowering, its thickly forested slopes screaming with insects.

The foreboding grew so powerful, I could feel it shivering down my spine and radiating out into my extremities. I lowered the glasses and looked around. I felt exposed, vulnerable, standing out in the open. I cursed myself for coming here with a teenager in tow. What was it? Sixth sense or hyperactive imagination? A warning note woven into the bush chorus or good old paranoia?

I raised the glasses again. The rocks and trees seemed to gather energy and pace, spin like a tornado or a cyclone. I stared into its eye, felt it staring back at me.

I caught a glint of reflected light. Reflected on what? Metal? Glass? I sensed its length, aim, intent. Its threat. Like Christie Looms' cat, I could feel somebody watching me. Worse – they were lining us up.

I dragged Possum down, trusting her supple young bones to carry her through the crash. As we hit the ground I heard a distant rifle crack, felt the air swivel and suck above us. How close was it? Too fucking close. I made an instinctive guess at the angles – it came from somewhere near the knoll.

Possum raised her head and I forced her back down. 'Somebody took a shot at us.'

'I heard a gun. But it could have been miles away.'

'It was close.'

The windrow in front of us offered a modicum of protection.

'Follow me,' I said.

We crawled on our bellies and came to what I hoped would be the shelter of a dogwood copse. I told her to stay there while I made a dash for the car and jumped into the driver's seat. I started her up and raced back to where Possum was sheltering.

'Onto the back floor,' I yelled. For once she obeyed, lying low as I threw the car into a wild spin and whistled down the High Line.

The SUV flew over the dirt on rubber wings. We hurried back the way we'd come, down Michaelmas, Crowcall. We hit the bitumen and I didn't ease off until we came within sight of the Bluehouse.

'I'm going in to report this to Vince Tehlich.' I dropped Possum off at the front gate and drove down to Windmark.

CHAPTER 33

The station was a worry – lights low, blinds drawn, not a vehicle to be seen.

There was a sign on the glass: *For emergencies, contact 000. For non-emergency events, call Greendale Police Station.* A number for Greendale finished the message. I knocked on the door: nobody home.

I heard a distant wail. A minute later an ambulance whirled through the town, lights flashing, siren screaming.

The fire station was across the road. Every other time I'd been here the trucks had been lined up and waiting, the bay doors closed. Today the tankers were gone, the doors open, men and women moving about with a busy, deliberate air.

I walked into the vehicle bay and came across a couple of guys in baggy yellows connecting a trailer-mounted pump onto a ute. Or trying to. One of the men smashed at the coupling with a rubber mallet and gave it a tug. He hammered it again.

'That oughta do it,' he said, then he noticed me. 'Hey, Jesse.'

It was Christie Looms.

'What's going on?' I asked.

'Fire up on Clayton's Lane.'

'Bad?'

'This time of the year, they're all bad. They've asked us to bring up the Big Fill.' He nodded at the pump. 'Means they need more water.'

The other guy – tall, thin, red-haired – took a call on the portable.

'Mate,' he said. 'We gotta go.'

They jumped into the ute. I watched them hurtle away, the trailer rattling behind them.

At least that explained the absence of emergency vehicles in town. Everybody was out at Clayton's Lane. Wherever that was. Somewhere to the north-east.

I glanced at the floor on my way out the bay doors, then stopped, my attention caught by one of the numerous boot prints on the oil-stained concrete slab.

I crouched down. There was a spider in the sole. A Redback – with a crack in the right place. Had it come from Christie? He'd said he only wore Blundstones. Maybe one of the other fireys? If the row of overalls hanging from pegs on the back wall was anything to go by, there were dozens of them. Did it mean anything? Probably not. Vince had told me Redback boots weren't that uncommon. But that crack ...

I returned to my car, drove to the north-east and spotted a column of white smoke. I pulled over and spent a minute or two observing it.

The smoke was billowing more or less straight up. I didn't know much about fire behaviour, but that seemed like a good thing – no driving wind, limited speed, spread. The white suggested it was slow-moving – black meant the fire was running faster than it could consume its fuel, the smoke full of unburnt particles.

I kept going and came to a police roadblock manned by Jace Gradey.

'What's happening up there, Jace?'

'There was an explosion in Johnny Blewett's workshop. Got into the paddock and started a fire.'

'Any casualties?'

'Johnny's a bit knocked about, I gather.'

'Bad?'

'Last I heard, ambos were looking for his fingers.'

'Erk. And the fire?'

'Fireys are getting it under control. They've got half-a-dozen tankers going at it.'

I asked if Vince Tehlich was around and he nodded at the distant fireground, said he was somewhere in there.

'I need to speak to him.'

He shook his head. 'Under the pump right now. Waiting for the bomb squad.'

'Bomb! Bloody hell.'

'Don't think it's ISIS. They're just playing it safe. Looks like an industrial accident – propane cylinders and chemicals in the shed, feller was welding – but they gotta be sure. There's ammo stored in there. We're keeping everybody back.'

A civilian SUV drove up and tried to barge past. Jace yelled at the driver to turn around, then took a call on his mobile. His radio crackled.

He had enough on his plate. I left him to it and walked

across to a nearby hillock. I could see the incident more clearly from there. The property was maybe five hundred metres away. There were threads of red on yellow grass, slow-moving, a trio of tankers working at the peripheries. I saw more vehicles arrive and an ambulance leave. An aerial-encrusted truck I took to be the bomb squad rumbled in, dropped a ramp and unleashed a rotund little robot that entered what was left of the shed.

I spent an hour or so watching the emergency crews going about their business, then drove back to town. I wondered if I was wasting my time. Whoever took a shot at us from Black Dog Rock would be long gone by now. Vince was hardly going to tear himself away from a real job to follow up on my phantom one.

There was still no sign of life at the police station, so I wandered over to Springhills and got a drink. Then I tried the station again. Still deserted. I sat in my car and waited. It was after dark when I spotted a police vehicle – moving at a surprising clip – barrel into the yard.

Vince Tehlich jumped out of the cab snapping at his phone.

'Everything okay?' I asked as he unlocked the door.

He ran his fingers through his hair. He looked lost, the colour drained from his face, his usual calm demeanour gone.

'Girls are missing,' he said.

'Which girls?'

'Karly and Possum.'

'Jesus.'

He told me they'd ridden up to a place called Sandalwood, a couple of k's south of Canticle, late this afternoon and hadn't been seen or heard from since. Both girls had strict family protocols for such trips – home before dark – and they always obeyed them. They would have had their mobiles with them, but reception up there was dicey.

His features grew sharp. 'Lucy tells me you were up the Michaelmas with Possum earlier on today. Orm Wilson's place?'

'I was, but I dropped her back at the Bluehouse.'

'What time was that?'

'Around three thirty.'

'Lucy wasn't home – she'd gone down to Greendale. Her mum's in a retirement village down there. Possum sent a message to Sam at four, said she and Karly were going for a ride up to the Sandalwood.'

Another vehicle appeared: an ultralight. A flustered Sam Kelly jumped out and came striding towards us, yellows flapping loosely.

'No word?'

Vince shook his head.

'We got another couple of crews,' said Sam. 'Maybe twenty vols. Not enough.'

He stood still for a moment, his face drawn, deflated. 'Why'd I let em go? The amount of shit going on round here.'

'I've called in back-up,' said Vince. 'SES from Greendale, some of the more experienced locals. Word's gone out for more. Don't worry, mate. We'll find em.'

I offered to help with the search but Vince just frowned. 'You're not a local. We'd end up searching for you.'

The message behind the words was clear: you've stuffed enough up already.

He began to walk into the office.

I put a hand on his shoulder. 'Vince, listen to me. I've done a lot of tracking. I can help. You know this – you're just too pissed off to realise it.'

He gazed for a moment into the darkness, then checked his watch. He said the staging area was at the Canticle Junction and that I should be there in half an hour.

He made to move away.

'Something else I have to tell you,' I said.

'Kinda busy here, Jesse.'

'It might be relevant. It's why I was waiting to see you.'

He turned.

'When Poss and I were up at the High Line,' I said, 'we pulled into Turner's Yard. I felt – not quite sure how to put this without sounding paranoid – but I thought somebody was watching us.'

I did my best to tell him about the incident, though it was difficult to explain my intuition to a meat-and-potatoes country cop. He didn't seem interested – until I got to the bit where somebody had taken a shot at us, then his jaw went slack.

'From where?'

'Up near Black Dog Rock.'

'How close was it?'

'Close enough for me to want to come down here and tell you about it.'

He ran a hand through his hair. 'Surely the girls wouldn't have gone back there?'

'They're kids. Who knows what they'd do.'

'What were you doing up there in the first place?'

I gave him a brief rundown. His eyes widened when I mentioned the Palomino vehicle running round the high country.

'What made you pick on them?'

'Saw the name on a calendar at the Dubica.'

'They're part of a wider investigation,' he said. 'This changes everything. I'm calling in the Special Ops.'

He spoke to Sam Kelly, filled him in. Sam's face grew even darker. The two of them discussed the situation and came up with a plan. Sam would lead a crew of locals up to Sandalwood and commence a search there. The second team would head up to Black Dog Rock with armed police in the lead.

I raced back to the Bluehouse. Lucy was standing at the gate, arms folded, eyes fraught. She and Nick had driven around to all the girls' usual haunts, but there was no sign of them.

'We'll find em,' I assured her. 'Where's Dad?'

'He's here,' said a voice from the shadows of the verandah. He came and stood beside me. 'You part of the search team?'

'Very minor part.'

He jumped aboard.

'What are we waiting for?'

CHAPTER 34

There were at least a dozen vehicles clustered around the water tank at the junction, most of them with lights flashing, motors idling. Police, fire brigade, State Emergency Services, even an ambulance.

Vince was addressing a crowd of maybe thirty people, some in uniform, others locals who'd turned out to lend a hand. Quite a few of them I knew by now: Nick and Sam Kelly, Geordie North, Christie Looms. Even the old and the lame had answered the call: Orm Wilson, carrying a torch not much smaller than he was, and Dom Talia, the bandages still visible under his yellow helmet. A crisis like this drew people out of the woodwork.

A clutch of desperadoes in black body armour – the Soggies – lounged against a heavy vehicle with an air of easy malevolence. They must have been choppered in.

We joined the crowd in time to hear Vince Tehlich's closing remarks.

'Our job is to find those girls. But we're not going to be able to do that if we're in trouble ourselves. So – first rule – look out for each other. Work in your allocated teams. This is a night search, and dangerous. Boots, gloves, all the torches and portables you can carry. Command Channel is three one four. Sandalwood team, report to Sam Kelly there. The High Line crews will be with me, but – I'll say it one last time – we don't know what's up there. There has been an unconfirmed report of shots being fired from the Black Dog, so the Special Ops will be going in first.'

When the crowd had dispersed, I introduced him to my father.

'Where do you want us?' I asked.

'All civilians to the rear.'

'I'm not exactly a civilian.'

'You are down here. When we reach the Black Dog, the Special Op guys'll check the area's safe. Then we'll bring you in, see if you can add to the story.'

By the time we returned to our car the rest of the team were setting out. We waited until they filed past, then pulled in behind them. Dad took the wheel while I kept an eye out for any sign of the girls.

We worked our way up into the hills, the strike team snaking ahead, its red-blue strobes casting an eerie oscillation into the bush. As we drew close to Michaelmas Road, I felt the tension beginning to stir inside me.

I asked Dad to pull over, then got out and examined the road and verges with my torch.

'Anything?' he asked.

'Too much traffic,' I said. 'All those trucks are wiping out whatever's there.'

We drove another five hundred metres and I repeated the action, with the same result. We did it three more times and then, at last, I found what I'd been looking for. A hoof print, elongated, broad, heavy on the outside edge with a straight wall. A line of others nearby.

'They've been through here,' I said.

'You're sure?'

'Been looking at Atomica all week. I know his tracks.'

I got a patchy connection through to Vince and managed to convey that information. He responded with what might have been a word of thanks.

'Terrible phone signal,' I grumbled.

We repeated the process every few hundred metres, and again, found more evidence that the girls had been there.

I made another scratchy call to Vince. 'We're heading in the right direction. Looks like they were riding up to the High Line.'

'Roger that,' he said, and I heard him pass the information on to his team.

We drove a little further then pulled up. I got out, took the torch from my pocket and swept it over the grass alongside the road. I knelt, then lay down, making a careful examination of the surface.

I came back and leaned in the window.

'Nothing.'

'Maybe the trucks have wiped them again?'

'Maybe. Keep going.'

I thought about Danny Jakamarra's approach to tracking – there's always something. If whatever you're after has been in the vicinity, there'll be a sign. It might just be a discolouration in the gravel, a bird call, a whiff of shit in the distance, but if you look hard enough you'll find it.

We continued for another kilometre, stopping every few hundred yards to examine the dirt.

Still nothing.

I stood up and stretched my back. Worried now.

'Doesn't make sense,' I said.

'Maybe they left the road?' suggested Dad.

'Maybe, but where?' There were no driveways or turn-offs that I could see.

Up or down?

I tossed a mental coin.

Down.

I walked back the way we'd come, criss-crossing the road, swivelling the torch onto the verges and into the ti-tree. What had I missed? Every so often I'd get down onto my knees and look for less obvious signs: crushed insects, stone rolls, horse hair.

Dad tagged along in the car. Two or three hundred metres back, the road dipped into a long depression where the bush was thick and dark. Surely they wouldn't have gone in there?

Somewhere near the lowest point I stopped, my attention caught by a fallen branch parallel to the road. There was plenty of timber on the ground round here, but this specimen looked out of place. It was too neat, as if it had been deliberately positioned. I scanned the nearby trees, but could see no damaged trunk from which it might have fallen.

I ran my torch along the branch and noticed a chainsaw incision at the base. I dragged it aside, then lifted some of the smaller limbs on the ground nearby. There was a set of tyre tracks turning in where the ti-tree was at its thickest. They'd been partially wiped out, but were still visible in places.

I pushed into the scrub and came across more branches attached to a wire line that had been fashioned into a rough bush gate. I unhooked it and pulled it back. A few steps in and I came across horse tracks – with wheel marks running over them.

I went back to Dad.

'They've gone in here,' I said. 'There's a track, but somebody's tried to conceal it.'

'I don't like the sound of that.'

'And there's a vehicle gone in after them.'

'Fuck.'

He climbed out and stood next to the door, looking around. We were alone. I peered into the gloom, felt my heart pounding.

'We need help,' I said.

I tried Vince on the phone again, but could pick up only fragments of his voice.

'You're breaking up,' he grunted in frustration.

I handed the phone to Dad. 'Walk up out of the hollow. See if you can get a better signal. Tell Vince what's going on. Wait here and guide him in.'

'What are you going to do?'

'Follow the track.'

He glanced at the shadows and clicked his tongue. 'No, you're not. Not on your own. I've got a bad feeling about this. Those girls would have come out if they could.'

'It's my job, Dad.'

'And you're mine.'

I gave him a harsh look.

'Somebody has to wait here to make sure we get back-up,' I said. 'Don't worry – I'm trained for this. I'm not going to do anything stupid, just want to see what's going on.'

I left him there and made my way down the track. I kept the torch in my pocket, not wanting to telegraph my presence, but that meant walking a gauntlet of scratches and snags from the overhanging trees and bushes.

The further I went, the more pronounced the track became. Even so, the darkness was terrifying, full of mysterious attacks and lashings. I could feel welts opening across my face, blood trickling into my eyes and mouth. Mosquitoes buzzed and stung.

Somewhere to my right a barking owl screamed. I stopped, spooked, alert, listening. Nothing. I pushed on. I jumped when a possum snarled – the bloody thing sounded like a lion in the night. Every root or branch underfoot was a snake until proven otherwise, every insect running up my leg was a centipede, every tussock a trip-stone. Was there an alarm? Was I walking into an ambush?

I pushed on. The track curved around a low hill – the remnants of an old mine?

All was pitch black until a weird orange glow shimmered through the darkness up ahead. I crouched low, moving towards what appeared to be naked flame hovering in the air.

I came to a clearing, at the back of which was a timber shack with a white van parked alongside. In front of the building was a mature candlebark that had somehow caught fire.

The blaze must have only just started – flames were still working their way up the long, loose strips of bark. Still, here at the business end of summer, everything was parched, primed and ready to burn. When the fire reached the suspended ribbons in the upper forks the tree lit up. The door of the shack flew open and two men tumbled out. I ducked into the bushes.

I'd spent much of the past week trying to work out whether the Gaunts or the Razics were responsible for what was happening here. I'd never considered a third possibility – that they both were. Standing in front of me, clearly identifiable in the firelight, were Benny Rork and Brock Gaunt.

I recalled Dom Talia's comment on his attackers' accents – one of each.

I'd been speaking the truth when I told Dad I wouldn't be tackling anybody on my own, an intention that only hardened when I saw they were armed – Brock with a rifle, Benny, a handgun. They were a good fifty metres away, ample distance for either of them to put a bullet into me if I tried crossing the clearing. I lay low. This was a job I'd be happy to leave to the Soggies.

The men stepped towards the burning tree, the expressions on their faces telling me they were as puzzled by it as I was. They scanned the bush, alert, weapons at the ready.

What the hell was going on? How had the candlebark caught fire? And where were Possum and Karly?

I received a partial answer to that question when I noticed movement at a side window of the building. I studied it, praying it wouldn't turn out to be what it soon proved itself to be. A shadowy head emerged, then a pair of shoulders and an upper body. Somebody was making a break for it.

The men continued to advance, eyes on the blaze, oblivious to what was going on behind them.

The escapee tumbled from the window, jumped up and set off running. I recognised the cascading red hair – Karly.

Brock must have heard something: he spun round, jerked the rifle to his shoulder and got off a quick shot.

Karly kept going. Another explosion and she pitched sideways.

The men walked towards her.

Karly lay on the ground, still as a stone.

CHAPTER 35

Whatever plans I'd made disintegrated. There was precious little cover between me and the men – the odd shrub, a rusty drum – but what there was, I made use of as I crept forward.

'Fuck me,' I heard Brock yell when they reached her. 'It's the copper's kid.'

'Is she dead?'

'Looks like it hit her in the shoulder.'

The next words I heard were Benny Rork's and they jerked me into a full-throttle sprint: 'Finish her off.'

'Jesus, mate,' said Brock, his voice cracking.

'You just shot a copper's daughter, you fuckin idiot!' He grabbed Brock by the shoulders and screamed into his face. 'You want to spend the next twenty years in jail? Buzz her, we'll bury her in the bush.'

Benny pushed him away and raised his pistol.

I was bolting now, balancing angles, time and distance. My footsteps boomed like thunder in my ears. How could they not hear them? Forty, thirty, twenty metres. A backward glance from either man and I was dead.

Then an offstage scream turned their heads towards a sight so astonishing that they both stood rooted: a big black horse burst out of the bush and galloped into them, its rider – Possum – swinging what might have been a mace.

Brock was bowled over by the horse. Benny leapt out of the way and raised his pistol – he had a clear shot at Possum as she wheeled round.

I launched into a flying back-kick that slammed into his ribs and put him down. I bounced up in time to knee him in the face and keep him down.

The gun fell from his hand. I jumped for it, then saw that Brock was regaining his faculties quicker than I'd expected. He began to raise the rifle, but stopped when my father cruised out of the shadows and smashed him in the skull with a lump of hardwood.

I snatched up the pistol and pointed it at Benny, who was trying to find his feet.

'On the ground, hands out, face down! You're under arrest.'

He snarled.

'Now!' I roared.

He obliged, reluctantly. Shiftily.

I risked a glance at Possum, who was tending to Karly.

'How is she?'

Corner of my eye, Benny's arm jerked up from his waist. Christ, another weapon there. He raised himself, loosed off a volley of shots, a zipping turbulence in the air about me.

I threw myself to one side. A curl and a roll then rising, lining him up, a reflex action. I pulled the trigger and Benny was gazing at his ribs in disbelief. He dropped the weapon, struggled to stem the blood, hands wet, fish-lips working emptily. He fell forward, his left leg at an awkward angle.

Brock, on his knees, fumbled for the rifle, changed what was left of his mind when Dad gave him another thump with the branch and ground his face into the dirt.

I told Dad to keep the pair covered and raced over to the girls. Karly was lying face down, blood pooling under her body.

Possum was doing her best to stem the flow.

I knelt down and made a swift examination. 'What have they done to you, honey?'

No answer.

The bullet had hit her in the shoulder. There was blood everywhere, soaking the grass, her back and shirt. I improvised a compression bandage from a sleeve and held it to the wound. Felt for a pulse.

There was one, but it was weak. I tried to speak to her, but she didn't respond; she was clearly in shock. At least she was breathing. I put her into the recovery position.

'She needs an ambulance,' said Possum.

'Should be one on the way,' said Dad. 'I got a message through to Sam – left the car with its lights on to show them the entrance.'

I heard a siren on the still night air, distant but growing louder.

Possum stared at me. 'How'd you find us?'

'Followed your tracks.' I looked around the clearing. 'The bloody fire helped. Was that you?'

'I was trying to distract them so Karly could get out.'

'What was she doing in there?'

'She thought it was a meth lab. Broke in through the side window.'

I knelt beside Karly, feeling for her vital signs. They were still there. The blood flow was diminishing.

I asked Possum what had inspired them to come here in the first place.

'We spotted a Palomino van heading up the mountain and followed it. Saw it coming out of this track, so we snuck in to have a look.'

Brilliant move, I was tempted to say, but now wasn't the time. I couldn't excuse them for the risks they'd taken, but I could understand them. Possum was as inquisitive an individual as I'd ever met, and Karly appeared to have inherited her father's bull-headedness. Maybe she was even trying to impress him; doubtless she would have heard numerous stories about drug busts and clan labs around the kitchen table.

'How did Karly get trapped in there?' I asked.

'I was meant to be keeping a lookout, but they came back so quickly. Karly was still in the back room. Then she tried to get away and I heard them say they were gonna shoot her.'

'So you attacked them with … what did you attack them with?' I glanced at the object on the ground. 'A jaffle iron?'

'All I had handy.'

A utility pulsing red and blue bounced into the clearing. Sam Kelly flew out of the driver's seat, assessed the scene in a moment.

'Geordie!' he yelled at the ute. 'First-aid kit!'

Geordie North was already on the way, big white box in hand.

'And check where that fucking ambulance is.'

'Tanker One's guiding it in behind us.'

They made a quick assessment of the damage – Karly first, then Benny and Brock. They began applying bandages and blankets.

More lights. Cop car. Vince Tehlich emerged, came straight to his daughter's side.

'She's been shot in the shoulder,' I said. 'We've managed to stop the bleeding, but she isn't conscious.'

He knelt down and spoke to her gently. She may have groaned.

The ambulance arrived, escorted in by a fire truck. Sam led the ambos across to Karly, and Vince watched anxiously as they examined her.

'How is she?' I heard him say.

'Give us a minute.'

'She's my daughter.'

The paramedic, a dark-haired woman, looked up at him.

'There was only the one bullet?'

'Two,' I said, 'but I think only one hit her.'

'That's what it looks like,' the woman said. 'It's a nasty wound – the bullet's still in there. She's in shock. But she's coming round. That's a good sign.'

Vince closed his eyes.

When he opened them he spotted the pistol in my hand.

'What the fuck happened here, Jesse?'

'She saved our lives,' said Possum.

Vince nodded at her, then spent a moment whispering to Karly before the ambo moved past him and got back to work.

Vince stepped away and looked around. Benny Rork was on his back, barely conscious, a second paramedic working to keep him alive. Brock, head in hands, spat out a muddy, bloody tooth. The cabin glowed in the tree-fire's light, a reflection of the flickering rays dancing in the windows.

'It's a clan lab,' I said. 'Karly thought so, anyway.'

'Makes sense,' he said. 'She's heard me talk about em often enough. I'll take the weapon.'

I handed it over. He emptied and examined it, then sniffed the chamber and frame.

'Only got off a single shot,' I explained.

'Whose is it?'

'Benny Rork's. I took it off him but he pulled another one, so I had to shoot him.'

He looked around, trying to take it all in, work out what had happened. The scene was illuminated by a maze of headlights and the burning tree.

'Who shot Karly?'

'Brock.'

Vince's expression darkened. He marched across to the men on the ground. Benny lay there, face up; the paramedics were trying to secure his airway.

Brock, nearby, glanced up, then away.

'You'd do this?' Vince snarled. 'To a child?'

He looked like he was about to kick Brock's head in. Managed to restrain himself. I was relieved. I wasn't too fussed about Brock's head but it wouldn't have been a good look. More spectators were arriving now, mostly men in yellow overalls, a few women. The search parties.

I felt breathless, wheezy. The tension, fear and physical activity were tightening my airways. I found an inhaler in my pocket and took a deep drag.

When I opened my eyes I spotted another figure, one that drove a spike of alarm into my heart: a tall, hawk-faced man with a broad forehead and a Nick Cave moustache. He was off to one side of the group, his arms folded. But when he caught my eye, he began striding towards me. Jesus, would this never end?

'Vince,' I gasped.

The sergeant looked around.

'That guy … he's one of them.'

The last time I'd seen those brutal eyes they'd been glaring at me from the front seat of the Razic Porsche. What was his name? Lev. He came closer and put a hand into his leather jacket. Was he going for a gun?

He pulled out a wallet.

'Rashid Melick,' he said, showing me a badge. 'Organised Crime.'

'Rash is a police officer,' said Vince. 'Working undercover.'

'Well, I was,' said the guy. 'Think I'm retiring now. How you doing, Jesse?'

I shook my head. 'Kind of speechless, if you must know.'

Vince Tehlich shook his hand. 'Mate. That's Benny Rork over there.'

Melick turned and saw the figure on the ground, the emergency service workers doing what they could to keep him going.

'What happened to him?'

'Jesse Redpath.'

He glanced at me. 'Makin a habit of Benny, are you?'

I may have nodded.

'Good habit to have.'

'Bastards shot my daughter,' said Vince.

'They tell me she's doing okay.'

'Seems to be.'

'Thank God for that.'

'Kingfisher gone in yet?' asked Vince.

Melick checked his watch. 'As we speak. Four squads across the northern suburbs. Others in Tatura. Wang. I was on the Palomino raid. Heard you had a disturbance up here.'

'They got the evidence to make it all stick?'

'Been working on that for months.' He nodded at the shack. 'This'll be the icing – pun intended. Picking up Razic's lieutenant in a lab raid. Very handy.'

A second ambulance arrived. Geordie led its crew across to Benny Rork. They did what they could to stabilise him while initiating a series of relayed radio calls to arrange an Air Ambulance evacuation.

The fireys rolled out a hose and extinguished the tree.

'Smother it with foam!' ordered Geordie. 'Warm weather coming up.'

Other firefighters ran a hose towards the cabin and began spraying water at the roof and walls.

'Christie!' yelled Vince. 'Dom! Careful. That's a crime scene you're drenching there.'

'Embers hitting dry wood,' said Sam Kelly. 'Your crime scene'll be a pile of ashes if we don't put em out.'

A couple of firefighters put on backpacks and moved around the building, pumping jets of water onto the emerging flames.

Rash Melick pulled a torch and camera out of his jacket, then slipped on a mask and a pair of gloves. 'Better get in first,' he said, walking up to the shack. 'Before the boys destroy the joint.'

More cops came, some in uniform, others in suits. The Special Ops guys stood around flexing their muscles and chewing gum.

Another ambulance entered the clearing. Benny Rork was loaded onto a gurney and whisked away. The remaining paramedics came over and checked out everybody else – including me. A woman with exceptionally powerful fingers managed to find aches and pains I didn't know I had. The encounter had been more bruising than I realised.

Karly was taken to the ambulance. She was followed by Possum, who had to be dissuaded from sitting in the front.

'You going with em?' I asked Vince.

'I'll follow in my own car.'

As they closed the door, Possum gave us a thumbs up.

'Unusual kid, that,' I said.

'I have noticed.'

I told him how she'd burst out of the bush swinging her jaffle iron around like a mace.

Vince stared at the vanishing tail-lights, the red reflected in his eyes. Then he patted my shoulder and went back to his car.

CHAPTER 36

I stepped out of the Windmark police station, yawned, blinked at the dazzling early morning light. They'd kept me there for hours. Vince Tehlich was still downtown with his daughter, but an inspector from Greendale had taken over the incident. I'd signed statements, answered questions, covered the events of the night before from every conceivable angle.

There'd be a Professional Standards Investigation, but the inspector was confident I'd be cleared of any wrongdoing. Right then, I didn't care. All I wanted was a moment to myself, hopefully some food, definitely some coffee.

A dog staggered out of a side alley, looked around and frowned, then returned to the alley. Wise move. The sun was low, but it lit upon the skin like a laser beam. It was going to be a prick of a day, an appropriate ending to a prick of a week. Temperature in the forties, wind rising, relative humidity less than 10 per cent.

This hour of the morning, though, things were still okay. The sky had a blue sparkle to it. There were white-limbed gums nodding over the median strip, a fountain bubbling in the town square, delicious smells wafting from the bakery. Windmark was waking up.

The Stoneground Cafe a few doors down looked promising – a ponytailed young man was out the front tackling the awnings and whistling.

I began walking along the footpath, ended up limping, my left leg apparently having come out of the previous night's exertions in worse shape than it had entered them.

I wandered in and eased myself into a comfy couch that had my name on it.

The young man took my order: bacon and eggs, mushrooms on sourdough, orange juice and a latte as strong and hot as the hand of man could make it.

'Big night?' he enquired.

'Words fail.'

He began to walk away, then paused.

'I saw you come out of the cop shop. You're the one from the Territory, aren't you?'

'Depends on what the implications are.'

'Main implication is breakfast on the house.'

'Sounds better than the Territory. Main implication there's a kick in the teeth.'

He said he was in the Windmark fire brigade and had been at the incident last night, heard we'd done well.

He disappeared into the kitchen. The breakfast came, and it was good. Too good. By the time I finished my second coffee I couldn't even contemplate walking, so I put my head back and let the headrest take me where it would.

When I came to, Vince Tehlich was standing in front of me. He had a black carry bag in his hands.

'Anybody ever mention you snore?' he asked.

'Not possible.'

He said he'd just returned from the hospital and that the girls were doing well. Possum had gone home, and Karly had been operated upon; all indications were she'd make a complete recovery.

He looked around. The cafe had acquired a few more customers, but our little corner of the room was still reasonably private.

He sat down and laid the carry bag on the table, said he had to show me something.

He opened the bag and removed another container, this one transparent plastic. Inside it was an item of clothing – a mud-stained silk hat. He asked if I recognised it.

'Only from a photo,' I said. 'And a painting. Looks very much like the one Daisy Baker normally wore.'

He nodded. 'Jace thought so too. She was wearing it when we arrested her at Echidna Creek.'

He explained that they'd had search teams going all night and they'd found this in a gully behind the drug-lab cabin, along with other incriminating objects: buttons that matched the top she'd been wearing and a blood-stained hair tie. They were on the way to the lab, but the Homicide investigators had come round to my way of thinking: Benny and Brock had killed Daisy, then set it up to make Adam appear responsible.

'The evidence is mounting by the hour. You were on the right track. The murders were about money – though more drug than timber money.'

'Maybe it was both?' I suggested. 'She could have stumbled across them, same as Possum and Karly did. Brock's got an itchy trigger finger. Did he have anything to say for himself?'

Vince went quiet as a trio of nurses in purple scrubs – just off a night shift at the Windmark Hospital – walked past. They took a table at the other end of the cafe and began talking softly among themselves.

'Not a word,' he said. 'They know the ropes, those boys: open your mouth and you'll find yourself at the wrong end of a shiv in the shower. We'll get em on attempted murder for last night, though – multiple witnesses.'

'Including me.'

'Especially you.'

I scraped the froth from my glass and finished the coffee. I thought about the case they were building, trying to see if there were any holes in it.

'So they've said nothing about taking a shot at us on the High Line?'

'Haven't said anything about anything,' he said. 'But it does look like they were moving out.'

He explained that they'd found some of their gear in a shed at Palomino Stockfeed, on Cinnamon Row. They were thinking that Brock had spotted me from Black Dog Rock and tried to scare me off, but then somebody higher up the chain – presumably Eddie Razic – worried we were getting too close and ordered him to relocate the lab. Benny had come along to supervise the operation.

'How's Benny doing?' I asked.

'He's gonna make it. Dunno if he'll walk again – bullet damaged his spine. But he'll have his day in court. Hopefully on a murder charge.'

'What about his mates?'

Vince explained that the Palomino raid was carried out under the auspices of a major task force – Operation Kingfisher – that had been going on for months. Twenty people had been arrested, prominent among them Razic himself, who was looking at a range of charges: manufacture and trafficking of liquid meth, heroin and cocaine, money laundering, possession of unregistered firearms.

I listened quietly to this litany of horrors.

A chough pecked at its reflection in the upper windows of the cafe. Watching its work reminded me of another, more dangerous attack.

'So how does Wolf fit into this scenario?' I asked.

He hesitated, clearly on shakier ground here. He said they were wondering if the target wasn't actually me. The working hypothesis was that Brock or Benny, or both of them, had followed me from Springhills and tried to fit me up for murder. Benny, in particular, seemed to have developed a deep loathing of me.

'The escorting officer said he's obsessed,' Vince explained. 'Even with a bullet in the guts, he was groaning: "She planted that piece on me, the little cunt."'

'Maybe it's an analgesic,' I suggested. 'All that aggro. Or a laxative. Better out than in. Make sure you check his boots.'

'For?'

'Spiders.'

A bemused smile softened his features.

'You've really got a thing about spiders.'

'Can you blame me? They're everywhere round here, from the flowers to the footprints. I still haven't forgotten Daisy's sketch. I'd love to know how that fitted in.'

'Unless the boys blab, we may never know.'

He stood up, adjusted his hat and said he'd better get back to the office. 'Appreciate it if you could lay off shooting people – paperwork's doing my head in.'

I settled the bill despite ponytail boy's protestations. As we walked out into the glare, Vince asked what I was going to do now.

'Dad has to finish a painting, then we're heading back to the Territory. I've had enough of Victoria. People keep trying to kill me.'

A sleek four-wheel drive pulled into the no standing zone, too fast. Neville Wallace climbed out and strode towards us, his face its familiar blend of bluster and aggression.

'Where do you think you're going, Redpath?' he asked.

'To my car – if that's all right with you.'

'And then?'

'The Bluehouse.'

'Then?'

Was this guy ever out of interrogation mode? 'The Territory.'

'The Sisterhood?'

'Mostly brothers actually.'

I made to move past him but he raised a hand and gave a smile that would have made hardened criminals blanch.

'Just heard from the DPP,' he said. 'They're going to charge Brock Gaunt with homicide. Two counts. Daisy and Adam.'

'Glad to hear that.'

'Benny Rork'll be next cab off the rank when he's well enough.'

'Congratulations.'

'Wouldn't have happened without you.' He reached out and engulfed my hand in his. 'Not often I have cause to say this, Redpath, and you're a bloody nuisance, but – you did all right. You and your old man. Those kids last night … They woulda been toast.'

I studied the ground, a little lost for words. 'Glad to have been able to help,' was the best I could come up with.

He drew a wallet from his pocket and passed over a business card.

'You ever get sick of chasing goannas, decide you want to do some real police work, there's a job here for you.'

Jesus. I must have heard weirder things in the past couple of weeks, but, right then, I couldn't think of any.

I mumbled a word or two of acknowledgement and farewell then made for my car. As I drove out onto the road I glanced into the rear-view mirror and saw Wallace standing there, stance open, hands on hips. I caught his eye and received a blunt nod in response.

There was something about that gesture, in the overall image of that man in the mirror, the light streaming around him, the shards of a smile, that gave me a peculiar sensation. It took a moment to identify. It was something I hadn't felt for some time.

Satisfaction.

CHAPTER 37

Friday afternoon. Possum and I were in the kitchen shredding lettuce, slicing carrots and avocados. We were on salad duty for the celebration her parents had organised to thank those involved in the High Line search and rescue. The weather outside was brutally hot, but the Bluehouse, with its earthen walls and high ceilings, offered a measure of protection.

The two of us chatted while we worked. We were firm friends now, the banter flowing easily between us.

She threw some mushrooms into a pan, fried them for a minute or two then sniffed.

'Grew these myself,' she said. 'Daisy gave me a kit for my birthday. I always figured fungi were some kind of plant, but she told me they're more closely related to *us* than they are to plants.'

Possum was her usual explosion in a fascinating information factory, but, right then, my mind was elsewhere. I was keeping a surreptitious eye on the studio door, waiting for the

VIPs to appear. The gallery curators, Clive Carpenter and Edgar Winters, had been in there for over an hour, viewing the new painting. How long can it take to look at a picture? I wondered.

Dad was the first to come out.

'Do your head in, these academics,' he grumbled. 'Trying to make you explain the obvious.'

He wandered down to the yard and whistled up the horses, then leaned on a fencepost chatting to them.

Lucy, Clive and Edgar entered the kitchen talking animatedly.

'How'd we go?' I asked.

'It's brilliant,' replied Clive, enthusiastically shaking his head. His jowls went one way and his Bo-Jo mop the other. 'Ben's developing a way of looking at landscape unlike anything I've ever seen. He's absorbed something of Takada's technique – the luminosity, the grace – and blended it with his own more technical reading of the environment. I'm honoured to be given the opportunity of acquiring the painting for the gallery.'

I assured him he'd made a great choice. 'Twenty years' time they'll be saying it's your *Blue Poles*.'

'All it needs now is a name.'

That didn't surprise me. Dad was always casual about titles – normally he just slapped on the name of the location he was depicting. At last count, there were over thirty paintings named *Nickel Creek*, each of them with just a number to distinguish it from the others.

I went into the studio, stood in front of the painting and lost myself for a moment in its convoluted particles and waves. It was like an illuminated manuscript – a search for integration in a crumbling world.

Dad appeared in the doorway.

'They're wondering what you want to call it,' I said.

'I was thinking *Canticle Creek*, but that's been taken. And *Canticle Creek 2* sounds almost disrespectful to Takada. He's cornered the Canticle market.'

I considered his dilemma and asked if I could make a suggestion.

'Sure.'

'*Donkey Engine.*'

He came closer.

'Say what?'

I told him the story Danny Jakamarra had given me, of how, when the wheels of perception were turning smoothly, things rolled along like the old donkey engine out at Mantulyu.

Dad threw his head back and laughed.

'Why thank you, Jess. I believe that's the nicest thing you've ever said about my work. Only nice thing, actually. You really think it's working?'

'I do.'

'I was being ambitious. Never know where that's gonna take you – success or disaster. *Donkey Engine* …' He glanced back at the house. 'We'll run with it. Don't tell em what it means, though. An air of mystery never did a feller's reputation – or his bank balance – any harm.'

'They're talking about Takada's influence.'

'They asked me about that. The man was a genius. Working with Lucy taught me a lot about the tricks of his trade. But you know the real inspiration, don't you?'

I looked back at the painting, struck by its vivid characters, the way they seemed to be at home in their environment. 'Adam?'

'He's in every inch of it. My god, I still feel bad about that boy. Tragic that he never got to do more of his own work.'

We went back to the house. If the curators were puzzled by the new name they managed not to show it. Clive nodded sagely, as if it was what he'd expected all along.

'*Donkey Engine* …' he intoned. 'Fascinating.'

When Lucy said they were welcome to stay around for tonight's party, Clive and Edgar glanced at each other uncertainly.

'Bit of punch might help you make up your minds,' offered Possum, leading them to a sideboard on which rested a bevelled crystal bowl full of colourful juice and fruits.

Clive leaned in close and sniffed. 'Interesting. Is it alcoholic?'

'No,' and 'A little bit,' mother and daughter answered simultaneously.

'Oh god,' said Lucy, pointing an index finger at Possum. 'You didn't?'

Possum looked around the room, as if searching for an escape route.

'Not the bloody Hurricane?' asked her mother.

'That does sound promising.' Clive began filling a glass.

'It's got a secret ingredient,' said Possum.

'What's that?'

'If I told you it wouldn't be a secret.'

'It's fridge cleaner,' said Lucy. 'Bloody Serge.'

'Serge?' I asked.

'Friend of Nick's. Barman in a local winery. Taught Possum all the tricks she shouldn't know.'

Clive had a little sip, then a larger one. A fruity smile played upon his lips. Clearly impressed, he said maybe they could stay a while and appointed Edgar the designated driver.

Possum and I returned to the kitchen while Lucy gave the curators a guided tour of Takada's sketchbooks. The sun went down and the guests rolled up.

A lot of them I knew, either personally or through their partners: Jace Gradey and his girlfriend, Tanya; Geordie North and a scary Mrs North. A recuperating Dom Talia and his wife, Sheree. Christie Looms and a bottle of whiskey. Others I was introduced to: Serge Garcia, the inventor of the legendary punch; the Kefala Brothers, wine-makers and sculptors in glass and steel.

A gang of rowdy reprobates setting up on the verandah turned out to be Sam's band, the Canticle Creek Boys, who charged their glasses and launched into a raunchy rendition of 'Wagon Wheel'. Serge retrieved a piano accordion from his car and accompanied them, then improvised a set of variations on a tune he described as 'Afro-Argentine candombe'.

Clive Carpenter flopped into a club lounge with a build not unlike his own – plenty of padding – hit the punch hard and told tales of his earliest, undergraduate encounters with Kenji Takada, about whom he'd written a book he described as 'the first and truest word on the great man'.

Possum was – unusually – acting her age, tear-arsing around with a bunch of mates. They set up a trampoline at the base of the flying fox, then went screaming down the wire and crashing into a castle of mattresses. They kept this up until they were distracted by the arrival of Karly, who was keen to show off her wounds. She was moving a little tentatively, but was clearly on the mend.

Later in the evening I stepped outside and listened to the music coming down from the verandah. The Canticle Creek Boys were doing a howling-at-the-moon version of 'Far Away Eyes'. I moved across to the barbeque and joined some locals who'd clearly been discussing the events up on the High Line. Not that there was anything unusual in that – the town had been talking about little else all week.

'So, Jess, you were on the money all along,' asked Sam Kelly, who was having a break from the band. 'About Daisy and Adam.'

'Looking that way, but we'll see what comes out at the trial.'

'Case seemed clear-cut to the experts,' said Jace Gradey. 'What made you think it wasn't?'

'I knew Adam. Never could imagine him doing a thing like that.'

'Last time I spoke to you,' said Dom Talia, 'you were wondering about some sort of logging involvement.'

'I was just covering all bases. Figured they were natural enemies: the logger and the greenie. Still might be relevant – he's a wired-up boy, young Brock. I'm no expert, but I'd say he's been overindulging in his own produce.'

Christie Looms, on the outskirts of the circle, as always, but listening closely, asked if they'd come up with anything definite about the death of Wolf Gunther.

I glanced at him in the semi-darkness, the reflected light flickering in his glasses. I thought about the morning I ran into him at Daisy's cabin, his anger tangible, burning. What was all that about? Wolf's death was the one piece that didn't quite fit into the puzzle. Could Christie have been responsible? I should pass my suspicions on to Vince Tehlich.

Best to stick with something noncommittal. 'They're still working on that,' I said. 'Might have been the same as the girls – wrong place at the wrong time. Or maybe they were trying to frame me. I was the one stirring things up, asking questions.'

'Kickin balls.' Dom smiled. He clearly hadn't forgotten the encounter on Cinnamon Row.

'They were just collateral damage.'

'What about the attack on poor old Dom here?' asked Sam.

'Pissed-off Collingwood fans,' interjected Dom.

'Payback,' I said. 'He helped me out when I first ran into the Razics.'

I caught Dom's eye, might have seen the shadow of a smile. I felt grateful to him for not revealing how Eddie Razic had learnt his name.

Sam was suddenly dragged away by the boys from the band for an all-hands-on-deck performance of 'Moondance'. The crowd joined in on the chorus – a surprising number of them could even sing.

Our little group dispersed. I wandered into the kitchen to top up my drink and spent an engaging half-hour listening to Geordie opine upon chimneys.

The party was a lively but short-lived affair, at least compared to the booze-ups I was familiar with from the

Territory, where we'd be dragging them out of the shrubbery for days.

Sam set the ball rolling when he glanced rather pointedly at his watch and said he was putting on a roof at seven.

'We've got a big day too,' added Lucy, explaining that she and Dad would be delivering *Donkey Engine* to the gallery tomorrow. Nick had offered to do the driving. He and Nadia were staying in his old room overnight.

People began drifting out to their cars, first in ones and twos, then in waves. Edgar and Clive were the last to leave, the former at the wheel, the latter clutching a farewell bottle of punch and distributing slobbery kisses to everybody within range.

I went to bed and stared at the ceiling. The music resonated in my head, especially the accordion and its lilting harmonies. He had a gift, that Serge. His instrument seemed to float around the melody, not just accompanying it but layering, exploring, expanding.

I should have felt better than I did. For some reason I was restless, rattled, ill at ease. Was it still adrenaline? The last couple of weeks had been the wildest I'd ever known, but the conclusion had left me feeling flat. I remembered a similar emotion as a kid when my basketball team finally won a premiership. Is that all there is? I couldn't help but wonder.

I lay there listening to the Teskey Brothers on my phone and fighting off a persistent mozzie. I tried to sleep, but couldn't manage it. Nothing unusual in that, alas. Sleep, for me, is like riding a wave. There's a fleeting moment when all the elements – energy, timing, momentum – come together. If I miss that, I'm history.

After a while I gave up and went across to the window. It was a warm black astral night. A fragment of rust-yellow moon hung in the sky. Somewhere a fox screamed.

On a whim, I crept out, sat on a branch of the paperbark. I heard a tiny *prrrr* from above, and climbed higher. Pendles was in residence. He was gazing at me, a glimmer in his eyes.

I looked down. From here, you could see the lights of Windmark. Beyond that, just, the golden glow that marked the distant towers and chain-lights of Melbourne.

The bird ruffled its wings and shivered.

'It's okay,' I whispered. 'Normal transmission has been restored. Why aren't you satisfied?'

I tore off a leaf, sniffed and savoured its rich green scent. Why wasn't I?

CHAPTER 38

I was woken the next morning by a punchy mechanical rattle from outside.

I grunted, groaned, dragged myself out of bed and to the door. Nick was down near the water tank, ripping into the earth with a jackhammer. He was decked out in the bushman's uniform: big boots, bush hat, singlet and shorts, a layer of sweat and crud. A shovel and pick lay on the ground beside him.

He spotted me and flicked off the drill.

'Morning, Jess. Hope I didn't wake you.'

'No, I love the sound of jackhammers in the morning. More than jackboots, anyway,' I added, thinking of Wallace and Vince's dawn raid. 'What are you doing?'

'Running a water line out to the fire bunker,' he replied. 'Been meaning to do it for months.'

The sun was yet to rise, but there was an unusual smell in the air: burnt almond. The sign of an ecosystem under stress, surely. It had been a torrid summer. A string of torrid summers, from all reports.

'Sure you want to be working outside on a day like this?' I asked.

'Day like this is why I'm doing it. If we ever do have to rely on the bunker, be a lot better off with a water supply. Gonna put sprinklers on the roof, install a fire hose.'

He rammed his shovel into the earth and heaved out an arc of yellow clay. Repeated the action. Did it again, at speed. Dirt whirled, dust rolled. He worked with a smooth, powerful efficiency, swiftly extending the ditch.

Rather you than me, I thought.

I went into the kitchen and made myself some toast.

The radio news reported the Wimmera fires were flaring up again, and there was a major blaze in East Gippsland.

I was pleased we were leaving this pyromaniac state tomorrow. We had fires in the desert, but they were altogether gentler, more grassy affairs. The Indigenous people almost seemed to regard them as love letters to their country.

I distracted myself by browsing through a copy of the local paper I found on the table. I skipped the lead article: 'Shootout on the High Line'. I had absolutely no desire to revisit that unsettling incident. The cricket reports looked more promising. Somebody named Bugg had brought up his century with a six through a car windscreen. Bridnok had beaten Windmark West. A Mr Cliff was whingeing about the quality of the pitches in the drought, predicting a rash of broken bones come footy season.

Possum staggered into the kitchen, carried along on an endless yawn. She splashed milk into a bowl of Vita Brits and bananas and took a mouthful. 'I needed that,' she said, licking milk off her chin.

She picked up a note from the kitchen bench and read it out loud: 'Bad day, stay alert.'

'From your dad?' I asked.

'Natch. He's a fanatic.'

Possum polished off her bowl and went to feed the horses.

Nadia appeared and gave me a quick hug and a fugitive smile. She was wearing a summery blue dress, with a leather belt and silver headband. Her bleached hair glowed, her face seemed sparkier, with more colour in it than I'd seen before. Clearly a weight had been lifted from her shoulders.

Lucy and Dad joined us at the table. We finished breakfast, then Nadia and I were left alone as the others went out to wrap and pack the painting.

'What are you going to do now?' I asked her.

This was the first quiet time we'd had together since the morning I barged into her house on Connolly Street.

'Just ... get by, I suppose. Something I hope'll be a lot easier now the Razics aren't on my case. Stay away from Melbourne, much as I can – not healthy for me down there.'

Out in the yard Nick was still going, hammer – jack – and tongs.

Nadia made more toast, spread blackberry jam onto it and took a bite.

'Nick and I were talking last night. We've decided – this might seem weird – we're going to visit Bosnia–Herzegovina. Not sure when or how – we can barely pay the rent right now, and I don't know if I've still got any family there, but –' her eyes flared, 'we'll do it.'

I touched the back of her hand. 'I don't think that's weird at all. It's terrific.'

Nadia and I talked for a good hour. She opened up even more, sharing some memories of Bosnia. She told me about her hometown, her friends and family. How her mother had been a hairdresser, her father a schoolteacher who dreamed of being a writer.

'And who knows? He may have succeeded,' she said. 'Had he lived. He had imagination. And the hands you need to bring such a thing to life.'

'The hands?'

She told me he'd built her a village of sticks and stones in the shade of an olive tree and populated it with clay figurines of contradictory characters from their community: the benevolent banker, the skinny baker, the one-armed mechanic, the rakija-slugging imam. He invented funny stories about them, gave them quirks, fears and fantasies, secret passions and kitchen-door romances.

'He sounds like a sweet man,' I said.

She stared out the window. 'Maybe too sweet.'

'Too sweet?'

'Too trusting.'

'In what?'

'Humanity.'

She took a swig of tea and studied the leaves at the bottom of the cup.

'Still,' she said. 'What can we do? We push on.'

'Like boats against the current?'

She gave no sign of recognising the line.

'Sometimes,' she said, 'surely, the current runs the right way?'

Her eyes rose to meet my own.

'Course it does,' I said.

Mid-morning Lucy reappeared and said it was time to go. Nick followed. He dropped his pickaxe at the laundry door and went in to have a quick shower.

'Did you finish your water line?' I asked when he came out towelling his hair.

'Getting there. Knock it off when I get back.'

'Please try to, Nick,' said Lucy. 'I appreciate you're doing it, but we don't want another one of your wretched ditches or potholes in the yard for everybody to trip over.'

If the wan smile on Nick's face was anything to go by, this was a familiar admonition. He was a guy who specialised in the ditch half-dug, the fence unstrung.

'What are your plans, Jess?' asked Lucy.

'Think I'll just take it easy,' I said. 'Big trip tomorrow.'

Dad and I were catching a plane at noon.

She repeated the question to Nadia, who gave a similar answer: she didn't feel up to running round town in all this heat.

Possum drifted in, a skink in her hands. She ferried it across to the back door and let it go.

'What about you, kid?' asked Lucy. 'I was thinking we could drop you down at Karly's place?'

'I'm staying here,' said Possum. 'Somebody's gotta make sure the animals don't cark it in this heat.'

She had a point. The mercury was rising rapidly, the iron roof generating a battery of stretching and groaning noises. The air on the other side of the window shimmered with vaporising eucalyptus oil. The cicadas were screaming blue murder.

'If Jess and Nadia are with you, that'll be okay. You know the ropes, honey.'

'What are the ropes?' I asked.

'Stay alert,' Possum replied drily, reciting what was clearly a family mantra. 'Listen to the radio, watch the horizon. Any sign of trouble, even a whiff of smoke in the distance, head for the bunker. Take shelter as the fire approaches, stay until it's safe to go outside.'

Lucy explained that if we did get caught, the bunker contained everything we were likely to need: smoke masks, air cylinders, protective clothing.

Dad came in, hat dusted and boots polished. 'Ready to roll,' he said.

We all went out to the verandah. Lucy and Dad waved goodbye and Nick followed them in the jeep, the painting secured in a trailer.

The three of us stood at the top of the steps as they drove away. There was a sudden lift in the wind that buffeted our faces. It was as if the elements had waited until we were on our own before showing themselves.

Nadia went back in, but Possum stared at the rippling vista and frowned. 'Better finish my chores.' She went down to the chook shed, collected some eggs, touched the tin roof. 'Ouch!' she yelped. 'Burning already. Girls need a bath.'

She found a mattock, scraped out a hole beneath a nearby wattle, rolled out a hose and filled it with water. She let the birds out of the pen and watched them peck and splash about.

We filled some buckets and moved about the garden topping up the numerous containers she'd left out for the more feral members of the household: possums and birds, kangaroos and echidnas, any creature that felt in need of a drink. She sprayed water into the trees overhead, explaining that everybody enjoyed the resulting shower. Even the rats and mice were welcome, those that had survived Sam's persistent attempts to kill them.

Worn out by the exertion in the heat, we sat on a rocky cairn in the shade of a large tree down where the front yard met the bush. Pendles came floating in and perched in the branches above us.

I noticed a line of wooden crosses at the foot of the cairn, a name painted onto each one: Alph, Digger, Finders, Keepers, MacBirdie.

'What is this place?'

'The pet cemetery.'

I'd guessed as much.

'So who have we got?'

'Alph was a blue-tongue,' she explained, beginning with the nearest memorial. 'Digger was a border collie. Finders and Keepers were a couple of joeys. MacBirdie speaks for himself – and he certainly did that.'

She gestured at the tree we were sitting under and asked if I knew what it was.

'Can't say I do.'

'It's a Japanese elm.'

'Grandpa again?'

She nodded. 'Mum says people laughed at him, bringing in seeds from his hometown – he had them in his bag when he first came here – but I love this tree. It's cool, in every sense of the word.'

I could see what she was getting at. With its thick limbs, spidery branches and deep green shade, the elm was an attractive, natural refuge from the heat.

Possum lay back, gazing up into the speckled leaf-light. She told me about her plans: the year after next she hoped to go to university, where she would study environmental science. We remained there until Nadia came down and invited us up for lunch. She'd prepared a salad and dips and mixed a jug of lemon barley water and mint.

We sat round the kitchen table. Possum and I hoed in, but Nadia only picked at her food.

'My god,' she said, 'it's so damned hot.'

'One of the problems with this house,' said Possum. 'Takes a long time to heat up, but when it does, it takes as long to cool down. We need a banana surprise.'

She dug out a blender and began tossing ingredients – ice, fruit, chia seeds and milk – in with gusto.

'What's the surprise?' I asked.

'No bananas.'

She did some heavy blending and passed round the drinks.

'Not bad,' I had to admit. 'In fact, friggin delicious.'

It was thick, sweet and cold. Nadia must have thought so too – she licked her lips and asked for more.

I switched on the radio. There were warnings and reports of fires flaring up and breaking out across the state, but none anywhere near Windmark. I presumed the emergency services would still be busy, dispatching tankers to false alarms and phantom wisps of smoke. On a day like this everybody would be jumpy.

Nadia crawled under a wet towel on the floor. Clearly, she wasn't a summer person. Either that or she'd had too much smoothie.

Possum checked the thermometer. 'Yoicks. It's hitting forty.'

She grabbed some water from the fridge and swallowed it in one go. 'Sweating it out faster than I can get it in.'

The phone rang. It was Sam, checking up on us. I heard Possum repeat the mantra: smoke, bunker, shelter.

'What's he up to?' I asked when she hung up.

'He's coming home early. Weather's worse than forecast. They're going on stand-by at the brigade. This calls for more drastic measures.'

'Such as?'

'Cold showers all round.'

She stepped outside, grabbed a garden hose and hit me with a jet of water through the screen door. Then she directed a fountain into the air and stood beneath it, soaking her dress.

'Horses could do with one too,' she said.

She dragged the hose across the yard and gave them a spray. I watched from the verandah for a minute or two but the wind was sucking the life out of me. My mouth felt like it was lined with hessian bags.

Back inside, Nadia had passed out on the couch, right arm drooping down. She was like the old FitzRoy storm glass my father kept on his bench: fine-tuned, fragile, sensitive to changes in the weather.

I flopped onto the floor and gazed up at the rotating fans. I held the water glass to my throat, found a brief respite in its coolness.

I put the glass aside and closed my eyes.

CHAPTER 39

I must have nodded off. I found myself dreaming about cool water and sweet rain, about gentle breezes and whirling fan blades.

I was snapped back to reality by a distant cry. I opened my eyes, heard a rush of hooves. I reached the verandah to see the horses bolting away, a frantic Possum sprinting after them.

Realising the hopelessness of pursuit, she stopped, put her fingers to her lips and let fly with a whistle to wake the sleeping owls.

Atomica knew the score. He pulled up and looked around guiltily. She'd trained him well. She hadn't done such a good job with Nutmeg, whose fat little legs kept pumping, propelling him out through the front gate. He galloped down the road and disappeared round the bend.

'You little bastard!' yelled Possum.

She reached Atomica, grabbed a fistful of mane and settled him down, then ran him back to the yard.

'Get a saddle!' she cried.

I went into the tack room, found some gear and brought it out.

'What are you going to do?' I asked as we threw on the saddle.

'Catch Nutmeg.'

'You know where he's gone?'

'Down to Windmark.'

'You're sure?'

'Pretty much. He's got a crush on Red. Gotta stop him before he gets out onto the highway.' She stopped and shook her head, close to crying. 'Can't believe it. All my life round horses and I do a stupid thing like that.'

'How'd it happen?'

'Went to get some chaff, mustn't have shut the gate properly. I'm filling the scoop when I hear bloody Nutty doing a bolt.'

She kicked the dirt and swore.

I put a hand on her shoulder. 'Don't crucify yourself, Poss. Day like this, everybody's brains are scrambled. We'll get him.'

I asked her how I could help and she suggested I take a halter and a bucket of chaff and try to get ahead of him. I helped her onto Atomica and she galloped out the gate.

I went in and told Nadia what was going on.

'Anything I can do?' she offered.

'Just take it easy. No point all of us dying of heat stroke.'

By the time I came back out the wind was really ripping it up, a blistering, blustery northerly, surely hitting sixty, eighty k's an hour. The trees were dancing around like a mob of stampeding cattle.

I grabbed the gear and set out in the SUV, but I'd only gone a few hundred yards when I came across Possum reined in on the side of the road.

'What now?'

She was staring forlornly at the scrub. 'He's taken the short cut.' I followed her gaze and saw fresh tracks disappearing into a gap in the shrubbery.

'That's bad?'

'It's terrible. Potholes, stumps, hazards everywhere.'

'So what are we gonna do?'

'I'll follow him, take it slow and careful. You drive down the road and try to get ahead of him. If you do spot him, lure him in with the chaff. Get a halter onto him. Main thing's to catch him before he gets out onto the main road.'

She turned Atomica towards the track.

'You be careful,' I said as she spurred away.

I drove slowly down the road, and was pleased to notice the binoculars in the well. Every few minutes I'd pull over and look around. Once I caught a glimpse of Possum and Atomica, heads down, ploughing into a gritty headwind.

The sight made me thirsty. I looked around the car. No water. Damn! If this ends well, I resolved, I'll take the girls down to Springhills for a refreshing drink on the back verandah, listen to a bit of Johnny Cash, swap insults with the Burns Boys.

As I drove, I was struck by the lack of people to be seen; the heat was keeping everybody indoors. Sensible. I spotted the odd cow sheltering under a tree, a windmill with a broken sail.

Finally I came out onto the flatlands at the bottom of Robinwood Road. I pulled over, grabbed the binoculars and studied the landscape. I was looking at the rear of the Robinwood Lakes Estate. Various items of plant and equipment – an earth mover, a grader, a bobcat – were dotted about, none of them moving. The workers must have taken the day off. The BMX kids had done the same thing. I'd be doing it myself when we caught this runaway nag.

A blur of movement to the south and I was pleased to spot Possum riding out of the bush. She was heading north-west, but then she turned Atomica's head and cantered towards a copse in the middle of the estate.

I swung the glasses onto the grove and caught a glimmer of water. That must have been the lake.

I studied it more carefully and saw what had made Possum head that way. A familiar ute was parked there: Geordie North's. Through the trees I discerned the man himself at the water's edge, and, more importantly, a small bay horse drinking from the lake and shaking its mane.

Possum spotted me and gave me an enthusiastic thumbs up.

'We got him!' she yelled.

I returned the gesture, drove round to the front gate and parked in the shade of the hoarding advertising the estate.

I looked out over the development. I hadn't paid it much attention until now, and I was impressed. It was more expansive than it appeared from the road, with a dry creek bed forming what I took to be its southern boundary.

And there was more to the positive impression than mere size: the project's defining quality was aesthetic. Robinwood

Lakes was a living sculpture, a skilfully designed landscape that had been carved into and out of the surrounding bush.

What had Sam said? They were going for the rustic look. They'd certainly got that. The massive swamp gums had been left in place, and the new bitumen roads seemed to shape themselves around them before undulating up into the adjoining slopes. I'd never been to Italy, but something about the scene brought to mind sun-washed tracks weaving their way up a Tuscan hillside.

So absorbed was I by the scene in front of me that I failed to notice what was happening behind me until I heard a car door close.

I looked around.

Shit. Allan bloody Gaunt. An under-the-weather Allan Gaunt, if the wobbly gait, flushed face and jutting jaw were anything to go by. His hair was like tightly sprung steel wool. He came close. Veins were popping in what little he had by way of neck.

'Afternoon, Mister Gaunt.'

'Don't fuckin Mister Gaunt me. Got what you wanted, did you?'

'Sorry?'

'Know where I've just come from?'

'The pub?'

His eyes flared, nostrils ditto.

'The hospital. Nancy's in there.'

Mrs Gaunt, I assumed. I said I was sorry to hear that, but he pointed a stubby finger at me. 'You put her there.'

'What?'

'The boy. You come looking for someone to pin it on, found Brock. Give her a heart attack.'

I considered reminding him that it wasn't that long since I'd seen his hard-done-by boy shoot a teenage girl, but decided against it. There's a time and a place, and standing out here on a lonely road with him half-cut was neither.

'That's nothing to do with me, Mr Gaunt. If you've got a problem, take it up with the Homicide Squad.'

'Homicide! That's the bullshit! Boy mighta been muckin around with drugs – show me a kid round here who hasn't – but kill that couple! No way.'

He came closer. He was three sheets to the wind, and, God knows, there was plenty of wind around today. His breath reeked, his eyes were shot with blood.

Vince Tehlich's comment came to mind. Brock wouldn't have the brains to plan something like the terrible events at Canticle Creek, but his father – a man who'd prospered in the cut and thrust world of small-town business – certainly would.

And I'd let myself be caught alone with him.

CHAPTER 40

Maybe not so alone. Another vehicle, a black BMW four-wheel drive, came cruising down the road. It turned into the drive and pulled up next to us.

The driver got out. It was, I was relieved to see, Dom Talia.

He stood there for a moment, sizing the situation up.

'Afternoon all,' he said.

Gaunt grunted. Dom came over and put a hand on his shoulder. 'Mate, I was shocked to hear about Nancy. How is she?'

I looked at the timber miller, saw the wheels clicking, if a little disjointedly, the rage draining from his eyes. Whatever he'd been planning to do, he wouldn't be doing it in front of Dom Talia.

'Looks like she's pickin up.'

'Family going through a tough time, Al,' Dom said. 'Never forget your friends – we're here to help.'

Gaunt nodded and wobbled.

Dom turned to me. 'Let me guess. You're looking for a fat little horse?'

'I was. But it looks like Geordie's got him cornered by the lake.'

'I know. I was there. He came bolting out of the bush, decided to stop for a drink. I've just been running around the neighbours to find who owns him. Don't tell me the bugger's come all the way from the Bluehouse?'

'Fraid so.'

Gaunt rubbed his eyes, then jerked his head, once, twice, like a swimmer trying to shake the water from his ears. He began to walk away.

'You right to drive, Allan?' asked Dom.

'Course I fuckin am.'

He gave me a lopsided version of the parting you'll-keep glare his family did so well, then climbed into the cabin.

Dom and I watched him leave.

'You do have a beautiful sense of timing,' I said. 'I wasn't sure what that guy was gonna do.'

'Neither was I. He's under a lot of stress right now – first the boy, now Nancy. Decent enough bloke, normally. Just gotta watch it when he's got a few beers in him. Anyway, let's sort out this runaway pony.'

I hesitated. Duty called. I asked if I could borrow his phone and rang the Windmark Police Station, got Jace Gradey. I told him Allan Gaunt was on the way to town, half-pissed, suggested he intercept. He said he would.

'Can't have him driving around in that condition,' I explained as I gave Dom back the phone.

'Course not.'

He returned to his car and cruised out to the lake.

I noticed a *Work Vehicles Only* sign on the gate. Unsure of whether this applied to me, or of the wisdom of driving onto a building site, I followed on foot. As I did so I wondered whether there was any way of checking whether Allan Gaunt might have 'had a few beers in him' around the time of the deaths at Canticle Creek. We had Benny and Brock in the frame, but there was plenty of room for an accomplice – or local organiser.

I drew close to the lake. Maybe a hundred metres in diameter, it was clearly the centrepiece of the development, the focal point of a series of overlapping slopes that ran down to its clear waters. The design of the landscape had something almost oriental about it – a subtle nod, perhaps, to the region's tutelary spirit, Kenji Takada?

The impression of Eastern sensibility was intensified by the two-metre-high glazed metal sculpture of a bird perched on a curved rock in the middle of the lake. That must have been the installation Christie Looms mentioned at the gallery.

The scene wasn't all oriental harmony, though. On the far side of the lake was a flushed and sweaty Scotsman holding onto one horse and a relieved Australian teenager mounted on another. Dom had parked under a stand of ghost gums. Possum jumped off and slipped a bridle over Nutmeg's head. She was securing him to a stump at the foot of a nearby rock formation when I joined them.

'Aye, I might have known,' said Geordie. 'Trouble always comes in threes.'

'Hope he wasn't too much of a nuisance,' I said.

'Nay, lass, doolally little bugger wanted a drink from the lake. Got a rope onto him, easy as.'

'Ah, Geordie,' said Possum. 'You're a lifesaver.'

'Oh, go on with you. Didn't want him getting out onto the main road.'

'What are you doing out here on a day like this?' I enquired.

'Concreters are comin' in Monday. Wanted to be sure the markers weren't damaged in this crazy wind.'

Dominic ambled over, a rolled document in his hands.

'Sorry about this, Mr Talia,' said Possum. 'Somebody didn't shut the gate.'

I liked the somebody.

Dom said not to worry, there wasn't much damage the horse could do here.

'Different story next week, though,' he warned. 'Construction's scheduled to begin Monday. Make sure you keep him out of the way then.'

'Of course,' said Possum.

'What is it you're constructing?' I asked.

Geordie answered for his boss. 'Why – the future, lass.'

'Future of what?' I enquired.

'The future of Windmark,' he enthused.

Dom suggested, with a slight smile, that Geordie was perhaps a little prone to exaggeration. They were starting on the clubhouse. But, long term, he wasn't that far from the truth. The local economy was stagnating, the drought was hitting hard – not just the farms and wineries but the businesses in town as well. A major development like this would give the region a genuine boost.

298

He unrolled the document, which turned out to be a plan of the Robinwood Lakes Estate. I examined it with interest, surprised at how substantial the development was going to be: there were dozens of dwellings, a clubhouse, parks and playgrounds, even a retirement home.

He made a sweeping gesture that suggested he'd caught some of Geordie's optimism. 'Have you ever seen a better setting?' he enthused. 'It's a natural amphitheatre. Our architects have captured the essence of the ranges and transformed it into something magical.'

He sounded like he was reading from a brochure. Maybe he thought so himself – he flashed a self-deprecating smile: 'In my humble opinion, of course. The lake's the key.'

I knew what he was getting at. I'd thought the same thing. The site was something of an oasis, a green paradise amid the parched yellow that had descended upon so much of the local environment.

'It's unique,' he continued. 'For this part of the world, at least, down here on the flats. Spring-fed. Collects the run-off from the ranges through a series of aquifers and underground streams. Never runs dry – even in the drought. Makes for some magnificent plant life.'

He nodded at the swamp gums and their adjacent grasslands, still green at the end of a long summer.

I noticed Possum follow the gesture, then pause and narrow her gaze. She turned her head and looked around the property.

A vicious gust of wind whistled in from the north, stirred up a willy-willy that spun away to the south and broke up as it hit the bush.

'I better get the boys back home before they do any more damage,' said Possum, clambering onto Atomica via a convenient stump.

'Will you be right with the pony?' asked Dominic. 'I could get one of my blokes to float him up to the Bluehouse.'

'No thanks. We've been enough of a nuisance,' she replied. 'He's actually pretty well-behaved when he's on a lead.'

'What can I do?' I asked.

'Just go home, Jess.'

Did I detect a note of insistence in her voice? What was she getting scratchy about?

She set out for the Bluehouse, Nutmeg falling into line behind her.

We watched until she gave a final wave and disappeared into the bush.

'Gotta go myself,' said Dom. 'You happy with everything here, Geordie?'

'Aye, I think so. I'll pop down again in the morning, have another look. I'll call you if there's any problems.'

The men made their farewells and returned to their vehicles. I began to do the same, then paused, my attention caught by a couple of wood ducks that drifted in and landed on the lake, the flurry of webbed feet, the subtly upward tilt as they hit the water.

I walked back to my car, squinting in the glare, regretting I didn't have my sunnies. I heard a car change gear and caught a glimpse of Geordie's ute running down the road to town. He gave me a farewell toot.

I paused for a last look at the hoarding. Robinwood was going to be a nice place, with its wide roads, generous allotments, prestige homes – not that I'd ever be able to afford one.

I climbed into the SUV and started up. Then hesitated. Looked around. Chewed a lip. Turned the motor off, puzzled. By what?

I could only describe it as silence. Not so much a physical silence – it was more an abstract one. An absence, as if a clock I was barely aware of had just stopped ticking.

Why did I find myself thinking about Danny Jakamarra, my friend and colleague back in Kulara? It was that comment of his out on the Gunshot Road: long as you hear the motor knocking, you haven't got it.

The knocking had just stopped.

I sat there trying to figure out what was going on inside my head. What subconscious forces were at work there.

I drummed my fingers on the wheel.

No good, I had to investigate.

I got out of the car and took a closer look at the hoarding. Its central feature was an aerial shot of the estate and the surrounding countryside. Its interconnecting colours and contours reminded me of Dad's painting. What had he said about the source of a country's energy? Down here it's all about water. You could see that here, the way the watercourses that shaped the topography came together at the lake.

I stared again at the hoarding. That damned thing was trying to tell me something.

Another comment of Danny's came to me. *It isn't always what you see.*

There was something in the photo that I hadn't seen when I was at the lake.

Some trees.

I walked back towards the copse, a dull throb tolling like a distant church bell in the backwoods of my brain.

I looked at the sculpture and was struck by its beauty: the blue metal breast, the bronze beak, the spray of gold in its wings. As Dom Talia had said at the gallery, it was a minor masterpiece.

As I gazed at the bird, I had a peculiar sensation – that I was looking at Daisy Baker. What was it? The friendly ripple across its face, the sweet green prism of its eyes? I'd never even met the woman but, over the past few weeks, I'd internalised a sense of her personality, felt a connection. I could see why Adam was attracted to her.

I understood what Christie Looms had been doing that day, out at Daisy's cabin, killing cats. And when he was working in his studio, drinking wine at an exhibition or standing around a barbeque.

He was mourning her. So overwhelming was his love for Daisy that she'd begun to colonise his art.

The poor bugger must have been devastated when she died.

But why did I feel as though somebody was looking at me? Was it just the bird? My gaze drifted down to the rock upon which the sculpture stood.

Not somebody.

Something.

Among the watermarks and weathering, the cracks and fracture-lines of the boulder, there was a shape which could have been an overturned eye. I tilted my head, made out a face, partially submerged, an ancient, oriental face, the visible eye turned to the horizon, the fingers shading it long and narrow.

I stood there for a moment, my brain struggling to corral the storm of ideas pelting through it.

I studied the terrain between the rock formation and the bush, then stepped out over the landscaped earth. I took some twenty paces to the west and came across a stump, cut close to the ground, visible only because the wind had whipped away its covering dust. I knelt down and touched its surface, recognised the grain, the colour. It was a manna gum.

The truth hit me like a bull-whip.

I began to trace out a path to my right, searching for the second stump, but I'd only taken a couple of steps when I paused.

A shot of iced water through the veins.

I wasn't alone.

CHAPTER 41

He'd come back – had he ever left? His car was still under the ghost gums. He'd climbed out of the cab and was standing at the open door. He had a phone to his ear but his shades were turned in my direction.

Dom Talia.

I gave him a quick wave.

'Everything okay?' he called.

'All good.'

'Forget something?'

'No – just admiring Christie's sculpture.'

'Brilliant, isn't it?'

He put the phone into his pocket. 'Word before you go, Jesse?'

'Yes, Dom?'

He came over and leaned against one of the wave-shaped rocks at the water's edge, gazing out over the estate.

'You understand what Robinwood means, don't you?' he asked. 'For the town? The district?'

'Sure. Like Geordie said, it's the future.'

He smiled. 'You're smart. Knew that the moment I met you.'

I returned the smile.

He cast his gaze around the property, the sky reflected in his shades. He seemed to be weighing things up.

I said goodbye, began to walk away but he spoke again.

'It's not just the future, this development. It's more … a buffer, you might say.'

I stopped and turned. 'A buffer?'

There was a sheen of sweat on his upper lip, a tightening at the corners of his mouth.

'World's a terrible place, Jesse. And it's getting worse. Pack of savages out there, desperate, hungry. Running amok. Like those Razics. Hunt in packs. Put a weapon in their hands, gun or a car, try to make you think they're something other than animals. Vermin.'

'I see.' I was seeing a lot of things: this guy was as cunning as a feral cat but a million times more dangerous. And out of his fucking mind.

Looking into his shades was like staring into an infinity of mirrors. He took the glasses off, but, strangely, the impression remained. His eyes were a void.

'You need some space between you and the … swarm.' He waved a hand at what, to his mind at least, was doubtless looking less like a luxury housing estate and more like a redoubt. 'That's what we're building here. A buffer zone. There's going to be two sorts of people in this country before much longer: those who've shored up their defences and those who haven't. You understand that, don't you?'

A pause. Only a few seconds, but those particles of time crawled by like decades. Within their parameters, the world changed: crows called, fluttered from the trees, rotted and blossomed into maggots and flies. Greeny-black ants scuttled for cover. Trees wilted and lost their leaves, dropped limbs, shed seeds, bark. Kangaroo shit disintegrated, gave birth to exquisite orchids.

'Don't you?' he pressed.

I swallowed. 'Sure I do. Well, I better be on my way.'

'Of course. Sorry to hold you up.'

He stood upright. I moved towards my car.

A disturbance in the air, the flicker of a shadow on the ground. I'd been waiting for it. He knew that I knew. As he jumped at me I swivelled and caught him in the right arm with my right foot. Which should have given me more time than it did but the bugger was left-handed. And a damned sight stronger than me. Not to mention quicker than I'd expected. He came at me again, something in his hand. A heavy spanner. Where had he been hiding that?

I rolled to one side as it swung down, attempted a roundhouse kick, but again, he anticipated – he deflected my heel, smashed me in the right leg. I doubled over in time to receive an almighty kick in the guts.

I found myself on my back, gasping for air and staring up at the wild sky.

Talia stepped towards me, his face radiating confidence; he had everything just where he liked it: under control. I tried to get up, stumbled and staggered away from him.

I heard his footsteps. How had I let myself get caught like this? How many clues had I missed? How blind had I been?

Then there were more footsteps. Rapid, rolling footsteps. Not feet. Hooves. I looked to the south and saw Atomica galloping at us.

The horse swung round, Possum in the saddle.

'Get up!' she yelled, her arm extended.

I grabbed the arm. I threw my body onto the horse's rump and my right boot into the face of the charging Dom Talia.

Atomica pounded across the paddock. I felt myself slipping off but Poss put an arm back and steadied me. I wrapped my arms around her waist.

I glanced back to see what Talia was up to, and was surprised to see that he'd disappeared.

I was horrified to hear the BMW burst into life.

'Head for the scrub,' I yelled at Possum.

The vehicle burst out from the ghost gums. As it drew close, Atomica veered to the left and jumped a fallen log. The Beamer wasn't as agile: it smashed into the obstacle and ground to a halt. I heard a crunch of gears as it reversed, but we weren't hanging around to see what he was up to.

Atomica reached the scrub and angled down into the dry creek bed that ran along the estate's southern boundary. We ploughed across a sand drift then came to a steep incline and pulled up.

Talia didn't. The four-wheel drive crashed over the bank and came at us again. Black wattle and wiry dogwood flew every which way. A rock pigeon shot out from the undergrowth and whirred into the air.

We wheeled away, racing along the creek. The vehicle came after us, bouncing over rocks and logs, spitting angry sand, roaring and revving.

Jesus, that was a determined man. And he knew how to handle a four-wheel drive.

'We have to get out of the creek!' I screamed.

We came to a dip in the bank that seemed ascendable – just. The horse hesitated, scraped earth. Possum leaned forward.

'Come on, boy. You can get up there.'

She kicked him on. The hooves struggled through tumbling gravel and crumbling clay, then began to slide backwards. The car was closing in. Atomica flung his great head forward, found a footing and we were over the slope.

I risked a backward glance. The vehicle rushed the bank, reared up so high its fat black wheels whirled dirt into my eyes.

Then it slipped back into the creek.

I heard a roar from the cabin and caught the dark fury on his face.

I remembered Sam Kelly's comment on Talia's football days: maybe not the most naturally talented player you ever saw, but definitely the most determined. I hadn't seen it until now.

We pushed through the bush. At the top of a low rise, we paused to look back. The Beamer was sitting down on the flats like a shiny black beast, gazing up at us with spotlight eyes. Waiting.

No going back that way. Straight up the hill was our only option. We had to get to the Bluehouse and call for help.

'Are we safe yet?' asked Possum.

'We won't be safe until that bastard's in jail – or the ground. What made you come back?'

'I never left. I was watching from the bush.'

'Why?'

'Something he said – about the waterhole being a good spot for plants. I remember Daisy said the same thing, one time we were driving past. It was Mr Talia, wasn't it? Killed her and the others?'

'It was.'

The final pieces of the puzzle flew together in my head. Daisy had been drawn in by the site's unique features and come across the orchid. Going across her sketches sometime afterwards, she'd puzzled at her inability to identify it. Suspecting that the plant was a new species, she'd gone down and asked him to stop work. Maybe she'd threatened legal action, maybe he never gave her the chance. Maybe she'd said something to him at the high-angle rescue on Crowcall Road.

Wolf Gunther must have made the same mistake. Perhaps he recognised the scene from her sketch when he was driving back from Johnson's Falls. Despite his reservations about the existence of a new species, he'd gone in for a closer look and run into Dom Talia.

Talia. Jesus, the guy was a fucking sorcerer. Misdirection, that was the key to his modus operandi.

Every move he'd made, every murderous act he carried out, he'd been careful to arrange the signs so that they pointed away from him. He'd torched his own vehicle to get rid of any evidence that it had been involved in running Adam off the road or attacking me at Demon's Leap. But he'd done it in a way that made him look like another victim.

It was the same with Daisy's shack. He'd burnt it down, presumably to destroy any evidence she might have gathered about him. Had he spotted her taking photos on his property?

That was the significance of the picture on the USB: not the fact that it featured a Gaunt vehicle, but that it suggested she was worried about construction works at the Robinwood Lakes Estate.

I looked back at the BMW. No sign of its owner. Then I saw him out where the grass met the scrub.

His gaze lifted to us and lingered for a moment.

Then he crouched down and put a hand to the ground. A wisp of smoke curled up from a tussock.

He moved a few metres to his right and repeated the process. Then he did it a third time. And a fourth. The first little licks of flame appeared.

'Fuck me,' I muttered.

Another quality of Talia's Sam had commented upon: his cunning.

'Bastard's going to burn us out.'

Talia knew fire. I'd seen him among the fireys on the High Line, which must have been when he'd planted the evidence that led to the charging of Benny and Brock. He knew the damage a runaway blaze could do on a day like this, the evidence – and witnesses – it could eliminate.

The fire drifted a metre or two at a time, thin red fingers reaching out for fuel, consuming. Heading directly towards us. Then the wind picked up and it shot forward.

Sparks and embers whirled overhead, came down to earth. Ominous little puffs began blossoming in the bush up ahead.

'Let's go,' I said.

'Where?'

'Home.' The bunker was looming large in my mind.

I looked around. 'What happened to Nutmeg?'

'I had to let him go. Last I saw he was galloping up the track. Hopefully he's headed for home.'

We kept to the track as best we could, working our way uphill. In the bushier sections we dismounted and led the horse. My right leg was aching, but I could still function.

Somewhere in all that chaos we crested a rise and I glanced back. No angry BMW to be seen, but something far worse.

A fat black plume was tumbling over the valley, clouding the sun.

An inferno was running up at us.

How the hell had it taken off so quickly?

Dad's words came to mind. *This country is ready to explode.*

We stared at it, transfixed – until a burning branch came spinning out of the sky and crashed to earth nearby, igniting another blaze that swarmed uphill.

'They're bloody everywhere,' spluttered Possum.

Not quite, but they soon would be. The escarpment was igniting above us. Small fires were linking up, being sucked back into the advancing front. We'd started uphill on a following northerly, but then the wind shifted and swung round from the west. A torrent of debris – twigs and sticks, burning embers – rained down around us.

A flaming messmate crashed to earth in front of us, whipping up a flurry of fires and, worse, blocking the track. The bush ahead of us was dense, dangerous, swiftly igniting.

We'd have to get around it, but how?

'Head for the Canticle gully,' said Possum, pointing to the left.

I followed her outstretched hand to see a rocky crevice that was fire-free running down the escarpment.

We dismounted as we reached the gully, and I saw what she was getting at. This was where the Canticle Creek emerged from the heights. Its tumbling waters provided a brief respite that gave us the energy to tackle the climb. The three of us plunged our faces into the water and set off. There was a wallaby path alongside the creek, and though steep in places, it had little of the undergrowth that was rendering the slopes impassable.

Possum grabbed the reins and together we pushed, dragged and coaxed Atomica uphill.

When we reached the top of the rise we remounted and rode along the track until we came into sight of the Bluehouse. Thick smoke was weaving through the branches and fountains of the garden. The Japanese elm was at almost forty-five degrees, its trunk straining at the base.

The full force of the fire itself, though, was yet to hit. Possum urged the horse into one last burst of energy and we galloped towards the house.

CHAPTER 42

I was dismayed to see Nadia on the back verandah – still in her blue dress and sandals, pathetic little mop in one hand, garden hose in the other. She was watching the deadly rain fall down around her, fear distorting her features.

'Thank God you're back,' she yelled.

I dismounted. 'Don't worry about the mop. Just get into the bunker. Have you called triple zero?'

'I tried, but the phone wasn't working.'

The fire had taken out the phone towers already. It probably didn't matter much. Everybody in town would have seen it by now. The question was would the strike teams be able to get up the hill? I doubted it. We had to assume we were on our own.

Possum rode Atomica down to the back paddock, where she spotted Nutmeg, up against the gate. She opened it and drove the horses in. Mowed grass, relatively few trees – that was as good as they were going to get today.

Nadia and I made for the bunker.

'Do you know how it started?' she asked.

'Dom Talia lit it.'

She stopped. 'Why would he do that?'

'He's the one doing all the killing round here.'

Her eyes widened and she put her hands to her temples.

'Daisy tried to stop his new estate. There's a rare orchid there,' I explained, which did bugger-all to reduce her bewilderment and not much more to reduce mine.

Possum joined us.

'Where's the fire pump?' I asked.

'Beside the workshop.'

She led me round there. I threw out a hose and gave the pump a burl. It rattled into life at the first yank of the cord. I began wetting down the verandahs and eaves. Possum tried to help but I pushed her away.

'Just get into the bunker,' I ordered. 'Take Nadia.'

I did what I could to hit the ember fires that were breaking out among the wooden beams and boards of the house, but unless help – preferably in the form of a fleet of big red trucks – arrived soon, I suspected I was wasting my time.

'Jess!'

Possum reappeared, gasping.

'Why aren't you in the bunker?' I yelled.

'We can't get in.'

I froze. 'It's locked?'

'You can't lock it. Door must be jammed.'

I flicked the nozzle off and followed her.

Halfway across the yard I paused.

'What's wrong?' asked Possum.

Was fear doing my head in, or was the wind running two ways at once? The air around my head seemed to be running in a southerly direction. Below my waist, though, it was flowing to the north. The nether wind was slower but more powerful, more dangerous, like an ocean rip.

How was that possible?

Was the convection column of the approaching fire creating a vacuum that was sucking the ambient air back in? I'd heard of such a phenomenon, never imagined I'd be caught in the middle of it.

There was a god-almighty firestorm racing up the escarpment. We had to get into the bunker, fast. I picked up the pace. Nadia was crouching on the bottom step, leaning into the handle.

I pushed her aside and tried to move it. Nothing. I shouldered the door, then grunted and kicked it in frustration. It was no good. The bloody thing wasn't budging. Something must have fallen down behind it.

I examined the hinges and latch. Maybe I could get round it with a wrench or a screwdriver.

'Where are your tools?'

'In the workshop,' said Possum.

I ran halfway across the yard and stopped. I felt a rumble under my feet, heard an approaching roar. I raced back and threw myself onto Possum and Nadia just as a mighty burst of flame flew out of the bush. It swivelled about, then dissipated.

'Is that it?' Nadia asked.

More fireballs fizzed out of the forest, inscribing crimson arcs through the air. 'Barely even the beginning,' I said.

One of the paperbarks on the northern edge of the clearing ignited, disgorging a shower of sparks. Spot fires blossomed across the lawn, took off, linked up. Embers came zipping in like bullets, singed our clothing and skin. The surface of the frog pond was hissing and sizzling like a rush-hour Chinese wok. A wooden sculpture of a woman by the pond – one of Takada's experiments – had smoke billowing from her hair.

'Back to the house!' I bellowed.

We were halfway across the clearing when the tsunami I'd been fearing – a wave of crown-fire swirling eighty metres into the air – roared over the rise and came leaping through the treetops.

I'd have thought I was past shocking, but the transformation of the front paddock shocked me. One second it was blown grass, the next it combusted, like a pool of petrol touched by a spark. A wallaby flew out of nowhere, tail ablaze, then disappeared into the smoke.

I grabbed hold of Possum and Nadia, hauled them into the house and slammed the door behind us.

I sat there for a moment, back to the wall, wheezing. I reached into my pocket for a puffer. Amazingly there was one there. I gave myself a blast, suspected I'd need a truckload of the stuff to get me through the next few hours. My companions lay on the floor rubbing their eyes and shaking their heads.

My kickboxing instincts – not so much the kicking as the thinking, the routines and strategies – took over. I dragged the others to their feet.

'We don't stand still,' I yelled. 'We keep moving. Anticipate. Watch your back and look out for each other.'

I struggled to recall the basic structure-fire training they'd given us when I joined the force. It was a balancing act: the killer outside against the killer within. Out in the open, radiation was the enemy; inside, it was smoke. Having the roof fall in on your head didn't look like it would do you much good either.

Nadia seemed smaller, shrivelled. She put her head in her hands and began shaking.

She was a threat to us all.

'Listen, Nadia.' I grasped her shoulders. 'You can't lose it now. All that work you put into getting yourself clean, telling us about the Razics. Bravest thing I've ever seen. It's all been for this. You understand?'

I wrapped her in a quick embrace and released her.

The smoke in the room was already building, swirling and sinking.

'Fill the sinks and baths,' I said. 'Put out the hot spots, block up the entrances with wet towels, keep under the smoke as best you can.'

I looked out the front window. The sky was a satin-yellow effulgence that rose and fell in intensity, as if great pulses of energy were blasting through it.

'Jess!' Possum was pointing at the ceiling. 'Up there!' Sharp little blades of flame, blue-edged, shone through the smoke.

'Towels!' I yelled.

We ran to the laundry. Hideous red roses bloomed in the window there. We found some extra clothing and scrambled into it. We soaked mops and towels, dashed up to the mezzanine and began swatting flames. They retreated to reappear everywhere else.

A wail cut through the fire's roar. One of the smoke alarms had gone off. Another joined it. Soon there were half-a-dozen of them, a nightmare choir screaming at us from every direction. I disconnected those I could get at, smashed others.

I ran past the front window and caught sight of something that puzzled me. Was it a trick of the light, or did the bunker door just move? How had that happened?

If we could reach it, our chances of survival would improve dramatically. But we had to do it fast, before the bunker filled with smoke or the yard became impossible to cross.

I went to the front door, opened it a millimetre or two and peeped out.

The door slammed into my face and a yellow monster crashed into the room. It was wearing goggles and a mask, carrying a jimmy bar in its hand. I staggered away, stunned.

The bar carved an arc through the air and smashed into my ribs.

The pain was like a bomb going off inside me. I gasped, went down, stayed down for too long. As I struggled to find my feet he leapt at me, delivered a massive kick to my guts.

I caught sight of Nadia, staring in disbelief and fear.

'They're everywhere,' she mouthed.

I knew what she meant: her Barleymen. She turned and ran from the room.

Sensible woman, I thought. The way Talia's going, we'll all be dead in seconds. Again, I struggled to my knees, again, he delivered a ferocious kick that sent me sprawling.

'Mr Talia!' Possum screamed. 'What are you doing?'

He jerked his goggled head in her direction and paused. Whether there was any reluctance or remorse there I couldn't say. I doubted it because he swiftly turned back to me.

He was Yama, the God of death, a juggernaut, rocked by winds, fuelled by fire.

I tried to crawl away, gain distance, room to manoeuvre. But he stepped forward, planted a foot in the small of my back and raised his arm for the *coup de grâce*.

'Enough!' screamed a voice I barely recognised.

I heard a thud and a grunt and Talia threw his arms out, then toppled forward onto me.

I wriggled out from under him. There was a pickaxe buried in his back. He shuddered and groaned, his face twisted in agony. He managed to remove the pick but couldn't do much more. We locked eyes, fleetingly. His were still a void. He tried to find his feet, but crumbled to the floor. He lay there, face down, arms out, breath fading.

Standing behind him was Nadia, a fierce expression on her face. She hadn't run away. She'd gone looking for a weapon and found Nick's pick.

There was a deep rumble in the roof. You couldn't see much of anything in the smoke but you didn't need to. We heard the crash of falling timber and screaming iron. The smoke pressed down on us like a black mattress.

Nadia screamed above the roar. 'We have to get out of here!'

I wanted to move, but my legs had other ideas.

She grabbed me by the arm. 'Come on, Jess!' I was surprised by the authority in her voice.

A beam collapsed and brought down the dividing wall next to us. I was pinned beneath a fallen panel and a pile of bricks.

I tried to free myself, tried to breathe. Failed on both counts. So this is how it ends, I thought: the sucking heat, the fucking weight. Bloody awful way to go.

I felt a pair of hands upon my shoulders. Nadia, grunting from the effort, pulled me from the rubble.

'Can you walk?' she yelled.

I tried to, but a searing pain along my right side told me I wouldn't get far.

'Possum,' she screamed. 'Help me.'

They took an arm each, dragged me to the front door and wrenched it open.

A wave of flame flew in at us: the verandah was engulfed. No exit there. Nadia slammed the door. Jets and sparks came spitting and fizzing in through crack and keyhole.

'Out the back?' she gasped.

I propped myself up against the fireplace while Nadia crawled into the kitchen. She opened and closed the back door on another slice of hell. The windows in the west side shattered and gave way to wild red winds that ignited curtains and furniture.

'We're trapped,' Possum said, despairing.

Nadia looked up at the ceiling: it was bowing, burning, about to cave in.

'The flying fox!' she yelled.

Out through the big bay window, in the upper level of the house, was a radiant steel line.

I saw what she was thinking. The external sections of the house – verandahs and porches – were ablaze, but if the fox held we could swing out over them. The yard couldn't be any worse than the death-trap the house was rapidly becoming.

She looked at the mezzanine stairs, then at me. 'Can you get up there?'

I took a few steps and stumbled. Nadia threw an arm around my upper body.

Somewhere in the storm of emotions raging through my head as she hauled me up the steps I found space to be amazed that scrawny woman like Nadia could muster such strength.

The window frame was smouldering but the metal bracket that held the fox was still in place. Nadia touched the cable. It was hot, but taut, angling off into the darkness.

I heard a scream of wood as a section of the roof caved in and the mezzanine floor gave way beneath us. The three of us clung to the frame.

Nadia wrangled me into the seat. 'Hang onto the chains.'

I may have nodded but I could feel my brain slipping away to parts unknown. She must have noticed.

'Possum,' she said. 'Can this thing carry two people?'

'Right now, I don't even know if it can carry one.'

'No choice. You go down with Jess. Hold her in place.'

Possum squeezed in beside me.

'What about you?' asked Possum.

Nadia pulled the leather belt from her dress.

'This'll do.'

She pushed us off. We whizzed down through smoke and flame, light bending around us. I began to slip away, felt Possum tighten her grip. A looming scarlet bloom told us that the wattle at the base of the fox was ablaze, so she let go early and we crash-landed in the middle of the yard.

Nadia came swinging in seconds later.

She dropped and rolled in the dirt, tearing off a smouldering shirt. We were still too close to the wattle. The heat was sucking the oxygen from our lungs. We had the house on one side, the bush on the other, both blasting out waves of radiation.

We crawled away until we came to a shallow trench and rolled in.

'Wait here,' said Nadia.

And she was gone, clambering off into the darkness.

She came back a minute later.

'Can't reach the bunker,' she said. 'Burning tree in the doorway. We'd cook.'

'How long till we cook here?'

She flipped her hands.

Nadia looked as bad as I felt: cheeks flushed, lips crimson. There were scorch marks all over her face and arms, black and red rings around her eyes.

What were we going to do now?

CHAPTER 43

Istared up into the firestorm, trying to gauge how long we
had. Sheets of corrugated iron cartwheeled by, coruscating
blades of light. Every breath was a short, sharp jab in the
throat, an asthmatic wheeze.

Then – some freak in the physics of wind or heat – there
was a break in the cloud. I saw something. A bird hovering.

I looked the creature in the eye. It was Possum's bloody
magpie, Pendles.

But a Pendles transformed into something grander, a wild
witness, an imagination on wings.

Through its eyes I watched the inferno's brutal run up into
the hills.

I found myself swept up in a tempest of emblems. I saw
robins and wrens, honeyeaters, mudlarks, their tiny bodies
broken on a wheel of pain, the fragile architecture of their
bones exposed. I saw falling koalas, smouldering kangaroos
and echidnas. I saw run-around horses, tails ablaze; cattle on
their sides, their skinny legs twitching and kicking.

Time was transformed from a navigable stream into an exploding stained-glass window and fragments flew everywhere. Winds ran backwards, clouds clipped away to the west, light warped.

I rolled over, face down. Felt the life slipping away from me.

Dying, I decided, is the loneliest thing you ever do. That bolt of useless wisdom flew through my head like a wayward arrow. For all the friendship and family, the moments of solidarity that bind our lives, when it comes to the crunch, you're on your own.

Or are you? I felt a firm little hand in mine. Nadia. She knew what was going on. She'd been doing this – fighting to stay alive – for most of her life.

That hand was the only thing tethering me to the planet. If it hadn't been there, I would have just floated away, another piece of space junk.

I found myself slipping into a dream world. Memories rolled through my head: myself as a young girl running wild through the streets of Laverton; my frazzled mother, driven out of her wits by my eccentric father, who'd been driven out of his own wits by his failure to find a voice.

I began to relax. Not a wise move, Nadia's grip warned me. The sleep creeps up on you, like fog. Like snow. But it's a sleep from which you never awake, a fog that doesn't lift.

An explosion snapped me to my senses. I opened my eyes to see a gas canister shoot through the air.

Nadia and I locked eyes.

'We need shelter!' She had to scream to be heard. 'We're going to die out here.'

I tried to speak and couldn't.

She put out an arm and felt around. 'This is the trench Nick was digging this morning.'

She looked to the house. It was barely visible, but sporadic hints through the gloom suggested that the south side was still standing.

'Goes back to the tank,' she said.

I could almost see the idea forming in her mind. And I saw something else, something Nick had told me about: her determination. In the world Nadia came from, when you decided to do something, you did it.

'You're not going back there?' I gasped.

'We need water. There's a tank full of it there.'

She made to move, then stopped. Possum had her by the leg.

'Don't go,' she pleaded.

Nadia looked back at her. 'No matter what happens, honey, you've already given me a life. All of you. You tell em that.'

She kissed the top of Possum's head.

Then she crawled off into the smoke.

Another wave of radiation ran through me. Where was that coming from? I raised my head. The mineral earth was on fire. Is that even possible? I asked myself. Can dirt burn? But there it was, creeping closer.

More than anything, I wanted to be out of the heat. Death would be a relief. I wanted cool, cool, cool …

Then I found it. Or it found me. Something foreign – water – came running down the ditch. It trickled under my legs, my waist, over much of my body. It bathed my back, soaked my clothing.

What had she done?

I rose to my knees, looked towards the water tank.

Then I was slammed backwards by an almighty explosion that tore the air apart.

Darkness. A thunderclap boom, rain, cooling, mega-smooth.

Sleep.

My dreams were a procession of unlikely characters: a white-haired woman in a wooden cage, her haunted eyes staring into the darkness. There was a boy on a donkey, an arrowhead in his hand, an ancient battlefield behind him. Then an old man with angular eyes moved along the peripheries of my vision, touched me with a wooden stick from which a bird – a hawk – emerged.

Then nothing.

CHAPTER 44

I woke to find myself tossed about on a sea of thumps and bumps. Somewhere a horse whinnied, a chainsaw screamed. Blue sky jounced about.

I felt my body then wished I hadn't. Pain everywhere, cross-hatched metal panels pressing against my back. I was on the tray of a truck. Somebody was crying.

I raised my head and caught sight of Possum kneeling, sobbing into her hands. A firefighter – a woman in ash and yellow – had an arm across her shoulders.

'What's going on?' I rasped.

The woman looked at me. 'We're taking you down to hospital.'

'Possum – you okay?'

'She's fine,' said the woman. 'You're our number one worry right now. I'm Jenny.'

I looked around the truck.

'Where's Nadia?' I asked.

'You just relax,' Jenny said in a way I didn't like; a tone I'd used myself when trying to break bad news gently.

Possum swung round, her eyes red-rimmed and wet. 'She's dead.'

I groaned.

'She was trying to save us,' said Possum. 'She did save us – filled the ditch with water from the tank. Then it all blew up.'

It was coming back to me now: the workshop, the ditch, the explosion.

'You're sure?'

'Just try to rest,' said Jenny.

'Are you bloody sure?'

Her mouth softened. 'Sorry, love. We found her body in the wreckage.'

I rolled onto my side, wishing that I could weep. Tears were a gift I'd never had.

The truck stopped. A couple of the guys climbed down and hacked at a tree that was blocking our way. I heard a whinny and looked up at a big black horse's head. Atomica.

'Feller insisted on coming along,' said Jenny. 'Wouldn't leave his boss.' She nodded at Possum.

I should be so faithful, I said to myself.

But this didn't make sense. Why, I couldn't say. Something I'd seen in a dream. The white-haired woman in the wooden cage.

Only one thing to do. I had enough fuck-ups on my conscience already.

I dragged myself up the sides of the truck and scrambled over onto the horse's back.

'What are you doing?' I heard Jenny cry out.

I didn't know how to answer that so I grabbed his halter and turned Atomica's head for home.

'You can't go back there,' she yelled. 'It's dangerous. There's things still falling.'

I urged the horse on.

CHAPTER 45

It was the silence that struck me hardest. Where were the burbling birds, the bolting wallabies? Even a frigging insect would have been a relief.

The rain had extinguished most of the open flame, but the stumps still glowed. From time to time I'd snap a branch and a shower of sparks would shoot forth. Smoke coiled away from the trees, slithered out of tuft and hollow. Little ash-clouds curled from Atomica's every step.

Trees and branches fell – mostly in the distance, but a couple close enough to make the horse jump. They'd be falling for weeks, months.

Fire like this, only thing to really put it out was winter.

I rode for maybe a kilometre, then reached the front gate and stopped, stunned. I muttered a prayer – to what I didn't know: the wind? The sun?

The Bluehouse hadn't just fallen in upon itself. It had imploded. 'My god,' I mumbled. The intensity of the destruction. Nothing had survived. That beautiful, rambling dwelling, with its cool corridors and vaulted ceilings, its patina of family memories and works of art. Gone.

The iron roofs were like torn foil, the verandah stones cracked and shattered. The mudbrick walls had been battered into blackened piles. The workshop – and the part of the house closest to it – had simply disappeared. You could trace the direction of the blast by the arrangement – derangement – of the debris.

Ghost objects loomed out of the wreckage. There was an iron lampstand, a Coonara stove, a piano's broken teeth and twisted strings. A trickle of silver that might have been an engine block ran out from a mess of twisted metal.

Even the massive centre poles were obliterated. How much energy did it take to do that?

I circled the building, the horse's hooves carefully picking their way through a sludge of ash and mud.

At the heart of the destruction, close to the workshop, I came across a scene that tore a piece out of my heart: a cleared space, a red woollen blanket over a body. A much-diminished body, from the shape of it. I remembered an arson investigator I'd spoken to once in Darwin telling me, *Sometimes there's nothing left*. A knuckle, a tooth, a bone. A handful of ash.

What had been in the workshop? All the flammables and explosives.

I'd been concussed by the blast myself, and I'd been in a ditch thirty metres away.

I slid off the horse's back and a burst of pain rocketed through my right leg. I found a piece of steel and used it as a crutch. I hobbled forward and knelt by the body.

And at last I found myself crying.

For all of them. Adam. Daisy. And, most of all, for Nadia. That poor bloody woman, the things she'd gone through, the courage she'd shown in trying to break away from the drugs and the Razics, then saving our lives.

All for this.

I touched the blanket. The bottom hem slipped away to reveal a distorted boot sole.

In the middle of a blob of melted rubber was a shape that might have been a spider.

I froze. Pulled the blanket away.

This wasn't Nadia.

I scrambled to my feet. Where was she?

I hobbled to the remnants of the workshop, dragged away sheets of corrugated iron, twisted pipes and machinery. Burnt my fingers, blew on them, kept going, the pain in my body strangely fading. I used my crutch to smash and tear the debris apart, dug deeper. I searched the rubble between the tank and the ditch.

Nothing.

I dropped to my knees and ran my hands across my face. On the ground, four of five metres to the north, something glimmered. I hobbled forward and picked it up: it was a fragment of scorched metal. I turned it over: barely visible beneath its blackened surface was a blue and yellow star.

Nadia's medallion.

But what was it doing on the north side of the house? I'd been looking through the wreckage between the ditch and the workshop. Had she gone round to the other side? Surely the fire there was worse?

I heard a bird call.

I lifted my head, found myself gazing at the Japanese elm at the bottom of the lawn. It had been blown over in the firestorm. Pendles was hovering above it.

I hobbled down the slope. The horse followed, slowly, fearfully. The ash on the ground was like blue snow.

The tree was a twisted mess. Not as burnt as its neighbours. Some of the leaves were still green. Maybe Takada had intuited more than they gave him credit for. All those years of sitting looking at the bush must have taught him something.

I struggled up to the tree: it was a tangle of branches and roots: a cage, of sorts. Deep in its heart was a pile of rocks in a shallow declivity. Possum's pet cemetery. I pulled the branches aside and peered in.

The wind-and-rain-blown ash was twisted into a myriad shapes: topographical maps, fossils, ice crystals. One of the shapes could almost have been a bare human back: the arcing spine, the ribs aligned, a cage within a cage.

I pushed through the prickly tangle then put out a hand and touched it.

What looked like a bare back was, in fact, a bare back.

I tore the branches aside. The corpse was perfectly still, at one with the scorched earth, the grey layers and blue flakes. The stone piles and the declivity had combined to form a narrow shelter.

I crawled in through the branches. Found myself looking at a face. An ivory mask, frozen, lifeless.

'Oh my god,' I whispered.

The eyes flickered open. All over the mountain grey turned gold.

A long pause, then a whisper: 'Mighta known you'd be here.'

'You're alive.'

'If you are. Possum?'

'She's fine.'

Nadia closed her eyes, moved her lips. 'Where is she?'

'Heading to town on the back of a fire truck.'

'Why aren't you?'

'Came back to look for you.'

'Isn't that the firey's job?'

'They thought you were dead.'

'I'm still not sure I'm not.'

She moved a hand, pushed some hair out of her eyes.

'There was a body,' I said.

'And it wasn't mine?'

'It was Dom Talia.'

Her eyebrows rose beneath their coating of ash. 'They confused me with him?'

'If you saw what's left of him, you'd understand. He made it out of the house. Didn't get much further. Why did you come down here?'

'Try crawling through fire,' she said. 'You take what's on offer. There was an opening. Turned into a corridor of sorts. Finished up here. Then a tree fell on top of me and that was that.'

Her eyes closed again.

My heart skipped a beat.

'Nadia. You're not going to cark it on me, are you?'

Nothing.

'Nadia!' I snapped.

The eyes opened. 'How long's it been?'

'God knows. A few hours.'

'There was rain,' she said. 'Some of it fell into my mouth. Sweetest thing I ever tasted.'

I put a hand on the trunk that had fallen across her legs; several branches had pierced her skin. One had impaled her thigh, another was stabbing her in the lower back.

'Lemme get you out of there.'

I tried to shift the branches, but couldn't manage it. She shuddered in agony at every movement. I tried to dig her out, but the ground was rocky and baked.

'Nadia, I can't move this friggin thing. I'm going to get help. Okay?'

'Okay.'

'Take this.'

I put the medallion in her palm and folded her fingers over it. She might have sketched a smile.

I heard the magpie scream. I looked down the road. There was a fire utility working its way up the hill, a tanker behind it.

'On second thoughts, maybe I won't have to.'

The convoy stopped. I called out, but they didn't hear me. Someone jumped out of the ute and went at a tree that was blocking their way. The someone looked a lot like Sam Kelly. The driver came and helped him. It was Nick.

'You be right for a minute?' I asked Nadia.

'Not going anywhere.'

I dragged myself onto the horse's back.

Sparks flew from the horse's hooves as I galloped up to the road yelling.

Ghost Roads

I leaned against the bull-bar and watched the mail plane touch down on the Kulara runway. She was out of the Cessna almost before it stopped. I braced myself as she leapt into my arms with an enthusiasm that almost knocked me off my feet.

'Jess!'

It had been a year since Possum and I last saw each other. I held her at arm's length.

'Look at you,' I said. 'You're taller than me.'

'That's not saying much.'

'How was the trip?'

'Oh my god, this country is amazing.'

'Wait'll you see it from the saddle.'

I threw her bags into the car and drove back to the house. I had lunch ready and we chatted while we ate.

Just as we were finishing up we heard a voice calling

through the back door. We went out to see Danny Jakamarra and his daughter, Milly, mounted on stockhorses. They had two other horses on leads and a pair of dogs prowling around behind them.

Our plan, hatched a few days before, was to ride out and camp at his family outstation at Janapula.

'Jess tells me you're a regular buck-jumpin champ,' said Danny when I introduced them.

'I said she loved to ride!'

Milly burst out laughing. She was about Possum's age, a skinny girl in a blue shirt and a big hat. She was the star performer of the Janapula All-Girl Cattle Crew, could ride before she could walk.

'This is your horse, Possum,' said Danny, indicating the lanky grey closest to him. 'You'll like him.'

She did. He had a spring in his step and a mineral gleam in his eye.

'What's mine like?' I asked, studying the last horse. The horse studied me back. Neither of us was impressed. He had an ugly demeanour and a matching head.

'We call him Porcupine.'

'I hope that's because he's slow.'

'It's because he's prickly.'

We loaded our gear, mounted up and headed towards the serrated purple ranges to the west.

An hour into the ride Milly spotted a trail of black bees sidling through the air. She followed the insects to a bloodwood and shimmied up its trunk from the horse's back. She put her hand into a hollow and scooped out a handful of thick brown goo.

'Sugarbag,' she called. She collected the honey in a pannikin and passed it down to Possum.

We resumed our journey, Danny and I ambling along as the girls got to know each other in a string of sorties out over the red-yellow plains. They chased goannas through the grass, gouged witchetty grubs out of rotten wood, smashed open termite mounds.

As we drew close to the ranges the ground beneath our feet grew harder. Mulga and feather-topped spinifex gave way to nuggety ghost gums and dolomite fuchsia. The iron oxide plains ascended into granite outcrops and scree slopes.

It was getting on for twilight when Possum raised herself in the stirrups and looked around.

'I can hear music.'

'We're nearly there,' said Milly.

We rounded a bend and came across a cluster of dwellings and stockyards strung out along a waterhole.

'Janapula,' announced Danny.

A thin layer of smoke floated over the camp. On one side of the community was a demountable with a solar panel on its roof, on the other a battered Toyota ute. Between the two was a line of campfires around which half-a-dozen women sat singing rough harmonies and thumping the earth.

One of the women got up and walked towards us. It was my old friend, Elsie Napanangka. She gave me a hug.

'Come say hello to the ladies.'

Danny had vanished. There were more fires flickering through the bush. Was that where the men were hanging out?

Elsie led us down to the waterhole and settled us into a group of women who gave us food and drink and swags to sit on. After a while they resumed their singing, and the songs seemed to shape themselves to the contours of the country we'd just traversed. In that ragged music you could hear hidden rivers and salt lakes; you could catch the scent of honeyed grevillea; you could see drops of water on fat green leaves.

I watched Possum sitting there, wide-eyed, and understood what the women were doing. They were welcoming her to their country.

An hour passed. Possum was looking tired so I suggested she get some sleep.

'Maybe I will,' she said, resting her head on the pillow and closing her eyes.

By the time she opened them again the women had retreated to their swags and the stars were in a different place.

I stoked the fire and asked how things were down in Canticle Creek.

'Dad's flat out on the house. Him and Geordie North.'

I'd heard Geordie was lending a hand. Mortified to discover what Dom Talia had really been up to, the builder had sworn he wouldn't rest until the Bluehouse had been rebuilt.

'How's that working out?' I asked.

'They spend all day arguing about chimneys.'

I had to laugh. 'Tell Sam not to bother. Geordie knows his chimneys. What about Nick and Nadia?'

'Still in Bosnia – getting to know her cousins. You heard she's having a baby?'

'Wonderful, yeah – your mum told me.'

'Mum! I forgot. She asked me to give you something.'

She rummaged through her bag and came out with an envelope. She passed it to me, trying to stifle a yawn.

'You go back to sleep,' I said.

Possum curled into the swag. In a few minutes her breathing blended into the sounds of the desert night, the crickets and curlews, the snoring women and big bass frogs.

I pulled out my torch and examined the envelope. The first thing I saw was a card from Lucy. *Hey Jess, Thought you might be interested in this.* The card was attached to a print-out of a magazine called *Muelleria*: *Plant and Fungal Taxonomy and Systematics.*

The second page featured an article: 'A new species of Caladenia'. There was a photo that looked a lot like Daisy's orchid and a lengthy description: taxonomy, distribution, habitat. The species was named *Caladenia Bakerae*; the listed habitat was the Windmark Ranges.

I tried to piece it all together. I knew that after the collapse of what turned out to be Dominic Talia's desperately overdrawn development, the council had resumed possession of the property at Robinwood Lakes and was in the process of turning it into a nature reserve.

Lucy had apparently taken the matter further and contacted the National Herbarium.

I re-read the name of the plant. *Caladenia Bakerae.*

They'd not only confirmed the existence of a new species, they'd named it after Daisy Baker.

There was something else in the envelope. Another envelope, smaller, thinner, battered about.

On the front were written the words: *To Jess Redpath, wherever you might find her.*

Inside was a handwritten card.

They're still here. Miracles happen.
What did I say about your boats and currents?
Love, Nadia.

Nadia was as enigmatically succinct as ever. What was still where?

I turned the card over. It was a photograph. I studied it by torchlight.

A gnarled olive tree, a white-washed wall, at its base, a collection of structures, most only a few centimetres high.

The toy village Nadia's father had built for her.

I stared at the photo for a while, then slipped it back into the envelope.

I lay back in the swag and turned my gaze to the sky, lost myself in contemplation of the Milky Way. The Ghost Road they called it out here. The moon was as thin as a lover's late-night whisper.

What was it Nick had said?

You don't choose love.

Maybe you don't, but, sometimes, amid the firestorms and whirlwinds of this treacherous world, if you're really blessed, it chooses you.

It had chosen him; it had manifested itself in that pale, courageous woman with the rocky past and the hopeful future.

For my own part, there was another emotion moving through my body. So rare had it been in my life, it took a moment or two to recognise: tranquillity.

The world around me seemed to glow. Not just the stars in the trees, but everything – the sand, the water, the rocks and songs. Like Danny's donkey engine, Takada's wheel, Dad's geological images, they connected.

For now, at least, things were running smoothly.

I listened for a while to Possum's breathing then turned onto my side and fell into the deepest sleep I'd had for years.

ACKNOWLEDGEMENTS

Thanks to the First Nations people of Central Australia, especially the Warumungu, who welcomed me onto their country and among whom I lived for ten years. The insights you gave me about life, language and land infuse everything I write.

Thanks to all the crew at Ultimo. Robert Watkins, Brigid Mullane, Deonie Fiford and Ronnie Scott for the editorial masterstrokes and the fine-tooth work. Emily Cook and Katherine Rajwar for finding an audience for my writing. Thanks to Josh Durham for the beautiful cover. And special thanks to James Kellow for your enthusiastic response to my creative endeavours – you got it better than I did myself.

Thanks to Melanie Ostell, for both your excellent editorial advice and for your advocacy on my behalf.

Thanks to Mary Cunnane, Bill Healy, Sally Hyland and Laurie Steel for your insightful feedback on the manuscript. Special thanks to Kristin Knorr, who read the book in its every manifestation and always found a way to make it better.

Thanks to Kevan Carroll, the first and best of my teachers.

Thanks to my colleagues at La Trobe University – especially Catherine Padmore, Juliane Roemhild, Paddy O'Reilly and

Kelly Gardiner – for giving me your friendship and support (and a place to hang my hat).

As usual, I seem to have been harassing every expert who crossed my path. My thanks to Karl Just, Tony Fitzgerald, Detective Senior Sergeant Paul Maher, Andy Knorr and David Nash. Thanks to Mark Franceschini and Ramesh Presser for the gangster language. Thanks to my colleagues in the St Andrews CFA, especially Jason Earl, Chris Henderson, Steve Gormley and Matt Ryan.

Thanks to Quinton Addison and Morgan Brown for the photography.

Thanks to Sae Ikenishi and Kaori Okano for the Japanese.

Thanks to the various watering holes that have given me warm inglenooks and hot coffee over the years, especially Debbie Granger, Karen Watson and crew at the St Andrews Pub, and Debbie Oakes and team at the St Andrews store. A special shout-out to the late, great Jordy Close.

Thanks to the Australia Council for the Arts and Creative Victoria for their support.

As always, my deepest gratitude is to my beautiful girls – Kristin, Sally and Siena – your love is the cocoon that keeps me going.